Everlasting

ANGIE FRAZIER

SCHOLASTIC PRESS / NEW YORK

Library of Congress Cataloging-in-Publication Data

Frazier, Angie.
Everlasting / by Angie Frazier. — 1st ed.
p. cm.
Summary: In 1855, seventeen-year-old Camille sets out from San
Francisco, California, on her last sea voyage before entering a
loveless marriage, but when her father's ship is destroyed, she and
a friend embark on a cross-Australian quest to find her long-lost
mother who holds a map to a magical stone, hoping to reach it
before her father's business rival can.

[1. Adventure and adventurers — Fiction. 2. Seafaring life — Fiction.
3. Supernatural — Fiction. 4. Shipwrecks — Fiction. 5. Fathers and
daughters — Fiction. 6. Australia — Fiction.]. I. Title.
PZ7.F8688Eve 2010
[Fic] — dc22
2009020519

ISBN: 978-0-545-11473-8

10 9 8 7 6 5 4 3 2 1   10 11 12 13 14

Printed in the U.S.A. 23
First edition, June 2010

The text type was set in Garth Graphic.
Book design by Lillie Howard

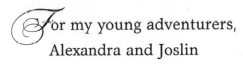

For my young adventurers,
Alexandra and Joslin

ONE

1855 SAN FRANCISCO

amille clicked the latches down on her trunk and glanced out her bedroom window. White haze choked the small seaport, and the fog bells sounding across the bay echoed in her chest. Fitting weather to mark the death of her freedom.

She ran her palms over the trunk's glossy redwood lid and took the handle. Camille had been sailing with her father since she'd learned how to put one foot in front of the other, and knew the value of packing lightly. With an easy tug, she pulled the trunk down the hall to the lip of the stairwell—the last trunk she would ever pack for a sea voyage with him.

The tallcase clock in the foyer snapped to the five o'clock hour, sending a persistent chime throughout the townhouse. Camille quickened her pace, careful not to nick the newel post as she maneuvered the trunk around it. Dropping the trunk near the front door, she turned and ran toward the recesses of the house, into the kitchen. The blackened hearthstones were cold and dormant, the tidy countertops waiting for the morning to begin with breakfast and tea. She liked being awake before anyone else. The notion that she was about to do something improper was an undeniable thrill.

Her heart gave a small flutter as a shadow rippled against the kitchen door's stained-glass window. Camille reached for the velvet cloak hanging on a peg and the woven basket stored on a shelf. He hadn't missed a Saturday morning in over a month. And now, even on the morning of her voyage, he'd come for her company. She opened the door, and Randall Jackson swept off his bowler. He raked his fingers through a tumble of glossy brown hair.

"You didn't forget," he said, his eyes drifting up to the second-level windows.

Camille stepped outside and closed the door, checking to be sure the crimson damask curtains were drawn across the windows of her father's room.

"Who would guide you through the markets if I did?" she asked. Camille put on her cloak for shelter against the predawn chill and brought the hood up over her black curls, drawn back in a loose chignon.

Randall extended his arm. Camille finished pulling on her ivory kid gloves and laid her hand in the crook of his elbow.

"If you recall, I was the one to suggest our secret market meetings," he said as they hurried through the back courtyard past the carriage house, and then swerved to hasten up the alleyway toward Portsmouth Plaza.

They emerged in the clotted white haze the port city knew well, so dense Camille could hear only the rattle of carts and kiosks setting up throughout the flat, grassy plaza her father's townhouse looked out upon.

"I enjoy a secret or two," she said though knew she really should have been taking a chaperone with her. The risk was slim enough. No one from the society her father or Randall cared about would be out at this hour, and certainly not in the markets. "Who knew buying fruits and vegetables could be so adventurous?"

Randall laughed freely as the vendors came into view. "I believe I'm having a negative effect on you, Camille. I should be careful not to fall out of favor with your father. I wouldn't want William to revoke his approval."

Randall stopped at a crate mounded with shiny, red-skinned grapes. He picked up a heavy vine and placed it in her basket.

"A treat for my future bride." A grin arched his eyes into half-moons. "I've noticed they're your favorite."

As he passed a few coins to the grape vendor, the perfection of his face awed her — his milky skin, wide smile, chiseled chin and nose. Randall truly was something grand to stare at. *Her future husband.*

The courtship had unfolded at an exhilarating speed the last two months, her father anxious to overcome gossip revolving around Camille's dismissal of a proper coming-out season. She couldn't have imagined staying in San Francisco for ridiculous balls and parties and lessons when she could have been on an eight-month trip with her father to India instead. It had been a simple choice for her. Upon their return, her father had learned one of the city's elite had died, leaving his son, Randall, a sizable fortune to invest where he pleased. To her father's pleasure, the young man had found an interest in shipping — and in Camille.

Randall released Camille's arm to help an older woman unhook a length of salt pork from a stall frame.

"I don't know your favorite," she said once he'd returned to her side.

Except for these brief outings, it seemed all their time had been spent in the presence of her father. Considering he and Randall were business partners, the conversation mostly revolved around shipping, trade industries, fleet growth, and money. Camille had started to wonder if their engagement was just another business matter to tend to. But then Randall had asked her to meet him on the kitchen's back steps before dawn one Saturday.

It took a few times to get used to rising so early, but soon she found the challenge of filling their baskets with the freshest pickings and getting back to the townhouse before her father rose from bed exciting. It became something she and Randall could whisper about throughout the week that didn't have anything at all to do with shipping.

Randall paused at a cart piled with cantaloupe, picked one up, and brought the rough rind to his nose.

"By far, my favorite. Especially when you can trace the musk of the inside right here." He tapped the apex of the melon, producing a hollow sound, and held it up to Camille's nose. She sniffed, feeling silly, but happy she'd learned something new about him.

"You know, Camille, as much as I adore your father, it is nice being able to steal some time alone together. I dare say once we're married, meeting secretly won't hold the same appeal." He paid for the cantaloupe and moved on toward a vendor of tomatoes and purple cabbage. Camille faltered as she followed. Meeting furtively was half the fun. Maybe even more than half.

"I'm glad I could be here today," he continued. "It's exciting to see you off on your last voyage."

Camille stopped walking, the fog swimming low around her heels. *Last voyage.* The words were a brigade of spiders creeping up her legs.

"Yes, I suppose it is very exciting." She hoped she'd sounded more enthusiastic than she felt. It was the right response to give, even if she didn't believe a single syllable.

As soon as Randall had started paying her calls, her father had swelled at the edges with relief. He'd smiled more, held his head up higher, and even started having full conversations with her again. For a long while it had seemed as if he'd lost interest in speaking with her. Only after Camille had officially taken the arm of one of San Francisco's richest and finest did she consider that perhaps her father had been embarrassed by her. The adorable little girl he'd raised aboard ships had grown into a young woman sorely lacking in the ability to attract acceptable suitors. Why Randall Jackson, the one suitor every girl in San Francisco swooned over, decided to call on Camille had perplexed her — and probably everyone else, too.

Randall selected a head of cabbage for each of their baskets. "In a few months' time all this hopping from port to port will be over," he said.

Camille's fair cheeks flared and she hardened the muscles of her jaw. "I do no such thing."

Hopping from port to port . . . like she was a child playing sailor. She'd once tried to explain to Randall how the sea and all its unpredictability, vastness, and mystery drew her. The idea that some other land, some other civilization lay out beyond that flat blue horizon intrigued her beyond any dinner party or invitation for tea. He'd only responded with a polite compliment on her sense of adventure.

"I'd wager your father's crew will be relieved, too," Randall said. He arched an eyebrow and looked at her. "Aren't women supposed to be bad luck on a ship?"

Camille picked up a vine of tomatoes. She pressed her fingers against the tenuous skin of one. That myth had irked her for as long as she could remember.

"My father refuses to employ sailors who believe in such absurd superstitions. He always has," she said, and then handed him the heavily laden vine. Randall picked off the tomato she'd bruised and returned it to the vendor.

"He shouldn't spoil you so blatantly. Darling, you should be spending your time here, on wedding arrangements. Because of this last voyage, we have to wait five more months to be married."

Five months. Was that all? She clasped a handful of her velvet cloak, her palm hot and damp.

"There." He topped her basket off with a fresh bunch of wildflowers. "I think we should be getting back. The sun is starting to rise."

She looked up into the fog and saw the sky trying to lighten to dewy pink. They'd taken longer than usual, talking more than any of the times before. They reached the back courtyard out of breath and saw a lamp glowing from the windows of the kitchen. A swell of panic stopped up Camille's throat.

"You can blame it on me," Randall said, not sounding the least bit worried.

"I intend to," she replied. The only figure inside belonged to that of her childhood nanny and cook, Juanita. The damask curtains in the second-floor windows were still drawn. Her father was certainly sleeping late for a voyage morning.

Randall removed his bowler again and held her back from the kitchen steps, out of sight should Juanita peer outside.

"I'll miss these mornings," he said softly. Camille knew she would, too. If she was going to marry him, she wanted to know him better. The opportunity just wasn't there whenever Randall paid her his more proper calls.

"It's only for a few months," she said, noticing he was drawing nearer, preparing for a kiss. He always closed their morning rendezvous with one. And with each Saturday that passed, Camille had begun to dread them. How could a kiss from a man as fine, intelligent, gentle, and handsome as Randall fail to produce a fire in the pit of her belly? It's what she'd always envisioned a kiss would do.

His lips grazed hers, holding on longer than normal, perhaps because of the impending voyage — or perhaps because he also felt a lack of fire and was determined to ignite it. Whatever the reason, he took her warm cheek in his chilled hand in the last second of their kiss.

He replaced his hat on his head and stepped back into the curls of haze. She pressed her lips together as she opened the kitchen door, searching for remnants of his kiss, perhaps a longing for another. Nothing. Standing at the tabletop, Juanita startled and spun toward Camille, her rolling pin ready to deal a blow.

"Miss Camille?" The rolling pin fell back to the tabletop, denting a disk of flattened dough. "What on earth are you . . . where have you . . . I . . ."

The plump, dark-skinned woman eyed the bulging basket of market goods on Camille's arm. She hiked up a brow. "So you're the one who's been vexing me with those baskets. I'd started to wonder if a secret admirer had taken to breaking in and leaving me anonymous gifts."

She sighed and turned back to her dough.

"It's Randall's fault," Camille said, smiling even though she was still disappointed by the kiss. What was wrong with her? Camille left the basket on the table and walked out to the foyer. She stalled midstep. A second portmanteau rested on top of her own.

"Is that you, Camille?"

William Rowen exited the study and hooked his thumbs into the pockets of his silk vest, each mother-of-pearl button stretched from the roundness of his waist.

"And how were the markets?" he asked. Her father watched her with amused curiosity as she widened her jade-green eyes and lost color in her cheeks.

"I don't know what you mean, Father." His curtains had been drawn! How had he known?

"Camille, I oversee twenty men at all times aboard my ship. I think I can handle keeping tabs on my seventeen-year-old daughter." He shook his head and turned away. "Come in. We're taking breakfast in the study this morning."

Breakfast together in his study, instead of in the formal dining room, was a practice she'd come to anticipate before each voyage. Perhaps in preparation for the lack of fine dining at sea. What she had not foreseen was her father's easy acceptance of her secret morning outings. She felt absurd for working so hard to deceive him.

The pocket doors to the study squeaked as she rolled them together, leaving just a crack for the aroma of a rich breakfast to trickle in from the kitchen. She could hear Juanita humming over the stovetop as she fixed heaping plates of griddle cakes, eggs, ham, toast, hash, and melon. It was Juanita's custom before each sail to fill Camille and her father up with as much food as their bellies would hold, as though her cooking could tide them over through the entire journey. Camille loved these little traditions, and her chest and stomach tightened knowing they were taking place for the final time.

She found her favorite chair, an oversized, bolted leather chaise, and sat in its firm grasp. Her father sat on a couch opposite her, the leather creaking beneath him. On the cushions were the scattered pages of San Francisco's daily paper, the *Alta California*. He picked up a loose page and grimaced at the type. He didn't need spectacles. She wondered why he was making such a face.

"Are you nervous about setting sail in this fog?" she asked.

He frowned and dismissed her question with a few rolls of his shoulders, as if loosening up after a long game of chess. "Not in the least. I've sailed through fog thicker than Stuart McGreenery's head."

He strained his mouth into a smile, but it didn't reach into his emerald eyes or crinkle the skin around his temples as usual. Perhaps he felt the finality of her last sail nipping at his heels, too. She hoped so at least.

"Have you heard from McGreenery lately?" she asked, hoping he had not. The mention of Stuart McGreenery always soured his mood. Her father's business rival ran an ever-expanding fleet out of Los Angeles and piloted one of the ships, a brig named the *Stealth*, just as her father did with the *Christina* out of San Francisco. The two men had been vying for ownership of the largest merchant shipping business in California for as long as she could recall, constantly trying to one-up the other. All rather boyish and immature.

Her father tossed aside the newsprint. "Nothing of a personal nature," he quickly answered.

Camille leaned forward and poured herself a cup of tea from the pot arranged on the table before them. She tapped her nails on her teacup as she blew on the steaming surface, the tallcase in the foyer chiming the hour. The dongs sounded a bit more melancholy than they had just the hour before.

"It seems you're nervous about something, Camille." Her father leaned back and propped an ankle over the opposite knee. She dropped her hand, hating to be so obvious.

He waited for a response, and Camille wilted under the pressure. Of course something was making her nervous, but speaking of it would make her sound as if she didn't want to marry. And she did. She *thought* she did. She leaned forward in her chair.

"What if Randall wanted to sail? He'd make a fine captain, don't you think?"

She and Randall would have so much more in common if only he would take to the sea and, of course, take her with him. Her father undid the buttons on his vest with a look of indigestion.

"Randall doesn't belong at sea, Camille. He's a man with a future ahead of him. You deserve a husband who can care for you every week of every month of every year. No sailor, no captain can do that."

She looked to the portrait of her mother hanging above the mantel, to the delicate red brushstrokes that had created her lips. Caroline Rowen's mouth was turned upward in a smile at one corner and remained straight and serious at the other. A smile Camille had never seen outside that portrait. Her mother had been dead for as long as Camille had been alive.

"But you were a captain when you married my mother," she said, twirling the sapphire gem on her left ring finger. Randall had presented it a few nights after proposing. She still couldn't believe she was actually getting married. Part of her felt ready, and if she waited much longer, every suitable man under the age of thirty would be married off. She pictured being stuck with a widower her father's age, with untamed ear whiskers, wrinkles, and a slew of motherless children. Yes, getting married now was a much more attractive option. She only wished she could force herself to be more joyful about it.

Things were perfect the way they were, just her and her father and their animated discussions at dinner about the next voyage and what they'd be transporting, whether it be lumber or ore or grapes from the valley. Grapes. She thought of the huge cluster Randall had placed in her basket. Now she'd be having dinner every evening with him instead of her father. What if Randall had asked for her hand only because of his investments? What if one day he arrived at the conclusion that choosing one of the finer debutantes, instead of the peculiar girl everyone whispered about, would have been a much better idea?

"Yes, I was away at sea most of the time," her father replied softly after a moment, his chin rumpling under his frown. "But you have no idea how often I wish I hadn't been. Things might have turned out differently. Trust me, Camille, distance like that breeds trouble. I've always told you I won't have you marrying a man of the sea, especially not when someone as fine and successful as Randall Jackson is completely smitten with you. My Camille," he said, his voice as soft and powerful as a blow from a bellows, "did you believe you'd sail with me forever?"

She wanted to say yes, just to be able to say yes. But she shook her head.

"This is all my fault," her father mumbled.

Camille sat back in the chaise longue and curled her legs beneath her. "What is?"

"I shouldn't have let you accompany me to sea all these years. I should have sent you to a proper finishing school, given you a chance to find your place here in San Francisco. Instead, I was selfish and wanted you with me every moment."

Camille relaxed her shoulders. "I don't mind your selfishness, Father."

He sent her a grin, but it was the one he used when there was a caveat attached.

"It did have to end sometime, Camille. True ladies don't belong on merchant ships, and it's high time you were a lady instead of a child."

He was right, though she wished he weren't. "True ladies" didn't sail on ships. Their palms weren't blistered from hauling line, the bridges of their noses and apples of their cheeks weren't bronzed from the sun, and they most certainly didn't associate with sailors.

Camille sighed. "Being a true lady sounds achingly dull."

Her father's contented gaze turned toward the oil painting. He had told Camille about her mother when she'd been old enough to understand. One year after their marriage, during a midnight hour, Caroline Rowen had given a final push, heard her baby girl's healthy cry, and collapsed onto sweat-drenched pillows.

"She was beautiful," he said, breaking the silence. "I wish she'd loved to sail. But like Randall, your mother became ill merely imagining the waves."

Bah! Anyone could overcome seasickness once they grew accustomed to the swell of the ocean. There was no reason Randall couldn't. Another grimace came over her father as he uncrossed his legs. He chewed the inside of his cheek.

"What's wrong, then, Father? I know you're not worried about the fog." She selfishly hoped he was in anguish over the prospect of her leaving home. What would he do without her once she became a wife and not just a daughter?

He snapped to attention and straightened his shoulders.

"I'm only concerned that you don't understand how a marriage works," he said, deflating her expectations. "You didn't get any examples from me, that's for certain. You'll be Randall's wife. If he's here on land, you must be, too."

She shook her head but stayed quiet. What could she say to that? She was aware of the rules required of her now. Heavens, she disliked rules. She'd always believed her father had, too, though lately he'd turned as starchy as the collars of his shirts. He was relieved she wouldn't turn out to be the city's eccentric spinster, yes, but something still seemed to nag him.

Her father sat forward, resting his hand on her knee. "I only wish you happiness, Camille. You will be happy with Randall, won't you?"

She licked her lips. If there was any way to explain how she felt about Randall, she hadn't discovered it yet. He was kind and generous, sincere and witty, with a smile that could probably charm the black off a grieving widow's frock. Girls fawned over him at every social gathering, even just passing by him on the street. So why did Camille feel nothing more than two lips on her own when he kissed her? No fire, no heat, no matter how hard she tried?

Her father's hopeful smile stretched across his cheeks, waiting for her answer. There seemed to be only one acceptable answer to give.

"Of course we'll be happy together, Father."

The pocket doors rolled aside and Juanita entered, balancing two silver-domed plates.

"Now, no more talk of the future," he said, clearing room on the shin-high table for Juanita to set the plates. "You won't see another breakfast like this until we reach Sydney."

Juanita lifted the domes, and Camille caught sight

of a cluster of Randall's red-skinned grapes on the edge of her full plate. She took a bite of toast and swallowed hard.

"I may have to leave for the wharf early to make sure the lading is finished. We have a few new sailors on for this voyage," her father said. He wiped the edges of his mouth and took a brass pocket watch from his vest.

Camille cleared her throat, feeling lightened by the change of subject.

"So, Oscar won't be along this time?" she asked, attempting to sound indifferent. Oscar Kildare had worked for her father for four years, but to William he was more like a son. To Camille . . . well, she didn't quite know what he was. Oscar had a way of sliding in and out of her mind with velvety ease, leaving a wake of improper notions behind. He hadn't signed on for this last voyage, and she thought it a bit out of the ordinary.

Her father returned the pocket watch to his vest and cut his eyes away from her.

"Does it matter if he won't be along?"

She picked at the hash on her plate, anxious to do something with her hands.

"No, I suppose not." She'd challenged her father's authority enough for one morning.

"I know you and Oscar have developed a kind of acquaintance over the last few years," he began. Camille furrowed her brow; she wouldn't have called it an acquaintance. She helped Juanita cook a birthday dinner for Oscar every September, and Oscar had once, for no reason at all, surprised her with a piece of intricate scrimshaw he'd carved on a shark's tooth. Acquaintances didn't do those kinds of things.

But then, Camille wouldn't have called it a friendship, either. Friends didn't sit in awkward silence if they unexpectedly found themselves alone in a room, with no one else present to carry the conversation. Camille saw herself and Oscar as somewhere in between, as if they were both heading in the same direction and might meet up someplace sometime and suddenly start laughing and feeling at ease with each other.

"However," her father continued as he forked up a pile of eggs. "After you're married, keeping acquaintances with other men, even Oscar, would be inappropriate. You realize that, of course? Your one duty, your one focus, is your marriage. You can't afford to have any . . . distractions." He said the last word softly, as if it might be taken as blasphemy.

The hash slid off Camille's fork, and the silver handle slipped in her suddenly sweaty fingers.

"Oh, of — of course. Yes, I realize that." Heat rushed to her face. Oscar had been her *private* distraction. Or so she'd believed.

"Of course you do," her father said. He left a last strip of bacon on his plate and replaced the silver dome. "Go on. Finish breakfast, and I'll meet you at the wharf in an hour."

He kissed her on the forehead before rolling open the pocket doors and disappearing into the foyer. Camille sat immobile. So now her father was not only banning her from the ocean but from the whole of male Californian society as well? The next thing she knew, he'd be telling her to hurry up, pack her things, and move out already. End of life as she knew it.

Lost of an appetite, Camille stood up and took a last look at her mother's portrait. She couldn't fathom that her mother hadn't loved the ocean. But it wasn't the sea Camille would miss most. The bond that really counted — the one between her and her father — had already started to weaken. It seemed all she could do was stand ashore and watch him sail away.

TWO

The *Christina* lay docked to the California Wharf, a fresh glaze of copper on the hull of the colossal navy blue, three-masted bark. Her father had crafted the hull out of superior white oak, the deck of hardy white pine, and the ship's insignia had been carved into the starboard side in deep, rich red. Camille had memorized every nook and cranny of the ship as well as she had the intricate brushstrokes of her mother's portrait.

The fog parted in gaps and started to lift, taking her apprehension with it. She stood on the edge of the wharf, activity stirring behind her. She raised the hem of her cornflower-blue silk dress and started for the gangway. All around, stevedores hauled crates and rigging to a great brig opposite the *Christina*. Despite its being a cool February morning, she smelled the bite of the workers' sweat as they hurried past. Sandwiched between the two ships, Camille felt comforted, like a swaddled baby.

She followed the two sailors carrying her trunk up the gangway. As she reached the top, an arm stretched out over the portal. She glanced up and saw Oscar waiting for her hand.

"Good morning, Miss Rowen." His voice was low and even, like someone trying to speak quietly in the middle of the night.

She grasped his hand delicately, and his coarse, chapped skin closed around hers. How many times had they touched over the last four years? Not many, but she was certain she could recall each and every time clearly. His touch always left a prickling sensation on her skin that was hard to shake. And hard to forget.

"Oscar, I thought you weren't coming on this voyage," she said, not surprised at the sudden buoyancy of her stomach. It seemed to float right up to her heart and lungs whenever she caught sight of him. Everything eventually settled, but it was that first glimpse of his broad shoulders, lean waist, and muscular legs that always made her breathless.

Oscar smiled, his blue eyes glinting in the coming sun. A perfect dimple formed in each smooth-shaven cheek, and she noticed his dark blond hair had grown a bit since she'd last seen him. His shirt, a crisp, checked fustian button-down, was new. Though his black, loose trousers were the same pair he wore on every sail. It had been weeks since Oscar had come for dinner or for a pipe with her father in his study. Camille liked to think that he'd been avoiding Randall. That perhaps he hadn't wanted to see Randall edge his way into the closest seat next to William, the one Oscar had owned for some time.

Oscar tightened his hand around hers. "Last-minute change," he said.

Camille's palms started to sweat; her breath came back to her in a choppy rhythm. She looked down, realized she hadn't moved from the gangway, and quickly stepped over the portal. She took her hand out of his, worried he'd felt the unladylike dampness through her silk gloves.

"My father asked you to change your mind?"

Oscar lifted a single shoulder. The half shrug. It was his silent way of saying yes to questions he wasn't sure he should answer. Especially questions posed by Camille. She squinted at him, appraising his expression. But he'd never allowed his expressions to give him away before, and he continued to stay true to that.

"No need for your help, Kildare." Randall stepped over the portal behind Camille, surprising her. They had said their farewells in the back courtyard, but perhaps Randall had wanted to bid her father a safe voyage as well. "I've never known a woman more able to find her way aboard a ship."

He straightened his jacket and eyed the water below, cheeks blanching from the slight roll of the harbor current.

Oscar hoisted the crate he'd set down to help Camille aboard. "And I've never seen a man lose his color from a few playful waves."

He turned and continued with his work, leaving Randall to smolder. The warmth of Oscar's fingers lingered on Camille's hand. If only Randall's touch could do the same thing. It would have made things easier. It would have been more acceptable. And then she could forget the way Oscar, a man from a world beneath her own, made her feel.

William walked over and patted Randall on the back, a salve that tended to work marvels whenever his future son-in-law and Oscar exchanged words. The two young men could argue about anything — the best ports for trade, the most efficient routes, news from the East, even the price of pipe tobacco. Oscar didn't have a refined way about arguing, either. He raised his voice, took low jabs, and even used profanity at times, though always with a soft apology for Camille on his next breath.

"You're right, Randall," her father said. "This girl could find her way around the *Christina* blindfolded." William then followed Oscar up to the quarterdeck, out of earshot.

"I don't know why your father insists keeping that harbor urchin on," Randall whispered to Camille.

"He's not a harbor urchin anymore," she said, thinking back to the afternoon she'd arrived home to find Oscar, then a tall, skinny fifteen-year-old, in the kitchen devouring Juanita's supper roast. Her father had been sitting beside him, fit to burst with the story of how Oscar had come to his rescue from some pickpocket. He'd taken him in on the *Christina*, given him work, and nurtured the malnourished boy into a capable, well-muscled sailor. Her father had cared for Oscar as if he'd been his own child.

"Your father should have left him on the streets where he found him," Randall said, as if he'd been peering into her memory. Camille pulled at the blue silk ribbon holding her floppy brimmed hat firmly atop her head. The ribbon cut into her throat, and as soon as the ship left the bay, she would rip the hat off and stuff it in her trunk with the rest of her proper, respectable things.

She walked to the railing and leaned out. Beneath her, moss-colored water slapped and sucked at the smooth hull.

"It's just Oscar's nature to have a sharp tongue," she said. "Don't take it personally."

"It's also the nature of the Irish to be lazy and fond of the ale tub," he said.

She shot him a warning glance. "I don't think it would be wise to let my father hear you speaking about Oscar that way."

"Of course not. I wouldn't want to insult William's protégé," Randall replied, the mockery—and envy—not lost from his tone. "Your father didn't do himself any favors by making Kildare first mate. There are plenty of other crewmen with more experience who deserved that post."

The recent promotion hadn't surprised Camille one bit. Her father had long been grooming Oscar for first mate and, ultimately, for a position in Rowen & Company as captain. The afternoon of Oscar's brave pickpocket rescue, her father had claimed he'd seen strength, bravery, and determination he'd rarely witnessed in another person. Perfect qualities for a man of the sea. Though it now seemed those sparkling qualities hadn't earned him a place within Camille's new life.

"Let's talk about something else," she suggested, not wanting to dwell on whom she would or wouldn't be able to associate with after her wedding.

"You're right," Randall conceded. He slid one hand around her waist, the other still holding his cigar. She hadn't put on a corset that morning and hoped he didn't notice the usual pleats and ridges of whalebone and steel were missing. "Let's forget it, shall we? I'm not going to see you for some time, and talk of Kildare isn't my idea of a romantic farewell."

He drew back a lock of her hair and allowed his thumb to travel down the curve of her neck. She waited for the fire of gooseflesh followed by a pull of sorrow over leaving Randall for so long. Nothing came except the creak of the ship's deck behind them.

"We're shoving off," her father announced. He wore indigo trousers and a white shirt with gold filigree buttons. The cuff links on his matching indigo coat caught the glare of the sun. He looked so smart, so handsome, and Camille beamed at him with unabashed pride.

"Randall," Camille began and, even though she knew and partly hoped he would decline, said, "you could come with us, too. You'd find your sea legs within a few days."

Oscar passed by them once again and snickered, intentionally loud. Camille pursed her lips, wishing he wouldn't spur her fiancé on so relentlessly. She didn't like to see Randall upset, the flare of his nostrils, or the absence of his easygoing charm. It reminded her that there was much about Randall she still didn't know. Sides of him that she might not enjoy.

"If we're to expand the fleet next quarter, I'll need to be here to take care of the arrangements," Randall answered her without more than a glance in Oscar's direction.

"You mean you'll need to be here to drink brandy, smoke cigars, and laugh at jokes told by a bunch of pompous old men," Oscar said as he passed by.

Randall threw down his cigar and ground it into the plank. "Clearly, there are some matters that are far above you."

Oscar stopped, turned slowly, and eyed the mangled cigar. "I run a tidy ship. You'll be needing to clean that up before you go."

Randall pressed back his shoulders and stepped forward, coming toe-to-toe with Oscar.

"You run nothing but your mouth, Kildare."

William stepped between them, placing a hand on Oscar's arm.

"Enough. I think it's high time the two of you got along. Randall is, after all, going to be a permanent fixture in the Rowen family, Oscar," William said. Oscar looked away with a hard glare, over to another brig, as if something more important was taking place there.

"See to your duties," William ordered him. Before Oscar turned and walked off, he sent an equally hard glare at Camille. His eyes flicked swiftly to Randall's hand resting on her waist. Her first thought was to peel Randall's fingers from her side, but she knew it was foolish to even entertain such thoughts.

"Randall," her father began. "I trust you have much to do in the next four months."

Four months? Camille turned to her father.

"You said we'd be back in two."

William coughed and leaned closer to his daughter, as if revealing a secret. "I've planned a brief extension in Australia for us."

She gasped and took his hand. "You have?"

Randall fished another cigar from his case and squinted at him. "You have?"

Her father simply placed a finger to his lips and walked off. She should never have doubted him. Of course he would have figured a way to make this last trip together special, and to surprise her like this made it even better. Too thrilled to contain herself, Camille threw her arms around Randall and kissed his cheek. He smiled wide, looking pleased by her attention.

"Perhaps you can use the extension to find pieces for the house," he said, curling his palm around the nape of her neck. His hand seemed to weigh as much as the ship's anchor rising noisily into the cathead. Why did everything feel like such a rush lately?

"Have a safe voyage," he whispered in her ear. "Once you return, you'll make me the happiest man in San Francisco. And I'm hoping" — he took her hand in his — "that I'll make you happy, too, Camille. You've always been so adventurous, so different from the other girls we grew up with. Really, it's what drew me to you." He twisted a dark ringlet of her hair around his finger. "But I do promise to make life — even life on land — an adventure for you."

She thought about her father's question earlier that morning, if she and Randall would be happy together. He truly was in love with her. As she took in his earnest eyes, the admiration in his gaze, Camille felt silly for being so worried. She and Randall *were* a smart match. She kissed him gently.

"Of course you will, Randall."

He smiled and kissed her once more, lingering a moment before turning to leave.

She walked to the port side as the men below unwrapped waist-thick hemp ropes from the wharf's bulbous cast-iron bollards. The ship rocked beneath her feet and made small pushes into the bay. The canvas mainsail unfurled and caught a gust of wind, flattening the brim of her hat against her forehead. Randall stubbed out his second cigar on the wharf, working it into the damp wood before raising his hand to wave. She waved back, invigorated by the unexpected yearning to return to him. Being away for so long might give her the slap of reason she desperately required. Of course she was fortunate to have Randall. How could she have ever thought otherwise? Even with all the genteel girls coming out of their season ripe and ready for the picking, this man wanted her, blistered palms, bronzed skin, and all.

The rooftops of San Francisco soon dropped from the horizon, and her worries cooled under a sharp westerly wind. As Camille untied the ribbon and pulled off her hat, she vowed to make an honest attempt to fall in love with Randall. She had four months to dig through her soul and unearth the feelings she knew were hiding somewhere. But right then, at that moment, she was a free woman. Camille breathed in deeply and turned from the rail.

THREE

*Y*ou wanna keep the rope taut. Like this, ya see?" Mickey, one of her father's seasoned mates, gripped a long length of rope between his calloused fingers. Camille watched his skilled hands twist and turn, forming a halyard toggle out of the hemp.

"Thank you, Mickey, but I know how to make a toggle. Do you think you might show me the French shroud knot instead?"

He yanked the rope straight. "Sure, but it's a bit more complicated."

She sat on the top of a barrel and waited for him to begin. Complicated was just what she needed. They were a handful of weeks into the sail, and Camille still didn't miss Randall the way she should. She needed something to distract her.

A half dozen sailors lounged on deck, enjoying the sunny Sunday afternoon and anticipating their arrival at the island of Maui that night. They gathered behind

Mickey, each calling out steps they thought he had missed or some other piece of instruction.

"Mickey, do I have to show you how to do everything?"

Lucius, a younger boy near Camille's age, rose up from the warmed planks of the deck. He had tossed his shirt aside earlier, as had some of the others, exposing his tan skin and narrow waist. Most of her father's young sailors cared little that a woman was aboard, and thought nothing of exposing chests and arms. The older men, like Mickey, kept their shirts on, either because they acknowledged her or, Camille smiled, because their bellies were not worthy of such display. Lucius strutted over, his hair, the color of beach sand, rustling in the breeze.

"Give me the rope," he commanded. Camille raised a brow as she handed it over. Out of the twenty men her father had signed on for this trip, Lucius Drake was the greenest. His smug grin and proud step had already started to rub Camille and the crew the wrong way.

His hands blurred in a flurry of movement, leaving the hemp a tangled mass. The men doubled over, howling with laughter. Red-faced, Lucius threw the rope at the snickering crowd and took back his position amidships. Mickey began to rhyme:

> *"Lucius Drake*
> *thought he could make*
> *a knot so tight,*
> *it would not break!"*

The rhyme grew louder and louder, with whistles and hoots thrown in. Lucius lay with his eyes closed, jaw set, until he finally bolted up.

"All right, you've had your fun. Now why don't you all shut—" He stopped and looked past their heads. They turned and fell silent. Oscar watched them from a few yards away on the quarterdeck, his expression as solid as his frame. The boys threw their white cotton shirts back on and spread out.

"We'll practice another time, Miss Rowen," Mickey whispered as he settled near a tall spool of hemp and began braiding more rope. The deck quieted. She glanced back at Oscar's towering figure and squinted into the sunlight.

"You certainly have a way with them," she said.

A smile cracked Oscar's stony cheeks. "So do you."

Camille scooped up the piece of rope from the deck and untied it.

"Mickey was only trying to help me with this knot."

Oscar rested his elbows on the rail of the quarterdeck, dimples still creasing his cheeks. "You need help with knots as much as I need help with sailing, Camille. I think the men just enjoy showing off in front of you."

Camille walked toward the stairs leading up to the quarterdeck, wanting to join him. Being at sea with Oscar was completely different from being on land with him. On the water, Oscar spoke to her without the stiff etiquette he showed her at home. He smiled more, too. At sea, Oscar's presence had a magnetic effect on her lips — the closer to him she got, the higher they curved into a grin.

"I think they show off for each other. It doesn't matter, anyhow. It would be pointless for them to flirt with me," she said, taking a few steps up. His presence also had an effect on her pulse, spiking it.

"It's never pointless to flirt with a beautiful girl. Especially one that's not married. *Yet,*" he added for emphasis.

Seawater misted her hot cheeks as the ship broke through azure waves. She tasted the salt on her teeth as she smiled, looking down at the rope in her hands, unsure how to respond.

A forceful voice from behind wiped the girlish smile from Camille's face.

"I'm glad you know better than to do so, Oscar."

She turned to see her father rising from the companionway. Oscar straightened and clasped his hands behind his back. He gave Camille a nod.

"Miss Rowen," he said, his cheeks stony once more. He turned to take his place behind the helm.

Her father walked over and took the rope from her hands. He raised a brow at her, holding up the hemp.

"He's right. You know every knot already."

He must have been hiding in the companionway to have overheard that part of the conversation.

"You mustn't encourage the men. They may begin to think they stand a chance with you, and making Randall jealous is not something you can afford. Oscar is correct. You aren't married, *yet*."

Camille resisted a sigh and held out her hand. He handed the rope back to her.

"We're docking in Lahaina tonight," he said. "Will you have dinner ashore with me?"

Instinctively, she glanced out past the prow of the ship, expecting to see the rise of land. Lahaina was lovely, warm and tropical, and the beaches were like nothing else she'd seen.

"Of course I will," Camille answered. "I'm famished for something fresh."

William eyed her dress and waved a finger. "I'm a lenient captain and father, but not *that* lenient."

She looked down at her dress, drenched from sea mist.

"And for once would you put some shoes on?" he asked, feigning exasperation, as he walked away. She hurried to the companionway and lowered her bare feet onto the rungs. Like the sailors, Camille kept her dress simple, with few layers and always light-colored fabrics to reflect the sun. She also preferred to walk barefoot, the soles of her feet as hardy as the leather tread of any boot. She admired her long, thin feet and toes, golden brown from the sun, and liked the feel of the rough ship timbers beneath them.

Perched on the rungs of the companionway steps, hands tight around the rope rails, Camille heard the voices of the dispersed sailors drift up from the fo'c'sle.

". . . and with a shatterin' explosion of water, eight tentacles broke the surface, high as the spanker sail, stretchin' from the prow all the way to the stern. Each sucker was bigger than the helm, and when they crashed down, four of the men lost their heads in 'em."

A breathy murmur moved through the large, arrow-shaped cabin at the bow of the ship, where the crew slept in narrow bunks stacked three high around a potbellied stove. Camille stopped to listen to the sailor's tale and wished she'd been able to catch the beginning of it.

"The serpent swallowed the ship whole, sinkin' back down into the deep, leavin' behind not even a twig of flotsam."

A snort broke the awed silence. "If the serpent ate everyone, how'd you hear about it?"

Camille grimaced at Lucius Drake's pithy voice and the way it ruined the story.

"Cap'n don't like us tellin' tales," another man added.

"That's just 'round his girl, is all," the storyteller replied.

Camille ceased breathing and widened her eyes. They were right about her father banning such rubbish aboard his ships, but she'd never known she was the reason for it. Why did he feel the need to protect her from them? The few parts of stories she had managed to overhear were entertaining but obvious malarkey to scare young sailors out of their wits.

"If he thinks she's too fine for them, he shouldn't bring

her along," Lucius said, his sneer reaching through to his tone of voice.

"This is her last time, ain't it?" another sailor asked.

Her stomach cramped at the unwelcome reminder.

"If it is, I wager it'll be Kildare's, too. He won't stick 'round no more," another chuckled. Camille's ears perked at Oscar's name, then reddened at the sailor's implication that Oscar was there only for her. It was absurd.

"Good," Lucius replied. "Who will be our new first mate?"

What were they going on about? Oscar was a perfect first mate. Her father had groomed him for it. Oscar couldn't just . . . leave.

"Well, it won't be you, Drake. You can't even make a shroud knot!"

The sailors in the fo'c'sle burst out in laughter. Grabbing her chance to leave, Camille took off down the corridor until their laughter faded with the sighs of the ship.

The crew craned their necks to gawk at a ruby sunset as they moored in the whaling town of Lahaina. Bodies filled the wharf and harborside as dories from the *Christina* splashed into the water. Sailors rowed across the shallow bay, schools of silvery fish darting off in jagged lines as the oars chopped the surface.

Camille and her father left the ship in Oscar's able hands and went ashore. Dark-skinned girls with long, brown legs, curvaceous hips, and voluptuous breasts greeted the sailors as they beached their dories on the white sand. Camille watched the men drape their arms over sun-kissed shoulders. She peered down at her own figure—boyish hips, the small rise of her own breasts—and felt closer to seven than seventeen.

Smoke curled up from an open-sided, thatched-roof hut near the beach, where coals had most likely been stoked and a feast prepared when the *Christina* appeared along the horizon. Colorful walled tents lined the shore, tables and chairs and beach mats spread out for them. During dinner, a native man drummed a slow beat on smooth pigskin stretched over a hollow jug. Camille reclined in a wicker chair, feeling the stillness of the land just as profoundly as the toss of the ship.

"There's something you're not telling me," her father said as he sipped a drink made of rum and guava juice. Camille turned her attention away from a young Chinese man basting a wild boar on an open spit.

"About what?" she asked, raising her cup to her lips.

"Randall."

Camille sipped more of her punch than intended. It burned her throat.

"I don't keep secrets from you," she said, but her voice caught on the way out. Was that the truth? She used to tell her father every thought that entered her head, every idea and every opinion. But how could she tell him how she felt about Randall, when she didn't even know herself? Camille stared at the plate of halved and seeded papaya, fresh octopus, and thick slices of pink ham. She heard her father sigh as she took a reluctant bite of octopus.

"My Camille. There are certain things you need to know now," he said with hesitation. "Things you need to be aware of with your wedding night coming up."

Confused, she glanced at her father, who always knew the right thing to say in any situation. He looked away, a bloom of red coloring his cheeks. She immediately understood what he was about to say. The octopus slid to a stop in her throat and she started to cough. Her father didn't seem to hear her hacking as he tumbled over his words.

"I wish there was a woman for you to speak to about it." He paused, staring out at the bay as Camille fumbled for her drink. "About the things that go on between men and women . . ."

With a final gag, the piece of octopus sailed out of her mouth and landed on the table between them. She stared at it, disgusted, and crinkled her nose. Her father finally turned back to her and saw her expression.

"Blast! You're horrified. I knew I shouldn't have said anything," he said, pushing back his chair.

"It's not that, Father." Camille quickly covered the mangled octopus with her napkin and whisked it to her lap. "It's just not the most comfortable of subjects."

"For either of us," he mumbled. "But I'm your father, and I must impress how important it is for you to take this marriage seriously. I don't like the way you act around

Oscar, and he is much too familiar with you. Randall should be the only man you pay attention to."

Having a chunk of slimy octopus stuck in her throat was suddenly preferable as her father searched her eyes. They were the color of the harbor, he'd often told her when she was still small enough to curl into a ball in his lap as he told her stories in front of the fireplace before bedtime. He had a matching pair, but a hint of distrust clouded them now.

"I don't know what you mean. Oscar is just Oscar," she said, feeling guilty for the lie. "Honestly, this marriage is beginning to sound more like a prison sentence." She sliced a crescent of papaya with enough force to send the knife screeching off the plate.

"Don't be dramatic, Camille. But I do wish you wouldn't fight this wedding. I've noticed your reluctance, and I worry Randall has as well. And if the wedding were to be canceled and Randall's investments pulled . . ." He rubbed the ivory handle of his fork with sudden aggression. Camille returned the knife to her plate and leaned forward.

"What *would* happen, Father? Randall's investment was hefty, yes, but we'd be fine without it," she said, inspecting him. The muscles in his cheeks flinched. "Wouldn't we?"

He avoided looking directly at her, but when she didn't waver, he gave in. "Camille, the truth is . . . the truth is that in the last few years, I've made some rather poor choices regarding my own investments. Whale oil that didn't deliver, companies that folded, ships that wrecked." He tucked his chin into his chest and fiddled with the napkin spread over his lap. "No, Camille, we wouldn't be fine. Randall's investment is the only thing keeping us afloat."

Her fingertips tingled with shock. She tried to swallow, but her tongue stuck to the roof of her mouth.

"I've only shielded you from everything because I didn't want you to worry," he said, correctly anticipating a demand to know why she'd been kept in the dark.

"But I could have helped. I could have —"

Her father waved a hand. "There was nothing you could do at the time. But now, Camille, don't you see how vital your role is? With Randall's support, Rowen & Company is impenetrable again. If you were to turn away from him or give him a reason to turn away from you or the company, we'd be ruined."

His words fell into her lap like wet sod. Ruined. Her father, herself, poverty-stricken. And their deliverance rested solely on her shoulders. On her wedding.

"Does Randall know?" she asked.

"No," he answered briskly. "He would have taken his inheritance elsewhere if he had, I'm sure. He isn't to know. No one is, if you don't want our name tarnished."

Like an oxidized copper penny turning a finger green, they'd be tinged with disgrace if anyone knew about their desperation. And Randall. He'd be furious about the deception. He'd cancel the wedding. They'd lose everything, and then no one — not even the flabby old widower with a horde of children — would want to marry her.

"I won't say a word," she promised as she thought of

all her father had worked for, all he'd done to build the company he cherished. To build a good, prosperous life for the daughter he loved enough to humiliatingly depend upon a twenty-year-old man.

She quickly took a big swig of her drink and shoved another bite of octopus into her mouth. They ate the rest of dinner in silence, each paying more attention than they normally would have to the beat of the drums and the whistle of woodwind instruments. Camille avoided any further conversation with her father as island men and women, along with members of the crew who had filled their mugs one too many times, danced. She didn't even notice him rise from his chair until he waved his arms about. He whistled to silence the crew and their singing.

"I'm glad you're all enjoying yourselves—and the rum," her father said. The men cheered, raised their mugs to him, and then toasted each other all around. Mugs slammed into neighboring mugs, dark rum sloshing over the brims onto hands and wrists as the men grunted incoherent things to one another. Once they quieted down, her father continued.

"I do have an announcement to make. The *Christina* will not be returning directly to San Francisco after business is completed in Sydney."

The men turned their flushed cheeks toward their captain, some even stopping mid-gulp. Camille considered their extended stay in Sydney, hoping she and her father could reconnect somehow while there. How could he have kept his financial ruin from her? Perhaps if they spent more time together, took in a performance at the Royal Victoria Theatre, or shopped in the Markets, or even just ambled through Hyde Park arm in arm . . . maybe time alone was all they needed for her father to realize he truly *could* depend on her.

William cleared his throat to continue his announcement.

"Instead, we'll be charting a course toward Port Adelaide. I understand this was not made clear to you beforehand, and I do apologize for that."

Camille uncrossed her ankles as his words trickled through her images of their Sydney holiday. Port Adelaide? He hadn't said a word about Port Adelaide.

"I am a fair captain, and so I will release any of you from your contract should you not wish to spend an extra two months aboard the *Christina*. There will be a ship leaving Lahaina for San Francisco the day after next, I am told. However, those of you who are on deck tomorrow morning will be paid a handsome advance. Good evening."

The men looked at one another, their glazed eyes reflecting their confusion and indecision. Disappointment soured Camille's belly as the men's grumbles set in. This extension of her father's didn't seem to have anything at all to with spending time with her.

"What is going on?" she asked, following him as he ducked out of the tent, leaving the men to their rum and decisions. "I thought you said we'd be taking an extension in Sydney."

The thick sand was difficult to tread, and her father had picked up his pace. She swiftly loosened the laces of her boots, ripped them off, and then hurried to catch up to him.

"I said it would be an extension in *Australia*," he replied, still heading for the beached dories. Cool, white sand filled the spaces between her toes as she grasped his arm.

"But why would you withhold this from me? I'm your daughter, not a member of your crew."

Blustery warm winds came in off the ocean, swaying the spiked fronds of palm trees skirting the beach. Her father's sun-streaked russet hair parted and flattened to the side as he finally stopped and faced her.

"It was a last-minute change, Camille. That's all."

He started again for one of the small boats they'd taken to shore, but she wasn't satisfied. Her father had purposely waited until arriving in Lahaina to inform the crew, knowing none of them would stay behind as they might have done if given the option in San Francisco.

"Why Port Adelaide? It's not one of your ports."

Her father motioned to a dory. Camille reluctantly climbed in and seated herself. He shoved the boat into the water, then jumped in, taking the oars and thrusting them below the surface. He looked past her, keeping his eyes locked on the *Christina* as he rowed. He wasn't going to answer her. She took deep, calming breaths of salty, flower-infused air as they rowed across the bay.

The dory knocked up against the hull of the bark. The

rope ladder swayed as she climbed, her father at her heels. Oscar appeared at the top, pulling her up and over with ease. He did the same with William.

"How did it go with the men?" Oscar asked him. Camille swiveled toward her father.

"He knew about Port Adelaide?"

Oscar took a step back and averted his eyes.

"Camille, he's first mate. Of course he knew," her father said, picking up speed toward the companionway. Again, she stayed on his heels.

"And I'm your daughter. Surely that position falls somewhere above the common swab."

Belowdecks, her father made his way toward the stern and his spacious cabin.

He sighed. "You're overreacting."

"Oh, I am sorry, but it's been an evening of shocking surprises."

He quickly glanced back at her, his lips tight. Perhaps it was the promise of solitude, or the prospect of a glass of sherry and a pipe, but as he reached his door, he turned around and gave her a shaving of an answer.

"I had a letter asking me to come to Port Adelaide. There is something I need to retrieve there." His expression remained blank, unreadable, and nothing at all like him as he stood in the entrance to his cabin. It was as though he purposely kept his expression that way to fend off her inquisition. He'd planned on this, she realized. He knew she would hurl a barrage of questions at him, and he'd been prepared for it. The floor creaked behind her. She turned and saw Oscar coming across the galley, toward her father's cabin.

"The men?" her father asked him.

"They're coming," Oscar answered. Relief spread over her father's unyielding expression. When he turned back to her, the veil came down over his face once more.

"Go to bed, Camille," he repeated. He shut the door, leaving her to stare at the lead-trimmed gold-and-red diamonds of the stained-glass window. Who had she just been speaking to? Certainly not her father, the man who had always been so open with her about everything, even attempting to discuss the goings-on of men and women behind bedroom doors.

Oscar poured a ladleful of water into a cup and held it out to Camille. She stormed up to him.

"Do you know who the letter is from? What it says?" she asked, ignoring the water. Oscar set the cup on the table. He took a step toward her, leaving only a small gap of space between them. She inhaled sharply and, for a moment, thought he might touch her. For a moment, she wanted to feel the prickle of her skin beneath the warmth of his hand. It would calm her, no doubt. Calm and excite at the same time.

"I wish I could, Camille, but I can't talk about it. I'm sorry."

He hesitated, still standing close enough for her to trace his ration of rum on his breath. He pushed the cup of water toward her and then moved back into the shadows of the corridor. Camille heard drunken sailors toppling over the railing onto the deck and a startled cry as one slipped off the rope ladder and fell back into the bay with a great splash.

She wrapped her fingers around the cup and stared into the water, furious with Oscar. Her father had always been so proud of him, first about whipping the devil out of that pickpocket, then about the way Oscar had so flawlessly taken to the sea. He trusted Oscar more than he trusted his own daughter. Of course her father loved her, she was confident about that, but she had never done anything to make him truly *proud*. And now that she was to marry and leave him for a new life, she'd never have the chance. Damn Oscar and his water. Camille emptied the cup back into the barrel and went to the welcome solitude of her cabin.

FOUR

$\mathscr{S}$itting on the maintop, one arm wrapped around the topmast, Camille stared out into the rippling green ocean. Rain spit down on the *Christina*, lighter than the previous four days of wet weather. The steady winds had died as well, and the sailcloth hung limp, suspending the ship as it made its way through the Tasman Sea. Camille had climbed to the maintop, a small square of planking midway up the mainmast. She wore trousers instead of her usual skirts. Climbing the ratline or shinnying along the footropes under the main yard would be too dangerous with skirts flapping about.

Camille watched as most of the crew shuffled below-decks to eat their beef stew and hardtack, the rain falling lightly on their shoulders. She wasn't hungry. She'd eaten by herself at each meal as the *Christina* cruised south of the equator past clusters of palm-covered islands studding the South Pacific. She'd avoided her father and Oscar as much as possible. Not even the passing of another vessel along their busy shipping route, or the exchange of letters and packages from captain to captain, had managed to lift her from her sulking.

She either stayed in her cabin sewing a quilt she'd been halfheartedly working on for years or sat on deck encircled by stiff canvas that needed mending. When her fingers tired, she opened one of the books she kept in the bottom drawer of her bureau and read well into the night. She attempted anything to avoid thinking about the secret her father was keeping from her and how much it hurt to be excluded. Often she found her eyes drifting from the pages. This secret about Port Adelaide was driving her mad.

"There won't be any supper left if you stay up here long enough."

Oscar popped his head up through the lubber's hole and rested his elbows on the platform.

"There's more hardtack on this ship than timber," she replied without looking at him.

"You should come down. Especially with that moving in." He nodded north of the starboard side. Dark clouds gathered a few miles away, close to the water's surface.

"It might not come south."

"It will," Oscar assured her. "Shouldn't be bad, though. Not the season." He started to move down the mainmast, hooking his boots on the metal rungs.

"The men are upset about the sail to Port Adelaide," Camille called as his head disappeared beneath the lubber's hole. He climbed up and sent her a satisfied grin, looking victorious that she'd spoken to him on her own accord. She started to smile in return but caught herself. Her father had noticed the way she looked at Oscar, and maybe Randall had, too. Before dinner on Lahaina's beach, before she'd learned they were completely dependent upon Randall, she might have brushed off her father's warning not to jeopardize the wedding. But now she couldn't risk it.

"Are you upset?" he asked.

Oh, if Oscar only knew the half of it.

"Of course I am. My father's treating me like I'm nothing more than a member of his crew."

Oscar looked out to the dark clouds. His eyes were the lightest blue Camille had ever seen, gray when the sun went in behind the clouds. The years he had spent at sea with her father had already weathered his skin, etching thin lines across his temples, making him look older than his nineteen years. But he was still handsome, in a rough, resilient kind of way.

Heat rushed to her ears as Oscar turned away from the darkening clouds and caught her staring at him.

"I don't like keeping secrets from you, Camille." Her heart skipped as it usually did whenever he called her by her given name. He only ever did so when they were alone; all other times, on land and at sea, he addressed her formally.

"Then, please, tell me who the letter is from," she said.

He pulled a black yarn cap from his coat pocket and stretched it over his head.

"You know I can't." He began to descend again. The wind drove her forward as she stood and grabbed hold of the mainmast. Camille passed through the lubber's hole, searching for the first rung with her toes.

"Not that you'll listen to me, but they do make shoes your size," Oscar called from below.

Camille lowered herself rung by rung, the metal wet from drizzle. Her toes curled around each rung where the soles of any shoe might slip. The thunderheads caught her attention as a bolt of serrated white lightning streaked through. The wind, pushing in from the north, grew stronger. Oscar had been right. The storm was moving toward them.

Camille looked down. Oscar stood on the deck with an expression of concern as he studied the storm. She resumed her descent, peering up every now and again at the clouds. Her feet hit the deck.

"Your father would want you to go below."

A strand of hair came loose from her braid and flitted into her eyes. The decks had quieted, the watch thinned out for evening.

"And what Father wants, Father gets," she sighed.

It wasn't prudent to say anything negative about her father to a member of his crew, but with Oscar she felt a sense of freedom from the rules. A freedom that sometimes edged near dangerous, especially when she allowed herself to enjoy his company too much. *He's a sailor,* she reminded herself. *A man of the sea.*

The renegade strand of hair nipped her eyes once

more. With a swift, steady hand, Oscar pushed it away from her face. His fingertip left a trail of fire along her cheek. Camille reached up to help him tuck the strand back, and their fingers met. She knew for certain the flush had returned to her ears.

Oscar dropped his arm and walked to the rail, wrapping his strong hands around the carved wood.

"He is used to having things go his way," Oscar said, his voice low and only for her ears. Camille moved to stand beside him.

"Have you always done everything he's asked of you?" She was cautious not to come off sounding snide.

His knuckles whitened as he gripped the rail tighter, as if to hold something back. Hold something in.

"No."

She hadn't expected him to give her an answer, and certainly not that one.

"No? I don't believe it. What have you done that's gone against his wishes?"

Oscar had been her father's shadow since day one. He'd watched and obeyed William Rowen with the kind of devotion any eager apprentice would show his teacher.

Oscar had been staring at the water, at the mounting churn of the waves. Now he shifted his eyes to her and fixed her with a look so strong and deep, she felt helpless beneath it.

"He asked me to stop associating with you," he answered, still hushed. Camille's eyes watered with mortification and dread. Her father had spoken to Oscar, too. She wiped her sweaty palms on the hips of her trousers.

"But clearly," Oscar continued, leaning toward her, "I didn't listen."

His gaze revolved out to the ocean again, releasing Camille. Air flowed back down her windpipe. This was beyond humiliation. Her father couldn't do this. He couldn't order people to stop speaking to her.

"Why not?" she asked, her breath uneven from a cross of fury and the steadfast way Oscar had looked at her. "He could fire you."

He moved away from the rail.

"If he wants to fire me for speaking to you, for looking at you . . ." He turned back to her on his way to the quarter-deck and held her gaze again. "Then I'll risk it."

. She watched in awe as Oscar took the helm from a sailor and placed himself behind the great spoked wheel. He'd risk everything he had to be able to speak with her, to just look at her. His bravery made her feel no taller than a hermit crab. She'd so quickly, dutifully, accepted her father's request to set her focus solely on Randall. But she mattered to Oscar. She *mattered*, and that one truth made her wish she was brave enough to risk everything, too.

A deceptive calm settled over the *Christina* as night approached. Camille came up the companionway a few hours after eating a bowl of cold stew in her cabin and entered the ominous air shared by those on evening watch. She walked toward Oscar, who stood at the helm behind the teakwood wheel that was centered with a hammered gold leaf sunburst medallion. It was the ship's solitary colorful ornament. The blackness of the storm had seeped beneath the water's surface, and gusty winds whipped up the canvas that had been still all day. Camille said nothing to Oscar as she reached his side. No words were needed. She could taste the strangeness of the storm. The sea was coming to life.

"We're in for a long night," her father said as he came to stand beside them. Shafts of lightning led the way for growls of thunder. "Oscar, give the order for oilskins. We'll need all hands on deck."

He started to walk away, then turned. "Camille, go below now."

She peeled her eyes away from the rippling ocean. In the peculiar yellow light, she noticed every line, every crease of her father's skin.

"I can be useful on deck, at least until—"

"Go below. To your cabin," he repeated. She dropped her shoulders as he cupped his hands around his mouth and shouted, "Lay the yards! Reef and furl!" The men on the main yard raced one another to hoist and lash the sails.

Camille took one last look at the skies before going below. She should have listened to Randall when he'd asked her to stay behind. Instead of cherishing this final snippet of time with her father, she'd come to feel like an unwanted guest. The cool, damp air made her shiver as she traveled the corridor toward her cabin. The last thing she wanted to do was go inside and while away the storm by paging through one of her novels.

Camille stopped in front of her door and peered down the corridor. Through the galley she spotted the diamond-patterned stained-glass windows. She'd always been welcomed into her father's cabin, invited to sit and read or take her meals and tea. But she hadn't stepped foot inside since Lahaina. Why didn't he want her to know anything about what or who had driven the change in his charted course? The letter her father had spoken of was inside the cabin, no doubt. In one of his desk drawers, amid cargo lists and bills, or maybe tucked safely inside his leather-bound ship's log. Perhaps somewhere in his bureau. His being so secretive only made her more curious. Why go to such lengths if it didn't have anything to do with her?

Camille looked over her shoulder, searched the corridor behind her, but it was empty. The men were all up top, including her father. Including Oscar.

I'll risk it, she thought.

Clenching her teeth, she breathed in deeply. Exhaling, she pushed out the shake of her limbs. This was a disastrous idea, she warned herself as she passed her cabin door and started for the galley. She would have to be quick, and she would have to take care to leave everything exactly the way it had been. The meticulous organization of her father's desk would not allow even a pen or piece of paper to be askew from its original place.

Pots and pans in the galley clanged into one another, and glass jars in the pantry smacked sides as the winds of the brooding storm arrived. The glass knob to her father's cabin clicked, and the sweet scent of old pipe smoke wafted under her nose. Four massive windows lined the back of the cabin, letting in the dusty, mustard-seed light. The storm clouds would swallow the light soon, she knew, so Camille shut the door and rushed to the desk.

As she yanked the center drawer open and started plundering through his papers, she felt like slapping her own hand. This was madness. Going behind her father's back, sneaking into his cabin. It was pure deceit, and it made her queasy.

Camille's fingers stumbled upon a few letters, but she dismissed them after harried scans. She shut the center drawer and moved to one of the side compartments, hoping for better luck. The mantel clock on a bookshelf in the corner of the cabin ticked softly, alerting her to her dwindling time. With shaky hands, she lifted a box of fine, bleached-linen stationery her father had shipped in regularly from New York City, and set it on the desktop. Underneath, she saw an envelope, its red wax seal crumbled.

Camille snatched it from the drawer and carefully slid two sheets of parchment paper free. She held it close to her eyes, the light almost too poor to make out the small, neat handwriting.

October 15, 1854

Dearest William,

Too many years have come and gone for me to begin this letter with any formal greeting. I owe you more than pleasantry. I owe you more than I can ever repay. Let me embark.

I am ill. Too ill to travel the great expanse of ocean I have put between us or else I would have come to you by now. Consumption binds me to my bed, and I am nearing my last days. Port Adelaide, Australia, has been my home for the last sixteen years. Though I am worthy of little for my betrayal of our sacred oath, I dare ask one final request.

I want to see Camille. I want to look at my baby one last time and beg her for forgiveness. She is grown by now, and I pray brought up by a better woman than I.

Camille's eyes smarted with tears. She could do nothing but stare at the inked sheet of paper, moistened at the edges from her palms. *My baby?* No. It was impossible. The story Camille had been told flashed through her mind—the dark winter night, the hours of difficult labor, and the blood. Her mother had lost too much blood.

"She can't be alive," Camille whispered into the gloomy cabin. Waves crashed against the wavy glass windows. Outside, the sea churned, and in her father's cabin,

Camille's stomach followed suit. Her throat tightened and she thought she might be sick.

With her head still spinning, Camille read on:

She is still a part of my soul no matter what I did to lose the man I loved, the life I wanted, and the little girl I have dreamed of for so many years.

Refuse me if you will. Crumple my letter if it brings you solace. Whether you come to ease my passage into the next world or not, understand that I must send what I carried with me in shame to Australia, back to San Francisco, to you. And so I've come to the most difficult, and most dangerous, part of my letter. You remember the map to Umandu, I am certain of that. After you returned from Sydney with it, I told

The knob to her father's cabin jiggled. Camille tore her eyes from the letter, but gritted her teeth and stayed put. She deserved an explanation and would demand one until her father relented.

The door opened, and Oscar appeared. He crinkled his brow, started to say something, but stopped at the fire in her eyes and the parchment in her hands.

"I told him to lock that up," he said. Camille came around the desk, brandishing the letter.

"How long have you known?"

Oscar motioned for her to quiet down. "William's going to be here any second, Camille. Put the letter back. We can keep this between us. I won't say a word."

Putting the letter back was out of the question. There could be no going back, not now.

"How long?" she repeated. Oscar sighed and rubbed his chin, looking back at the door. He didn't want to be in the middle of this, she could tell.

"Just before we shoved off," he finally answered.

Camille turned and threw the letter onto her father's desk.

"Why did he tell you?" *And not me,* she added to herself. The floorboards behind her dipped with Oscar's weight.

"He wanted someone he knew and trusted as first mate in case the men didn't take to the idea of Port Adelaide."

So that was the reason Oscar had changed his mind at the eleventh hour about joining the voyage.

"You should have told me," she said, sickened and shaking. His hand rested on her shoulder, barely rustling the fabric of her dress, his touch was so light and hesitant. She couldn't even feel the warmth she knew she shouldn't be yearning for.

"I wanted to, but—"

"But you're loyal to him, and only him. Isn't that right?" She moved out from under his touch. She closed her eyes and battled tears. She didn't want to cry, not in front of Oscar.

"He *is* my captain. And I knew he just wanted to protect you," he whispered.

"Let him make his own excuses."

Camille brushed the parchment lying facedown on the

desk with her fingertips, longing to drink in the rest of the words. It didn't seem real, this letter — her mother.

"What's going on in here?"

They turned at her father's voice. Oscar took a substantial step away from her. William stood inert in the doorway. His frown over walking in on his daughter and first mate together, alone, in the dim light, changed into trepidation as he saw the sheets of parchment under Camille's fingers. He narrowed his stare onto Oscar.

"I asked for your confidence, Oscar," he said, slamming the door behind him. He grabbed a box of matches and struck one, lighting a lantern by the door. A golden glow brightened the cabin as Camille stepped in front of Oscar.

"He's done nothing. I found the letter myself. The only person guilty of betrayal is you."

Her father breathed in, inflating his chest and pushing up his chin until he was looking down his nose at her.

"You don't know what you're talking about, Camille." He shoved past them and gathered the letter into his hands.

"I've read enough to know my mother is alive," she answered, her voice trembling. "How could you lie to me?"

Her father sent Oscar a tight nod, dismissing him. He moved toward the door.

"Captain. Miss Rowen." Oscar ducked to pass under the doorframe.

Her father knit his fingers together as he walked toward her. She saw his hands shake; his thumbs dug into the chapped skin of his knuckles.

"Camille, please." He tried to take her hand. She leaped backward.

"Leave me alone!" She wanted to hit something, to pick up the glass paperweight on his desk and send it crashing to the floor, to make more noise than the chaos inside her head. "All these years, you told me she was dead. How could you?"

She turned away from him and moved to the tall, leaded windows. The waves were no longer visible, but the lantern light reflected off the glass and illuminated her father's image behind her. She watched him rub his palm over his mouth and chin. Usually she wouldn't have been able to bear seeing him so distraught. But right then, Camille didn't care.

"Why is my mother in Port Adelaide?" she asked as ten more questions formed.

Rain lashed the windows, the shrieks of wind intensifying. The lantern swayed violently, and the contents on the desk slid at steep angles. She turned around and saw her father had leaned against the edge of the desk for support. In the smoky lantern light, his cheeks had turned sallow, his skin tired around the jowls.

He refused to look at her. "The reasons are complicated."

He ran his hand through his wave of hair and grasped a fistful, squinting his eyes as if in pain. "And as you can see, this is not the best time for me to explain them. There is a storm I need to sail through right now."

He tried to move toward the door, but Camille hurried from the windows and jumped in front of him.

"The storm can wait. You've spent the last seventeen years lying to me, and I want to know why. You told me my mother was dead! But she's alive and she wants to see me, and you never planned to tell me at all, did you?"

A growl built inside William Rowen, climbing from the base of his throat. He let out a guttural roar and swiped his arm over his desk, scattering papers and books, overturning an inkwell. A thick black pool spread over the wood and bled into the fibers of a sheet of paper.

"She left us! There it is. The very truth you've been begging for. Your mother left us." He slumped down into a chair and, after a pause, searched her face for a reaction. But she didn't believe him. Camille eyed the envelope, still clenched in his hand.

"Let me finish the letter," she whispered. "I want to know everything, and I don't trust you to tell me the truth anymore."

Her father tightened his hand around the envelope. He got up from the chair and took from his pocket the key to his safe box.

"There's something in it you don't want me to see," she said, following him to the box built into the wall next to his bunk.

He stuck the envelope inside and shut the door. The other keys jangled around on the hoop as he locked the safe. The ship rolled from the storm, jerking Camille side to side. She held on to a bureau and chair, her legs abnormally unsteady.

"There's more in it than I can tell you about right now. She left when you were hardly a year old. I never knew —" He pressed his palm against the metal door of the safe box as if another hand might be pressing against the opposite side. He shook his head. "I never knew where she went. She never wrote. Never contacted me. Until now."

Until she lay dying halfway across the world, Camille added silently. She ran her fingers through her messy black locks.

"Did you even try to search for her?" she asked. Her father let his hand slip from the safe box door and wheeled around.

"Of course I did. She was my wife, the mother of my child. Don't you think I wanted to know why she'd left us? If there was anything I could do to bring her back?"

A squall pummeled the *Christina*, and Camille lost her footing. Her father leaped forward to balance her, but she pulled out of his arms.

"Why didn't you just tell me the truth from the beginning?"

He sighed and rubbed his temple with the heel of his palm.

"There were other things," he said. "Other things that happened."

The *Christina* tilted on the rise of another wave. The spilled inkwell eddied and rolled off the desk, splattering ink onto her father's pant leg.

"Things you still don't want to tell me about?" Camille asked. He wiped the ink with a handkerchief, but the gesture was worthless against the blooming stain. He threw down the blackened cloth.

"Yes, things I needed to protect you from! And I won't apologize for doing so," he answered. Camille flung open the door, ready to be free of him and his secrets and lies.

"I don't want your protection. I want the truth!" She slammed the door behind her, the sound drowned by the storm. A gesture as futile, it seemed, as she.

FIVE

*C*amille lay in her bunk. It had been an hour since the storm winds had ceased. The lantern in the corner of her cramped cabin swayed gently on rusted chain links, a small flame sputtering inside. The storm had passed and so had her rage. The only thing left to feel was hurt. Her father had deceived her, and Oscar had signed on to protect his lies. Misery seized her and bound her to her bunk as effectively as the consumption had bound her mother to her bed in Australia. At least, that is what her letter had said. *I want to see Camille. I want to look at my baby one last time. . . .* The words struck out at her. If only she could have read faster, before Oscar had come in.

She squeezed her eyes shut, too frustrated to think straight. Other parts of what Camille had read returned now. What had her mother carried with her in shame, and what was all this about a map? The name of the place escaped her. The bell on deck clanged, signaling the change in watch. With the final clang of the bell, the name burst into her mind and flew like a bullet to her tongue.

"Umandu."

In the enclosed air of her cabin, her voice sounded louder than it truly was. In its wake came another sound. She pricked her ears and listened to a low, breathy murmur. She propped herself up on her elbows. It sounded like someone whispering outside her cabin.

The murmuring grew louder, seemed to pass through the solid pine of her door and swirl around her head. Twists of hair framing her face fluttered on a chill breath of wind smelling of something heavy and earthy. A scent Juanita had often worn. Myrrh. What was it doing on the *Christina*? The cold, cloying wind reached under the collar of her nightdress and fanned out down her arms, her chest, and stomach, rippling the blankets as it curled around the tips of her toes.

A scream gathered in Camille's throat, but before she could release it, the cool wind tunneled inside her ears. A raspy mumbling in a language Camille hadn't heard before took shape out of the wind. She held her breath as the voice intensified, as clearly as if some invisible person were shouting right beside her. The irregular beat of a drum ate up the words, and then the murmuring abruptly stopped. The cool wind swirling around her spun away and raced to the corner of the cabin. The flame in the lantern there flickered wildly and was snuffed out. Camille stared into the darkness, too frightened to do anything but blink.

The only sound that came was that of the wind, strangely picking up again. The rocking of the ship set in as well, and Camille clung to her bunk as a powerful gust bullied the *Christina*. She widened her eyes as opaque water, sloshing against her porthole, brightened to iridescent jade in sudden flashes of lightning. Another gust and then another attacked the ship, pushing the vessel farther onto its ribs. The howl of the wind sounded like it could rip the canvas from the rigging, not to mention a sailor straight into the night.

A sudden, deafening crack left her ears ringing. Lightning had struck the *Christina*. With the next violent swell, Camille's arms failed her and she flew from her bunk. Her knees scraped across the cabin floor and her head slammed against the edge of her bureau.

She heard the dark lantern crash and shatter. Her temple stung from the bureau's sharp edge, and her stomach lurched. She leaned into the pitch of the ship and retched. Reaching for the brass knobs on the bureau, she pulled herself up as the cabin door sprang open, exposing a mad rush of sailors. Orders and curses fused with the clamor of this second, unanticipated storm. With every roll, the *Christina* sounded ready to snap in two. The ship rose on another turbulent wave and crashed, sending Camille to the floor again. With every throb of her temple her vision pulsated. The doorway grew faint, then bright, small, then large.

"Camille!" Her father lumbered toward her, his body rocking with the ship. He tipped up her chin and inspected the wound. "Can you see straight?"

Camille nodded and got to her feet. "I'm fine," she answered, though her father's outline blurred. "Did lightning strike the mast?"

He gripped her shoulders, his oilskins dripping little rivers of seawater. She turned her head toward the companionway, where water rolled off the deck and splashed into the galley.

"Stay below," he said, responding to the curiosity in her eyes. "No exceptions, Camille. I don't know where this gale came from, but it's too dangerous up there."

She feared going back into her cabin alone. She wanted to be up there, with them, not stuck below, a bad-luck curse hidden away from the sea. Randall's voice barreled into her head as her father kissed her just above her bleeding temple: *"Aren't women supposed to be bad luck on a ship?"*

Her father turned and fought for the companionway.

"Be careful!" she shouted, but before she could go back into her cabin, Camille's ears nearly burst from a second shock of lightning. Her teeth ached and her ears rang. And that's when she heard the sound of splintering pine and the groan of wood bending and twisting. The world above her exploded as the topgallant mast speared the ship like a dagger. Water surged inside and swept away two sailors near the break.

"Camille!" She felt her father's hand before she saw him grab her—knew she was running but felt as if she were trapped in a tide of molasses. Water rushed around her ankles, and debris slammed into her shins. Wind slapped her in the face as her father hauled her up on deck, where the storm growled and slashed at them. Her feet slipped and she landed on her side, sliding as the ship pitched higher. But her father, his hand still wrapped around her wrist, heaved her back up. He brought her near, and she clung to his neck and shoulders. He hooked his arm under the roof of the companionway, and they looked out at the horror.

"Secure the line!" her father shouted to Mickey and Lucius, who were hugging the spiked stump of the mainmast as the ship tipped at a near ninety-degree angle. Loose rigging snapped in the wind, as lethal as the blade of a sword. As Mickey reached for the whipping line, a contrary wind sent the rope lashing toward him. It flayed his arm with such ferocity, he arched his back and dropped into the dark waters chomping on the ship. Water gushed into the break, filling the *Christina* and killing her buoyancy.

Camille searched the quarterdeck and found the helm where Oscar should have been gripping the wheel. The spokes whirred unmanned, the center medallion glinting in flashes of lightning. Her panicked eyes swept the deck, fore and aft, but she saw nothing but madness.

"Oscar!" she yelled to her father. "Where is he?"

Her father held her tighter.

"My Camille," he whispered in her ear, and even through the bellow of the storm she heard him clearly. "My Camille."

She stopped and listened, her father's voice calm, lucid. She closed her eyes to the rising water, to the wind and rain and lightning.

"Try and stay above the waves. Hold on to me when we go under. I've got you," he told her.

She dug her fingers into his back. Hot tears warmed her cheeks against the cold rain and biting sea spray. Camille opened her eyes, needing to see her father's face. But the mountainous waves spooling around the *Christina* crusaded for her attention. The jade breakers lit up in quick flickers, as if the water itself roiled with the electricity of the storm. In the translucency of one wave that reached taller than any other, the water glowed a vibrant chartreuse green. Camille watched it from the crest of her father's shoulder. The unnatural wave seemed to pause, unyielding as the others around it crashed and rolled and built up again.

"Father," she whispered as black gaps started to poke through the green wave. Two oval voids side by side, like empty eye sockets. Then centered below them grew a triangular void.

"Father!" she screamed, as a series of vertical and horizontal lines sliced through the wave directly below the triangle, like grinning teeth. Her father followed her terrified gaze and turned in time to see a black skeletal face looming in the green wave above the *Christina*. She felt her father's grip loosen as the giant skeletal jaws parted and the wave reared back to strike.

"Hold on!" he yelled as the teeth of the wave ripped into the ship. The green water engulfed Camille's scream as it crashed. Torn from the rail, Camille and her father plummeted down the steep slope of the deck into the water. All was black and cold. She clutched her father's arm as they floundered, the chartreuse wave now gone. What had that thing been?

She heard the ship, the gut-wrenching sound of bending metal and snapping wood. Through the pulses of darkness and flashes of lightning, she saw debris on the swell of every wave, the pale faces of sailors screaming and gasping for air, arms and legs thrashing. Her eyes craved the glints of lightning, to be able to see something, anything, even if it terrified her. And then, with the next flicker of lightning, she saw the last sliver of the *Christina* plunge below the surface. Her heart felt like it would burst — and then she suddenly comprehended she was slapping the waves with both hands.

A wave struck her, pitching her below. "Father!" she cried, gurgling on seawater as she rose up, thrust out by the next surge. She turned in all directions, but every angle looked the same. Cold, rushing water took her. She clamped her mouth shut, fighting the torrential surf with flimsy arms and legs. The sound of the storm muted as water filled her ears. She didn't know if she was sinking deeper into the fathoms of the sea or rising to its surface. The water numbed her, and she stopped slapping. Her legs quit kicking. Camille's hands floated weightlessly above her head. She went in every direction, a rag doll forced back and forth. But she refused to open her mouth and give up the last ounce of air in her lungs.

A warmth brushed Camille's hand. Its firm grasp closed around her freezing fingers, working its way down to her elbow and hoisting her up. She landed on something hard, away from the waves.

"Breathe!" Oscar's muffled voice shook her senses back into place. A warm shock of water flowed from her mouth, and she coughed as the rest of it rushed out her nostrils. Oscar's fingers bored into her arm, hurting her.

"Get down!" he screamed.

Camille gripped the edge of the dory as they rose on a crest and crashed on the opposite side. She coughed up more salt water and tucked herself into the belly of the boat Oscar had miraculously recovered.

Bile rose into Camille's mouth as orange and yellow dots burst before her eyes. A flash of heat spawned sweat on her neck and chest despite the frigid water. The dory felt like it was spinning, caught in a whirlpool. She lay on her side, her head cradled in her arms. Water sloshed in the bottom of the boat, sliding in and out of her ear.

Camille heard a groan and a *thunk*. Fighting through a fast-enveloping sickness and the searing pain of her injured temple, she lifted her eyes.

"Father?" she moaned. But the face next to her was long, pointy, and young. Lucius Drake lay on his back, chunks of sopping hair sticking to his face.

"Oscar, my father!" she screamed, but if he heard her, he gave no sign of it. Oscar kept rowing and ducking beneath the waves as they crashed down. In her dizziness she felt for her temple. The gashed flesh burned, and when she pulled away her hand, darkness coated her fingertips.

"Find my father!" she cried. A rush of water flowed into her mouth and choked out the words. She closed her eyes to the walls of water looming over them. Behind her eyelids, she saw a rapid burst of magenta lights. Camille had never fainted, but right then she felt unconsciousness nearing. A sharp ringing in her ears overtook the wind. The soft pillow of shadows pulled her in, tugged her under, away from the dory, and away from her father, still somewhere inside the storm.

SIX

Prodding hands tugged and yanked at Camille, rousing her to consciousness. Beyond her will, her legs and arms remained limp. *What's happening to me?* She tried to open her eyes, but without success. Even her lids were unresponsive. She heard voices at her side — men's voices. A pair of hands gripped Camille under her arms, and another set of fingers squeezed and pulled on her Achilles tendons until her ankles burned. The odor of sweat and tar and the scrubbed wood of a ship elevated her awareness even more. People were carrying her, but aboard what ship? A blazing ache tore through her skull, from her temple to the sockets of her eyes.

"Put her there," an unfamiliar voice ordered. Her back landed in a net, then her feet fell, too. God, she was so worn, so exhausted. A cool hand pressed against her forehead.

"Camille?"

She forced a single lid open at the sound of Oscar's voice. She saw his glistening wet forearm, lit by the soft glow of an oil lamp. Everything above his arm was lost in the dark fringe of her lashes.

"My father," she tried to say, her mouth a ball of cotton.

"She's awake," another voice said, this one chirpy and light. It belonged to a woman. "Make way, make way. Giv'er room ta breathe."

Camille's lid dropped shut and wouldn't budge, no matter how hard she tried. The incessant pain behind her eyes throbbed, churning her stomach, raw and empty.

"She'll survive," the woman said, her voice moving closer to Camille's side. "Best get this nightdress off'a her 'fore she catch ill. So, get on now. Get out."

Oscar's palm slipped from her forehead. The moment his hand fell away, Camille felt lost in a foreign world. She wanted him back, wanted him to stay with her.

"I'm just outside," he said, but his voice was fading, as was the oily smell of the room, the sensation of her dress being tugged at. The base of her head felt laden down with iron grommets, and once more Camille fell back into nothingness.

———

"Drink," she heard the woman's chirpy voice. "Drink it down, miss."

Camille startled awake to find a tarred ceiling and a woman with coal-black hair hovering over her. The woman pressed the rim of a cup to Camille's lips. Water dribbled down her chin. She swallowed and coughed, and water streamed out her nostrils.

"Who are you?" Camille coughed again. The woman batted thick lashes, which shielded deep-set blue eyes. She smiled, her teeth blackened and missing in spots.

"I'm Daphne," she answered. "You've been out most'a the day."

Camille struggled to rise from the hammock strung from two hooks in the ceiling. Daphne coaxed her back.

"I doubt your legs'll hold you upright."

"Where am I?" Camille asked, pressing her bandaged temple with the tips of her fingers. The soft, swollen skin beneath the gauze protested with a sharp burst of pain. She looked down at herself and saw she wore nothing more than a simple corset, with minimal hooks and eyes, along with a pair of cotton drawers. They were not her own. Shocked, Camille pulled the blanket back over her.

"Spotted you at dawn, we did. The three of you in that lit'l boat, just driftin'. This here's the *Londoner*." Daphne wrung tepid water out of a cloth and pressed it to Camille's cheek. Her dress sleeves, capped at the shoulders and cinched with string, cut into her doughy arms. Red lesions flecked her pale skin. Camille twitched her nose. Scurvy.

"Just three of us?" she asked, her voice scraping along her dry throat. In her blurry mind, she attempted to do simple addition of the people she'd seen in the dory. Her father would have made four. Tears stung her eyes and anguish swallowed her. Her chest felt as though it might cave in. Daphne touched Camille's hand lightly.

"Your Irishman told us 'bout the wreck. 'Bout your father. Poor thing, you've been through more'n a girl should."

Daphne tipped the cup to Camille's lips again. Her arms shook as she tried to take the cup and drink on her own. She cringed at a stranger fussing over her. Turning her head, she saw a second hammock. Dingy white sheets stuffed a wooden cabinet in the corner, and the rest of the small cabin was spotless and stark. She assumed it was the sick bay.

"Is Oscar all right?" Camille asked, wanting to see him right away. They had been on a busy shipping route. Maybe her father had been rescued, too. Maybe he wasn't gone. Oscar would know. He'd be able to reassure her.

Daphne bit her lower lip.

"Oscar, he the Irish? Well, heavens, he's all right. He's on deck. Didn't want no mollycoddlin'. Got right to work with the crew," she said, then winked at Camille and looked over her shoulder as if someone might be standing in there with them. "Now that other'un. The wily buck, there. He's been down in the orlop deck with me girls since the cap'n plucked you from the water."

Daphne chortled, displaying reddened gums. She must have meant Lucius, but Camille didn't understand the rest of her sentence. Gripping the blanket to her chest, she swung her legs over the side of the hammock.

"Stubborn, now! What's the rush? The *Londoner* won't be pullin' to port for 'nother week."

Camille lost her balance when her feet hit the floor. Daphne caught and steadied her with a strong shove of her hip.

"What port?" Camille asked. The muscles of her arms ached from just the weight of the blanket she held to shield her. Daphne swiped a pair of boots from a chair and handed them to Camille.

"Melbourne. Been bound for it nigh twelve months," she answered. "Haven't seen land for a fortnight."

That explained the pallor of her skin, the decay of her gums and teeth, and the scarlet spots of scurvy. Camille's whole body shook, and her fingernails were purple with cold. She wanted to see Oscar. She wanted to know what he had seen, if he had witnessed her father getting into another dory. She needed to know if there was a thread of hope, even one as thin as gossamer, to cling to.

"Men from all over the world are makin' their destinies in Victoria, what with the gold they've been diggin' up and all," Daphne continued. "We figured why not make our own destinies? So, 'bout ten of us women rounded up the money and here we are."

Destiny and money. Camille now knew that having the second didn't smooth the path for the first. *In the hands of Providence,* she could almost hear her father's voice whisper in her ear. It was a saying of his, often mumbled when something had not gone according to his well-laid-out plans. Her father had always been able to assuage his disappointment by knowing that everything, in the end, would be left to fate.

Daphne reached for the doorknob.

"And what is your destiny?" Camille asked as she drained the rest of the metallic-tasting water from the tin mug. Daphne, whom Camille put at thirty years, crossed her arms under her heavy bosom. For the first time, Camille noticed Daphne's cleavage mushrooming over the trim of her exposed corset.

"Come down to the orlop when you've dressed. The girls want to meet you," she answered instead and closed the door behind her. *Strange woman,* Camille decided, and shed the blanket.

By the time Camille finished pulling on a striped homespun cotton dress, her body swayed with fatigue. The hideous material drooped around the waist and ribs and exposed too much skin below the neck. A cylinder of bottle glass, lodged in the floorboards on deck, permitted some greenish daylight to enter the cabin. The ship's bell clanged on deck, signaling a change in watch as she unwrapped her bandaged head and tried to smooth her tangled hair.

She laced up her boots, and even though her head felt like a bowl of runny jelly, she stepped out of the cabin. She expected to see a darkened corridor like the one on the *Christina,* but instead, a whole level of the ship spread out before her.

More hammocks, some occupied by snoring sailors, stretched down from beams running along the ceiling, and two long tables with benches had been nailed to the floor near a potbellied cookstove. She glanced twice at gun ports, boarded up and sealed shut on both the starboard and larboard sides. This was no merchant ship like the *Christina*. Cannon had once sat before each gun port, though now the deck was clear of artillery. A ladder led to the upper deck, and beside it another ladder led below to the lower decks.

With labored movement, Camille‚ climbed the ladder, thighs shaking. She emerged on deck and lifted her face to the sun, drinking in the warmth. Golden evening skies and three ship-rigged masts loomed above her. Crewmen crawled along the bowlines and foretop, as far out as the jibboom. They were so high up they looked like little black flecks. The deck of the *Londoner* blurred with activity, the change in watch nearly complete. Camille spotted Oscar easily, his feet on the starboard rail, both hands wrapped around a taut line.

She waved her arm to gain his attention. He made his way toward her, sweat and grease streaking his chin. He looked tired and beaten, but relief brightened his eyes. Camille wanted to throw her arms around him, hold him, and tell him how relieved she was that he'd survived. But the closer he came, the more nervous she grew about actually touching him. It would be too bold, and she felt Randall's eyes on her from all the way across the Pacific.

"Daphne was supposed to come get me when you came to." His heaving chest told her he, too, needed more rest. He inspected her wound, furrowing his brow.

"I'm all right," she insisted. "But, Oscar, my father. Did you see him? We were holding hands, and then he was gone. I didn't even realize I'd let go. I thought . . . I was hoping maybe you saw him get into another dory before you were able to rescue me?"

Camille forced herself to take a breath as Oscar's look of concern for her wound changed to discomfort. Then despair.

"Camille." His hand fluttered down the side of her arm. He parted his lips to say something, took a breath, but exhaled and shook his head. "No, I didn't see him."

Camille bit the inside of her cheek until it hurt, and stared out over the railing. This couldn't be happening. Her father couldn't be gone. The waves knit into one another, smudging into a hazy blue-green as she fought back tears. The sea, the very thing he'd loved so much, couldn't have taken him. Just picturing him beneath the waves, struggling for air, his lifeless body sinking into oblivion . . . no, no, *no!*

She gripped the railing and hunched her shoulders, taking deep breaths to keep from hyperventilating. She didn't know what to do, not without her father. She wanted him back, she wanted him safe and with her and Oscar. She wanted him alive.

"Camille." Oscar laid his hand on the small of her back, though his touch did little to stir her. It seemed as if nothing ever would again.

"You were delirious all night in the dory," he continued. "I was worried about your head. But you look better. I'm glad."

She didn't feel glad. She didn't feel much of anything,

except scared and weak. But she couldn't show that. She'd never been weak, at least never outwardly. Camille had always been the captain's daughter, Rowen's girl, the young lady who wasn't really a lady. And although no list of rules had been written for the only child of a widowed sea captain (or whom she had always believed widowed), Camille had created one herself. Showing weakness, needing aid, playing the damsel in distress were not on the list.

Camille straightened her shoulders and wiped her eyes and nose as gracefully as she could. "We're on a frigate," she said, avoiding Oscar's eyes. They'd hold too much sorrow, and she didn't want to tear up again. "What are women doing aboard a warship?"

"The *Londoner* isn't with the Royal Navy." His answer explained the lack of cannon on the gun deck. "Her captain deals in cargo. You've met Daphne?"

Camille squinted up into the rigging. "She seems nice. A little odd, but she invited me to the orlop."

Above her, a pair of men oiled the topsail. Camille's boots slipped on a few drops of grease. Oscar braced her.

"To the orlop? Camille" — he leaned close to her ear and lowered his voice — "they're prostitutes."

She gasped, and finally looked at him full on. "Prostitutes? Are you positive?"

Oscar nodded as a few passing sailors gave Camille the once-over and then scoffed. She tried to quell the flush creeping up her neck. A surge of nausea clouded her vision. Her heart pounded and a cold sweat broke out on her back and chest.

"You're still weak. Go rest in the hammock." Oscar gently urged her toward the ladder. Then carefully he added, "You should know, the captain and crew prefer the women stay below."

Camille halted. "I'm not weak, Oscar. I'm recovering."

Oscar nodded to the companionway. "Go. I'll bring some food soon."

She felt empty, not hungry. Camille shinnied down the ladder, out of the superstitious eyes of the crew. In the quiet, sterile sick bay, the hammock cradled her tender limbs. Even her bones ached. She sipped more water and felt it cool her lips and throat, seeping into her empty belly. Sleep welcomed her, and she rocked gently with the playful toss of the frigate-cum-cargo ship.

Four hours later, the first watch poured onto the spar deck with the clangs of the ship's bell. Camille was lifted from a deep sleep, in which she had pictured the crossroads of Kearny and California streets back home in San Francisco. A few blocks from their townhouse on Portsmouth Plaza, California Street led straight to the wharf where her father's ship had always docked. She'd traveled that street so many times, down to the cove, anticipating a great voyage, a remarkable adventure.

In her dream, Camille stood alone on the corner of Kearny and California. She could see everything as clearly as if it were right there in front of her. The redbrick homes, the cast-iron lamps, the cobblestoned walkways and dirt-packed street. Even the drying laundry pinned to a clothesline between Dr. Jensen's and Mrs. Washburn's houses. She could see the square, glassed-in cupola of her father's townhouse rising above other roofs. Everything looked the same, and yet it felt empty, as if it had lost its soul. Camille knew she could not go back to it, not yet. The crossroads beckoned her to step out into the street and go down to the harbor.

She opened her eyes to the sound of the cabin door shutting. The light from the bottle-glass skylight had faded, but she still watched as Oscar lumbered to the hammock parallel to hers.

"Did you bring food?" Camille asked, a pang of hunger kinking her stomach. Oscar propped a foot up in his own hammock as he settled down and let the other brush against the floor.

"The bread is weevily, the meat's turned, and the cabbage is soft."

Camille grimaced. "Is there anything?"

"Boiled potatoes," he answered, then pointed to the cabinet where a bowl waited for her. She swallowed the grainy, flavorless lumps by the soft light of the oil lamp. She then collapsed back into her hammock. The heaping breakfast Juanita had fixed for them before the *Christina* departed came to mind, followed by the memory of browsing the morning markets with Randall. What would he say if he saw her right then, wounded and exhausted? Maybe those superstitions about women being bad luck

on ships weren't such poppycock after all. She remembered the voice that had echoed in her ears, and the chill
wind, infused with the scent of myrrh, that had swirled
around her just before the resurgence of the storm.

"Oscar," she said, turning toward him. He had closed
his eyes. "Do you think it could have been my fault?"

He didn't answer, and she wondered if he'd already
fallen asleep. *Better off,* she thought. She crossed her arms
over her chest and tucked them under the blanket.

"What do you mean 'your fault'? The wreck?" he
asked, sounding like he'd risen from a light doze.

"I heard a voice just before the storm returned, but no
one was there. And there was drumming and chanting in
a strange language." She knew she wasn't making any
sense. It had been late, she had been tired, and her mind
was overwhelmed with thoughts of her mother's letter.

"You must think I'm mad," she whispered, wishing
she hadn't said anything. But then she thought of the skeletal face in the chartreuse wave. Her father had seen it,
too. How could a wave just hover like that, waiting to
strike?

"I don't know what you heard," Oscar said, the tail end
of his sentence consumed by a yawn. "But it wasn't your
fault. None of this seems real. I have to think of a way to
get us back home."

Home to what? Nothing represented home more than
her father, and he was gone. So home was gone, too.

"We'll send word back to the company," Oscar said,
yawning again. He draped his arm over the crown of his

head, his eyes half open, and turned up toward the blackened bottle glass. No crewmate, not even Oscar, had been permitted inside her cabin on the *Christina*. She'd never been in the presence of another person while sleeping, and the idea of Oscar lying just feet away from her all night in the dark awakened an awareness inside her, destroying all prospects of sleep.

He glimpsed her looking at him.

"What is it?" he asked. Camille quickly turned away.

"Nothing," she answered. Guilt started to settle inside her for not being more eager to return to San Francisco. For all Camille cared, she'd be happy to remain in the sick bay's hammock forever. She again heard her father's voice in her head. *That doesn't sound like my Camille. She's stronger than that.*

Two levels below the sick bay, confined to the orlop deck, Daphne probably dreamed of her destiny awaiting her in Melbourne. She was making her destiny, not allowing it to be made for her. That took true strength.

Camille jolted up in her hammock, a spark igniting inside her chest.

"Oscar, how far is Port Adelaide from Melbourne?"

He lifted his brawny forearm.

"Camille, we barely made it away with our lives."

"How far?" she insisted.

"Too far. Especially with empty pockets." He tucked his arm over his eyes again. "Let's just get to Melbourne first."

Camille was certain that Oscar knew everything about the letter, every detail she hadn't been given the time to read. A slight wheeze in his breath stopped her from asking. He needed rest as much as she did. She listened to him breathe in rhythm with the creaking ship, comforted that he was there with her. He'd saved her life. Pulled her from the waves and certain death.

"Thank you," she whispered. "For saving me."

He didn't answer, except for a low moan, an acknowledgment that somewhere inside his fresh dream he'd heard her.

SEVEN

PORT MELBOURNE, AUSTRALIA

*C*amille peeled back the curtains, and sunlight streamed in through a pair of grimy windows. Outside, in Melbourne's harbor front, an endless line of schooners, sloops, barks, and brigs slanted from the incoming wind. Charcoal-colored waves rolled ashore, smashing into the pilings and wharves, sending up towers of white frothy spray.

Free of the *Londoner* and days of monotonous life belowdecks, Camille stood in a small room with white-washed walls and a single narrow bed. A sense of freedom both invigorated and frightened her. There was so much to do—so much to take care of. Insurance . . . her father had it on his ships, but how to lay her hands on it? She nibbled on her fingernail. Then again, maybe they didn't have it. They'd been going bankrupt, after all.

At least they had found a place to stay. Teaming up with Daphne and her "girls," Oscar and Camille had come upon a slew of TO LET signs that had covered doorways and fence posts of homes whose owners had headed into the gold-embedded countryside. In fact, most of what

Camille had seen of Melbourne felt like a ghost town, with its empty storefronts and abandoned vessels in the harbor.

Knuckles rapped on the door to her room. Oscar entered, a cracked porcelain bowl in one hand and a spoon in the other. She noticed the hard lines of his jaw and launched into the defense she'd already used twice that day.

"Oscar, we're alive and in Melbourne and that's all that matters."

The door clicked shut behind him. He placed the bowl on the dresser and dropped the spoon into the soup. "We're alive, in Melbourne, and living in a whorehouse."

Camille caught a glimpse of herself in a vanity mirror fogged in spots with age. Her disheveled hair embarrassed her, and the ugly gash on her temple had purpled and swelled. It would leave a scar, a permanent reminder of the instant her life changed forever.

"We should think of Daphne as our ally," she said, turning back toward the harbor. Few people milled about the wharves and streets muddied from rain. From their second story window topmasts bobbed at eye level. Dozens of ships, as far as she could see, were tied to piers, and among them she spotted the *Londoner*. Camille was relieved to be rid of the frigate and its cold crew and skipper.

"Besides saving us, no one else on that ship offered any aid," Camille continued. "They didn't even ration us enough food. Daphne convinced the other women to help feed us. We should be grateful."

Oscar walked toward Camille at the windows and looked out at the ships. "I am grateful," he said. "But we can't stay here. This isn't any place for you."

Camille polished a smudge of dirt near a bubble in the glass windowpane. It had never been Oscar's duty to look out for her reputation; she didn't want him to worry about it now. Right from the beginning, just after her father had given Oscar the loft of the carriage house to live in, Camille had known reputation would never place high on Oscar's list of important things. The reserved, cautious way he had carried himself, hardly able to look anyone, especially Camille, in the eye, had revealed that he already knew there were more sensible things than reputation to worry about. But perhaps living in Melbourne's newest brothel was pushing the limits for him.

It was only their first day, but Camille had yet to venture past the doorframe. She was too embarrassed to chance running into a patron and become mistaken for a trollop. Space was limited, and since they were lucky to be getting a room at all, Daphne had paired up Oscar and Camille. Lucius had been offered another portion of the floor opposite Oscar, but he'd declined, licking his lips and rubbing his palms together before catching up with one of Daphne's curvaceous girls. Camille hoped she could sleep better than she had aboard the *Londoner*, but with Oscar on the floor, she was sure his light, rhythmic breathing would make it difficult once again.

Oscar cocked his head and crossed his arms. Camille had grown gaunt over the last trying week, but Oscar had kept his bulk working aboard the *Londoner* for what little food they did receive. His forearms bulged just below the elbow, and his biceps stretched the cuffed sleeves of his checked fustian shirt. She'd started to take note of his fine build a few years before, when his lanky form had begun to fill out with the help of Juanita's cooking and daily ship's duties. But now without anyone around to watch her watching him, she allowed herself to admire the shape of his arms and imagine the way they might feel wrapped around her. A twirl of her stomach jumbled up the image and she forced her eyes away from him.

"I've already told Daphne we won't be boarding with her long," Camille said, proud she'd kept her voice steady.

"And where did you say we were going?" Oscar asked.

Camille clasped her hands in front of her. "Oscar, my mother is right here, in Australia."

He paced a threadbare rug by the bed and gripped the back of his neck. "It doesn't matter, that's hundreds of miles away."

"How can you say it doesn't matter? It matters even more now than it did before. My mother has been dead to me my whole life. Now she's the one alive and my father . . ." Camille took a breath and fought the clamp around her throat. It still didn't feel real. She couldn't say it, or even think it, without sending her pulse into a mad sprint.

"I didn't mean it like that," Oscar sighed. "But Port Adelaide is too far away, and we don't have a cent between us."

Camille traced the biting scent of turnip mush in the bowl on the dresser. It gave off a cloud of steam but did little to whet her appetite. Dark circles colored the skin beneath Oscar's eyes, and she guessed he hadn't slept much on the *Londoner*, either. He backed up against the bed and lowered himself onto the mattress.

"I disagreed with him, you know. About not letting you read her letter," he said.

She arched an eyebrow, surprised he'd been on her side. But then, he'd also gone against her father's request to stop associating with her. She'd been furious with her father. But being angry with him now that he was gone was impossible. Camille stomped down a lump in the rug.

"I wish I'd been able to read the whole letter."

Oscar ran his fingers through his short hair. "He read parts of it to me."

A spark of jealousy simmered through her as she sat beside him and gripped the edge of the mattress.

"What did it say?"

Oscar shifted uneasily. "That she's got the consumption and wants to see you before she dies. That she's never forgotten you."

His rendition of her mother's letter lacked the satisfaction Camille yearned for. She wanted to know each and every word, see them on the page, feel their effect, and then read them all over again. Oscar nodded, as if remembering something else.

"And that another letter had been sent to Stuart McGreenery."

Camille's grip on the mattress loosened.

"Stuart McGreenery? Whatever for?"

She had only met her father's business rival a handful of times. The deep, dark cleft in his chin was always the first thing she thought of whenever his name came up.

"Your father told me that before you were born, he and McGreenery ran a business together. Pacific Shipping, out of San Francisco," Oscar said.

Camille stared at him in disbelief.

"My father and McGreenery were business partners? But they detested each other."

Oscar shrugged, as if he couldn't believe it, either. Camille rubbed her uninjured temple. So many times her father had talked about Stuart McGreenery with never a mention of this other life. Another lie. Another cover. And something else he'd shared with Oscar instead of her.

"Things went badly with your mother after William won a map in a poker game while in Sydney. She ordered him to get rid of it, that it was dangerous."

A map. Camille could almost see the words scrawled in ink on her mother's parchment. *And so I've come to the most difficult, and most dangerous, part of my letter. You remember the map to Umandu.*

"Your mother disappeared soon after," he continued. "And so did the map."

The sun slipped behind dark clouds and the room dimmed. Camille became aware of the short space between her and Oscar on the mattress and of a spicy, citrus scent replacing the odor of the turnip mush.

"She took it?" Camille asked, distracted. Dizzy. Oscar got up and moved toward the door, taking his intoxicating scent with him.

"That's what William always believed. But I don't know for sure if she —"

"She mentioned the map in the letter," Camille interrupted as the sun came out and lit the room once again.

"Your father never told me why it was dangerous or what it was supposed to have led to. But it must have been important. Apparently, your mother thought so, too."

Camille walked to the bureau and poured a glass of water from the pitcher. Her hands trembled as the water cascaded into the cup. All she wanted was to crawl beneath the covers of the lumpy bed and submerge into a black, thoughtless sleep.

"It was to a place I've never heard of before. A strange name." She took a sip of the water and swallowed before continuing. "Umandu."

Oscar flinched and stared at her. "What did you say?"

Camille set the glass down. "Uman —"

"No!" He held his finger up to his mouth to shush her. "Don't say it."

"Why not?" she asked. "Have you heard of it?"

The wind picked up, and tree branches outside the windows thrashed against the side of the house, knocking a few loose clapboards into one another. Oscar covered his mouth with his hand and paced the rug.

"What's wrong? What is this Umandu place?"

He cringed at the word again and squeezed his hands into fists. "It isn't a place. It's a thing. A stone."

Camille crinkled her brow, unimpressed. It was almost comical to see a man as substantial as Oscar Kildare turn timid at the mention of a stone. He rubbed the back of his neck.

"The map was *the* map? That's . . . that's impossible. It's just a legend," he said to himself.

Camille finished her water as Oscar repeated in a whisper that it was just a legend, just a story.

"Why are you acting so afraid of a map and a rock?" she asked. Oscar snapped out of his mantra. He cocked his head to the side.

"You've never heard of the two stones? Of the immortals?"

Camille arched an eyebrow, wary of the turn their conversation had taken. "Uh, no, I — I suppose I haven't."

Oscar blinked a few times and scratched the back of his head, looking at her as if she'd just admitted she didn't like to eat or would rather not breathe.

"It's a legend, Camille. Everybody knows it. It's about an Egyptian goddess who stole two stones from the Underworld to create her own civilization of immortals. The stones made her more powerful than the Underworld's gatekeeper. She could do more than just turn a living human being immortal. She could actually take any soul the gatekeeper escorted to the Underworld and pull them back into the land of the living," Oscar explained, his words picking up speed. "Each time the gatekeeper tried to get the stones back, the goddess outsmarted him. Finally he succeeded, but was only able to recover one of the stones. The legend says the other stone is still out there somewhere, waiting for someone worthy of its magic. All the stories I've heard say the goddess made an enchanted map leading to the other stone. A map . . ." Oscar explained, again looking toward the floor in thought.

Camille couldn't restrain the amusement on her face. He sounded like one of the sailors in the fo'c'sle, telling a tale about a giant, ship-eating sea serpent.

"An immortal race of men? Do you have any idea how ridiculous that sounds? Certainly, there's no such thing."

A slight blush crept into Oscar's cheeks, and Camille wished she'd kept the laughter out of her voice. Oscar walked to the bureau and poured himself a glass of water.

"Of course there's no such thing. But your mother said the map was to one of the stones. Why would she say that?" He took a large gulp of water and swallowed. "Why would she mention it if it wasn't real?"

She hid her smile, but not well. Oscar set the glass down with more force than necessary and crossed his arms.

"Go on, laugh at me if you want. But according to the legend, the gatekeeper to the Underworld put a curse on the missing stone. Even just *saying* the stolen stone's name—which you just did—brings the curse on you." He raised his eyebrows at her. "So you'd better hope it is just a fairy tale."

Camille sighed. A curse from a rock seemed as plausible as a man losing his head in a giant octopus sucker. No wonder her father had never wanted those kinds of stories told aboard the *Christina*.

"Well, now that I'm cursed, what should I expect?" she asked, smiling again. She hadn't seen Oscar so enraptured before, and it was a side of him that was completely adorable. He was acting like an awestruck boy, when all he'd ever let her see was a mature, serious, stoic man.

"Disaster and bad luck, until you either lose your life or somehow manage to find the stone. But I'm glad you're amused," he said, sour about being poked fun at.

Disaster. Like the sinking of the *Christina*. The death of a beloved father. Tears formed along the rims of her eyes. Camille raised her hand to her lips and began nibbling on a fingernail. *If you say one of the stone's names* . . . Umandu. She'd said it before. On the *Christina*, just before the storm returned from out of nowhere. The chill wind . . . the rippling bedcover . . . the voices, and then the chartreuse wave and the face within it. No. The legend couldn't hold any real weight. It was absurd to even consider it.

"How is it you know this legend so well when I have never heard of it?" Camille asked, leaning against the bureau as she lost a bit of strength in her legs. Before Oscar could even reply, Camille had the answer. It hadn't just been tales like the giant octopus her father had tried to protect her from. What if he'd asked his sailors to refrain from such myth telling for fear of their tongues wagging about Umandu? He could have been manipulating her from the very beginning, working to hide the truth as diligently as a squirrel hoarding acorns in its burrow before the snows of winter.

"Never mind," she whispered. "But what makes Uman — what makes it so extraordinary?"

Even more curious to Camille was how this stone played into her mother's disappearance sixteen years earlier and why she'd also sent a letter to Stuart McGreenery.

Oscar adjusted the wide leather belt at his waist, looking like he'd taken a spoonful of the turnip mush.

"Because the first person to find and touch the stone can . . . bring someone back."

Camille held her breath tight in her lungs and shoved herself from the bureau. "Back from where?"

He sighed and hung his head, as if he regretted opening his mouth. "Back from the dead."

EIGHT

ow? Tell me how that's possible," Camille whispered, unable to believe she'd heard Oscar correctly.

"I know what's going on inside your head and it's not a good idea," he said as he picked up the soup bowl, still full, and opened the door.

"If it can bring someone back to life, and if my mother has the map, we could find the stone and then I could—"

Oscar disappeared into the hall as she spoke. He probably counted on her being too prim to walk among Daphne's girls to come after him. She pushed back her shoulders and took a ginger step into the hallway. Oscar wasn't getting away from her that easily.

He had already reached the top of the stairs.

"You should get back into the room," he said as the brothel's front door opened. Daylight spilled up the stairwell. Camille heard Daphne cooing over someone and nearly retreated. But she was tired of doing what she was told.

"Tell me more about the stone," she said. A door down the hallway creaked open and Camille darted forward, toward the stairs.

"It's just a load of nonsense treasure hunters get stagy over," Oscar replied as he descended the carpeted steps.

Camille caught up with him, her eyes avoiding the man removing his hat and cloak in the foyer. She didn't want to see his face, but more important, she didn't want him to see hers. Oscar headed toward a room out back, Camille on his heels.

"I saw the look in your eyes the moment I said the stone's name. I heard the way you spoke about it. I shouldn't have laughed at you. I'm sorry. But you don't have to act like you don't believe in it, Oscar," she said as he threw open a door and crossed into the kitchen.

A butcher's block centered the stuffy room, a headless chicken splayed out on top of it. A girl with an indecent lack of clothing on plucked the limp bird, white and brown feathers matting her hands and cheeks. Camille swiped a few out from under her nose as Oscar returned the bowl of turnip mush to the stove.

"All right, the legend's always intrigued me. And yes, I still don't think it's wise to say its name." He glared at her a moment, as if to let the bit of advice sink in. "But is it likely? Not a chance."

A woman stirring the pot of mush saw the fruits of her labor had not even been touched.

"What'sa matter wiv it?" she asked. Oscar turned to Camille.

"Too busy talking to eat," he answered as the kitchen door sprang open. Daphne came in, her makeup done up as brightly as sunbeams reflecting off a mirror. She grinned at Camille with her gray-toothed smile.

"Haven't seen you in a bit," she said, eyeing the hem of Camille's skirt. She swept it up, revealing Camille's legs from the knee down.

"Do you mind?" Camille took the hem from Daphne's hand and covered herself, her cheeks reddening.

"Needs a washin', is all. Your hair, too," she added, scrunching up her nose. A brothel madam was telling her to take a bath? Mortified, she caught Oscar stifling a laugh from around the butcher's block.

"Let me get the tub ready. It's in the back pantry there," Daphne continued as casually as if she were about to add salt to the turnip mush.

"Stop grinning," Camille hissed to Oscar. He took her by the arm and led her away from the kitchen, into the front hallway again. The man at the door had disappeared, thank heavens.

"Listen," he said, then lowered his voice. "No one can come back to life. Your father's gone, all right? He's *gone*."

He practically spit the word in her face. Gone. Up until that moment, nothing but raw grief had overwhelmed her when she thought of her father. Now, for the first time, Camille felt something more. Something unanticipated. She felt *angry*.

"He is gone. Don't you care about that? After all he's

done for you, you should be willing to do anything to help him."

Oscar's shoulders dropped. It was a low jab, and Camille knew it. As if Oscar didn't already know he owed everything to William Rowen. As if he didn't know he'd be indebted to him for life.

"Of course I care," Oscar answered. "But that stone might not even exist and we need to get out of here *now*."

As if on cue there came a giggling from the top of the stairs. Camille looked over Oscar's head and saw a man's and woman's legs descending.

"What do we have to lose?" Camille asked. "If it doesn't work, there's nothing lost. But if it does work, if this stone really does what it's believed to do . . . Oscar, we have a chance at getting him back."

She wanted to grab his arms and shake him until he understood how much she needed this. In the Tasman, in the center of the storm, she had let go of her father's hand. How could she have let him go without even realizing it? And if everything Oscar was saying about the stone was real, then the storm was her fault to begin with. This was it — her chance to finally do something substantial, to do something that would awe her father as much as he'd been awed by Oscar. She needed to prove that her greatest accomplishment could be more than just a mouthful of wedding vows.

"I know it sounds crazy. It seems as delusional as the voices I heard inside my cabin before the storm. But I can't leave Australia without so much as trying. Can you?"

If they didn't try for Port Adelaide, she'd never meet her mother, either, though finding Umandu had stolen precedence. The thought of coming face-to-face with the woman who had abandoned her was actually more upsetting than it was exciting. It was only now when her mother's life was fading that she wanted to see Camille again. She'd had sixteen years to right her wrong, and yet she'd stayed silent until the time suited her.

Camille saw the resignation in Oscar's expression as the couple from the staircase hit the foyer and turned for the kitchen. Lucius Drake had his arm wrapped around one of Daphne's girls, his cheeks pink and shirttail drooping out of his trousers.

"Making good use of that room?" Lucius asked them, having a laugh with the trollop at his side. Oscar stood unwavering in the center of the hall, forcing Lucius to skirt around him.

"You're a pig," Camille replied, but he only squealed and snorted like a sow.

"Either of you figure out yet how we're going to get home?" Lucius asked. "Don't get me wrong. I'm perfectly content here for the time being."

A pair of sloppy-looking men stumbled through the front door, obviously drunk, and howling like wolves. Oscar stepped up beside Camille, blocking her from their view. His shoulders and chest were the perfect shield against whatever misguided attentions the men might show her.

"When did you become concerned about the three of us sticking together?" she asked Lucius. "We haven't set eyes on you since you disappeared into the orlop deck of the *Londoner*."

Lucius nodded over his shoulder. "I'm being nursed back to health, can't you see?"

She glared at him. Why someone like Lucius had survived the shipwreck instead of a worthier person like her father angered her. Maybe she really *was* cursed.

"You don't have a plan, do you?" Lucius asked Oscar, who continued to block Camille from the two men anxiously waiting by the front door for someone to greet them. Lucius snorted a laugh. "Should'a guessed as much."

Oscar took a step forward, pressing Camille between his chest and Lucius's.

"What do you mean by that?"

Lucius laced his fingers together and bowed them, cracking his knuckles. "Just that everyone knew you were only good for dishing out orders that came from someone else."

Camille placed one hand on Oscar's chest and the other on Lucius and shoved them apart.

"Stop it," she said. "I liked it better when you were out of sight, Lucius."

He chuckled, bouncing on his heels, and entered the kitchen.

Oscar kept his heated stare trained on the braided hallway runner. "Go find Daphne," he ordered her. "Take your bath, and we'll talk after."

Without even waiting for her reply, Oscar stormed away. His feet pounded the stairs, and a moment later the door to their room slammed.

Oscar could object to finding the map and her mother to his heart's content. Camille had already made up her mind. And her mind was set on Port Adelaide.

Camille sat in a steaming bath, gagging from the turnip mush Daphne had insisted she eat to restore color to her cheeks. The woman had stood in the washroom, watching her spoon in the mush, until Camille scraped the bottom of the bowl with a groan of relief. The soap's sharp lye odor bit her nose and mouth now, and Camille wondered if anything would ever taste good again.

She leaned against the curve of the metal tub, and the muscles in her back relaxed. The washroom was a cramped pantry in the rear of the first floor. It felt like a miniature sanctuary, away from Oscar and the way her mind had mutinied when she'd looked at him earlier; away from Randall and the promise of poverty should she not marry him, away from her mother and the stolen map. It was also a haven from the memory of her father refusing to let Camille read the rest of her mother's letter. There had been things he hadn't wanted to share with her. *Things I need to protect you from.* He'd only meant to keep her safe from the curse of Umandu. And she'd lashed out at him, not understanding. How she wished she could go back and stop herself from hurting him.

Behind the slatted double doors that latched with a hook in the center, and behind lace curtains that diffused the glow from an oil lamp in the alley, Camille worked to erase every thought from her head. Her skin softened with the warmth of the water. She concentrated on loosening each muscle, beginning with her toes. Then up to her ankles, calves, thighs, hips. By the time she reached her shoulders, sleep tugged on her eyelids.

Camille filled her lungs with air and dipped below, saturating her hair. She stayed there, eyes closed. The thin walls of the boardinghouse instantly grew thicker as water muffled the sound of a man's hacking cough and the constant clank of something metal from the kitchen. Warm and hidden from the rest of the world, she thought of her father and the last moments of his life. Of icy, turbulent water rushing over his face, sucking him down, pouring into his lungs.

All of a sudden the bathwater started to hiss, as if hot coals had been tossed in. And then, just like they had on the *Christina*, the drums began, loud and fast and uneven. Still underwater, Camille's eyes startled open. On the surface of the bathwater, swirled into the soapsuds, was the same black, skeletal face that had lunged upon the *Christina* within the green wave.

Camille gasped underwater and took in a mouthful. She broke the surface, coughing up water and trying to take a breath at the same time — a taste of what her father had gone through. Her nose and eyes stung and her throat burned as she smoothed back her hair and rubbed her eyes. She blinked twice, and when the water cleared her lashes, the chanting stopped.

A man with a straggly beard stood at the end of the tub. Camille parted her lips to scream, but he held up a long, curved blade. It was probably the knife he'd used to slip between the double doors and unhook the latch. She couldn't move, couldn't speak, her jaw locked open. Her mind raced to calculate how far away Oscar was and if he would reach her in time if she screamed. If she could even manage a scream.

"Yer to come with me," the stranger demanded, without the slightest acknowledgment of how the clear water exposed every inch of her body. He picked up a towel and threw it to her.

"Put somethin' on. And not a peep outter yer."

No more than five minutes later, Camille and the stranger walked in and out of the yellow glow of globe lamps lighting the harbor docks. She wore only what she'd taken with her to the pantry: a pair of drawers and a chemise, covered by a nightdress, and over that a robe. Each time someone passed them, Camille wanted both to cower in humiliation and to scream for help. The man kept the point of his knife firmly to her side, as if he knew her plans.

"Who are you?" she asked for the fifth time. "What do you want?"

Again he gave her no reply, but this time he nipped her in the side. With his hand curled tightly around her arm, he forced Camille to turn onto a darkened wharf. A single lantern lit the slip, the sound of a ship gently creaking and sloshing to her left. Her eyes adjusted to the dim light, and she saw that the ship was a three-masted brig, sails lashed, fenders out.

"I know this brig," she whispered. Its insignia glimmered in the lantern light as the stranger pushed her up the gangway. The *Stealth*. This ruffian was leading her onto Stuart McGreenery's ship!

When had he arrived? Camille surely would have noticed if the *Stealth* had been in the harbor when the *Londoner* tied off in one of the slips. But Melbourne was one of McGreenery's ports, she remembered, and he had also been the recipient of one of her mother's letters. He'd come all this way for her mother? It made no sense, unless there was something he wanted, too, like the map.

The quiet decks alarmed her, and she presumed the crew had been dismissed. The only light that could be seen came from the windows of a cabin tucked below the quarterdeck.

The stranger's heavy fist rapped on the door.

"Enter," came a cool voice. As they stepped inside, Stuart McGreenery rose from his chair. His shoulder-length black hair looked the same as it always had — stick straight, slicked back, and tied at the nape of his neck.

"Camille," he greeted her, extending his hand toward the seat in front of his desk. He gave no notice of her appearance, including her bare feet. She might as well have been completely nude.

"Captain McGreenery," she replied, her repugnance for him brewing. She ignored his offer to sit, clasping the robe around her neck and wiggling her cold toes.

"Accept my condolences on the death of your father and the loss of the *Christina*," he said. She had forgotten the way he chiseled every syllable to a jagged edge.

"Is that why you had this beast break into my bath and force me here at knifepoint?" she asked, the shoulders of her robe wet from her loose hair. McGreenery nodded to the man, and the door clicked shut as he left.

"I apologize," McGreenery said with a definite lack of sincerity. "Some of my sailors have no tact."

Stuart McGreenery matched the name of his ship, *Stealth*, perfectly. His legs were long and lean, dressed in navy trousers and ivory silk stockings. A red sash, tied around his stomach, revealed a cut waistline, and his broad shoulders might have paired evenly with Oscar's. But mostly, he displayed stealth in the way he spoke. Smooth and fast, he chose his words and laid them out with confidence.

"You were injured in the gale," he said, noticing her bruises.

"I'll survive."

McGreenery flashed a set of perfectly white, even teeth. Camille recalled a warning of Juanita's that had once made her laugh. *Never trust a man with perfect teeth. He has too much time and money on his hands.* Camille didn't smile now. She took the warning to heart.

"Indeed, I see that you did survive. Along with that Irish ape." McGreenery raised a brow as he mentioned Oscar. "Forgive me if you find his company . . . pleasing."

Camille crossed her arms over her chest and gripped her shoulders. "How did you learn of the *Christina*?"

McGreenery closed his fingers around a glass of cognac and swirled the liquor.

"Lucius Drake. He signed on with me less than an hour ago."

The traitor! She should have let Oscar wallop him outside the kitchen.

"You'll regret that soon enough," she said.

McGreenery chuckled and stepped closer. Camille smelled his heady cologne, felt heat radiating off his body. She stopped short of breaking eye contact. It was what he wanted, and she wouldn't give it to him.

"Why have you brought me here, McGreenery?" She dropped his proper title purposely in an attempt to make him back off.

He interpreted her meaning and took a step away. "I'm curious as to what you and Kildare will do now," he answered.

"The same as you, I suspect," she said, wanting to sound as confident as McGreenery acted. "We're going to Port Adelaide."

A fire pulsated in a small stove in the corner of McGreenery's cabin but did little to heat the room.

"You know of the letters, then," he said, still standing too close for her comfort. She glanced at his desk, at the neat piles of papers and logs, but didn't spot her mother's red-wax-sealed envelope. Camille wondered what the rest of her father's letter had said. What her mother could possibly have written to Stuart McGreenery.

"Why did she send for you?" Camille asked.

McGreenery's lips thinned into a heartless smile. "She has something of mine."

Camille sensed his vague challenge. "The map isn't yours, McGreenery."

He arched a black, handsomely full eyebrow and turned his back to her so that all she saw was the seam running down the center of his jacket and the pressed high-neck collar of his shirt. In a glimpse of his profile, she watched the flesh of one cheek rise into a grin.

"So your father told you of the map to the enchanted stone."

Camille moved to the chair he had offered her earlier. McGreenery's harsh cologne invaded her nostrils once more as she passed him. Without warning she remembered Oscar's smooth scent, the rind of a peeled orange, the intensity of cloves. She forced herself to refocus.

"My father didn't have a chance to tell me." A painful knot formed in her throat. "But Oscar did."

McGreenery sighed heavily and leaned a hip against his desk. "Of course he did. I should have guessed William would tell that donkey everything."

She hungered to defend Oscar but suppressed the urge. It would do little good. A man of McGreenery's station would never change his mind about someone of Oscar's. Her father had tried in earnest to improve Oscar's life, but society wasn't as compassionate.

"In her letter to you, did my mother say why she took the map?"

McGreenery's lips lingered on the rim of his short-stemmed glass, the tip of his nose so close to the liquor, Camille thought he might accidentally dip it right in. But from what she knew about him, nothing he did was ever accidental.

"You didn't actually read the letter, did you?" he finally said, and extracted his nose.

Camille bit the inside of her cheek and felt the tips of her ears burn.

"I did read it. Half of it. Enough to know my mother's secret." She paused. "And yours."

Her legs went numb, Camille fearful he would call her on the bluff. She had no idea if he even had a secret, though a voyage across the Pacific did point to some kind of reward.

McGreenery's smug grin fell. "Tell me what you think you know."

She started to tremble and hoped he couldn't see it. "I think not, McGreenery."

It was all she could say without revealing the tremor of her voice. She hated to be so nervous, but something about him had changed. A deep chill now seared through his gracious, charming cover. He *did* have a secret.

"The stone is not a plaything for little girls, Camille." He hardened his stare. She tried to keep her eyes equally fierce. "The path to the stone is said to be riddled with traps, endless holes in the earth where you fall forever. Deep caves shelter a species of enormous beasts that protect the stone. Men who set out to find it are usually never seen again."

She sat back, surprised by his intensity and passion.

"Well, then," she said, and watched him puff out his chest victoriously. "I do hope you set out to find it."

He glowered at her. "Oh, I most certainly will. The map and stone will be mine."

Camille stood, pushing her chair back. "It looks like you have some competition, then. I won't give up until I've brought my father back to life."

McGreenery flashed his white smile and roared with laughter. "Bring him back? Oh yes, you would actually *use* the stone."

She lifted her chin. "And you wouldn't?"

He laughed at her again. "Dear child, you don't know a thing about it, do you? You don't have the faintest clue how the stone will work. If you think this is some short journey without risks or sacrifices, you should sail home right now. The magic of that stone is but a fraction of the everlasting power it leads to. A clever businessman would sell that power to the highest bidder."

McGreenery goaded her with a barbed stare. Camille didn't know how to respond. It was true. She didn't know much about the stone, just that it was one of two and that it would bring her father back to her. *How* her father's body would return eluded her as well. The truth of his death was irrefutable. He was dead, his body somewhere in the depths of the Tasman Sea. To believe in Umandu required Camille to believe in magic. It surprised her that she so readily wanted to.

"Once you touch it," she said hesitantly. "You have the power. How can you sell that to someone else?"

She immediately wished she hadn't exposed her lack of knowledge. McGreenery rubbed his smooth chin, his cleft as striking as it had been the first time she met him. He was the only man she'd ever seen with such a finely chiseled indentation cutting perfectly down the center of his chin. If it hadn't been on McGreenery, she might have actually thought it handsome.

"Really, Camille, you shouldn't trouble yourself with such details. After all, you have no means of traveling to Port Adelaide. I hear you don't even have enough money to let a respectable room. Drake tells me you're boarding in a whorehouse."

His eyes drifted to the rise of her breasts. He took a step closer, brushing against her shoulder as he rounded her. His fingers trickled down her arm.

"I do hope you don't resort to the tactics of your housemates to earn money. Your father would be terribly disappointed."

Camille pulled her arm away and walked toward the door. "Oscar and I will make it to Port Adelaide, and we'll get there *first*."

Voices rang from the deck as McGreenery's sailors clambered aboard. Probably back from dinner ashore. Camille remembered Oscar. He'd be looking for her.

"Am I free to leave?"

He waved a hand toward the door. "You were never a prisoner."

"You might have told that to the man with the knife before he abducted me."

McGreenery moved past her and turned the knob. A breath of fishy air wafted inside. She met his dark eyes, still uncertain why her mother had summoned him. Perhaps she wanted to give back whatever she took from him. Perhaps it was something else altogether. But what? He seemed to relish in her bewilderment.

"Good night, Camille."

She left without parting words. The sailors quieted when they saw her and her indecent lack of clothing. She searched their surprised faces for Lucius and spotted him near the bowsprit. He tried to avoid her stare, pretending to converse with another sailor. *That snake,* she thought to herself as she hurried down the gangway and toward Daphne's.

NINE

*W*hat the hell do you mean he had you taken to his ship?" Oscar shouted loud enough for the whole second floor at Daphne's to hear. His eyes traveled down Camille's skimpy nightdress and robe to her bare feet. "And please tell me you weren't wearing that."

Oscar had come tearing up the stairs just a few moments before, throwing open the door so hard he crumbled the plaster of the wall with the knob. He'd been out searching for her when Camille returned.

"Well, not at first," Camille answered him, wanting to avoid the whole stranger-bursting-into-her-bath part altogether.

"What happened? Did McGreenery harm you?"

Camille moved to one of the windows in their room and pushed the curtain aside. On the way back to Daphne's, she had gotten the feeling someone was trailing her. Sure enough, two men stood under the lamppost just beyond the boxwood hedges.

"McGreenery had some ruffian bring me to the *Stealth* at knifepoint. And no, he didn't hurt me. He brought me there to gauge how much I knew about the letter. If I even knew anything at all. When I told him we'd be going to Port Adelaide for the map, something changed." Camille pushed her nearly dry hair out of her face and began pacing the rug near the box stove. "He got angry. He seemed obsessed with the stone."

Oscar gripped the back of his neck, looking as if he would throttle anyone put before him. "Did he say why she wrote to him?"

Camille shook her head. "But he already has plans for the stone. He plans to sell its power. Can you even imagine what someone would pay for that kind of miracle?"

Oscar nodded. "I can also imagine what McGreenery would do to keep us from reaching Port Adelaide."

Camille looked outside. "He's probably sent them to watch us."

Oscar threw the curtain down after he saw the men.

"Word traveled fast about the *Christina*," he said.

"Lucius signed on with the *Stealth*," she said, preparing for another outburst from him. Oscar only rubbed his neck until it grew pink and red, a new habit that seemed to keep his temper under control. He stoked the embers in the hearth before kicking the pillow from his blankets on the floor.

"I can't think straight," he said, rolling out a rag quilt to sleep on. "We'll figure out what to do tomorrow."

Camille put out the light, untied her robe, and settled under the covers across the room from Oscar. She closed her eyes on what had been one of the longest days of her life. Her mind felt clogged, and sleep sounded like the best remedy. Darkness always had a way of making every noise seem louder, and Camille listened intently as someone snored down the hall.

"Are you sure you're all right?" Oscar asked.

"I'm sure." The sound of their voices disturbed the night, and her dishonesty disturbed her. How could she be all right? She'd been abducted at knifepoint. She'd heard the chanting again and seen the eerie black skeletal face on the bathwater's surface. What were those things, if not part of the Umandu curse?

"Are you sure he didn't touch you?" Oscar asked, the softness of his question poles apart from the anger and irritation he'd shown all day. It was obvious he didn't want to go chasing after Umandu, but she couldn't imagine the prospect of bringing her father back to life would make him so sour.

Camille sat up, holding the thin blanket around her neck. An odd thought struck her: They were on land, alone in a room, and they hadn't yet struggled with an awkward stretch of silence. Camille liked the change and hoped it stuck.

Oscar lay on the floor, beneath the double windows. He had one arm over his chest, the other behind his head. He saw her and pushed himself up, his own covers loose around his waist. He still wore his clothes, and she grinned, knowing it was for her benefit only. He'd be sweating rivers tonight in the heavy heat. Oscar wrapped his arm around one knee.

"You have no idea what went through my mind tonight when I found that bathtub empty," he whispered. "I can't let anything happen to you, Camille."

She sat up a little straighter, hoping he wouldn't pledge his protection just to honor his dead captain. "I didn't mean to make you worry, Oscar. But my safety isn't your burden."

Though she couldn't see him clearly in the shadowed room, Camille felt his eyes on her.

"You're not a burden, Camille. Not to me."

She searched his dark outline. A patch of moonlight fell on a swath of bare skin on the curve of his neck. It glistened with sweat, and she felt her own skin fire with the charged silence growing between them. She didn't know how to respond; he wouldn't look away.

"He didn't touch me," she whispered instead, answering his original question. She lay back and turned onto her side, disappointed she hadn't found something more to say. Something to make the moment last a hair longer.

Oscar's covers rustled as he settled back as well.

"That was smart of him," he replied, and said no more.

Waves melted on shore, seeping into wet sand, beneath rocks, shells, and seaweed. Dawn's high tide had riddled the beach with shimmering seashells and stubbly pink starfish. The gouge on Camille's temple had started to scab over and peel, making her self-conscious about how it looked as she walked beside Oscar toward the post office.

"What does it say?" Oscar asked, nodding to the letter clasped in her hand. She had scribbled a short note to Randall before sunrise, pausing her pen so long above the paper that it had dripped blotches of black ink.

"I told him about the wreck, my father, McGreenery . . . Port Adelaide." She'd left out details about Umandu, Daphne, and where they were staying. Even thousands of miles away, she worried about what Randall might think and all the explanations she would have to finesse when she returned.

"He'll get it in about two months, give or take," Oscar said, then looked over his shoulder. The two men McGreenery had posted outside Daphne's followed them at a safe distance.

"I'd like to beat them all the way back to the *Stealth*," Oscar grumbled.

"McGreenery just wants to know the second we've left Melbourne," Camille said. "And I think we should. Soon."

Oscar opened the door to the post office. They stepped inside, leaving the two men trailing them in the blaring sun. The office smelled of sweat and seaweed, and behind a counter stood a gangly man with badly kept whiskers.

Oscar held Camille back.

"We don't even have our own clothes." He nodded to the pants he wore. Daphne had scrounged them up while the rips in his others were being stitched. The borrowed ones rested well above his ankles. "How do you think we're going to pay to get to Port Adelaide? Even if I could set something up with a captain and work for our passage, we wouldn't have control over the ship's course. If the winds are right, it'll take McGreenery three weeks at the most to get there. A regular passenger ship may take up to a month."

Camille cast her eyes to the old man behind the counter, who watched them whisper in the corner. She hadn't thought of how they would pay for their tickets to Port Adelaide. Daphne had given them the money to post Randall's letter, but they couldn't ask her for much more than that.

"Your father's insurance company has a branch in Sydney," Oscar continued.

"It does?" she asked, still unsure they'd find anything there due to them.

"I thought you knew that."

She squeezed her eyes shut until the desire to scream unintelligibly at him passed.

"It doesn't matter. Sydney is in the opposite direction," she said. "You're more than welcome to go back to San Francisco, Oscar, but I'm going to Port Adelaide."

He pursed his lips, no doubt to seal off an objection, and looked up at the cobwebbed ceiling. Camille fidgeted, rubbing the gold band on her left hand. She swept the engagement ring up to her eyes; the sapphire sparkled.

"We don't need my father's insurance. This is as good as money!"

Oscar looked away from the ring as she tugged it off. "Randall gave that to you."

Camille stared at the sapphire, wanting to feel a connection to it. She had been overwhelmed when he'd presented it to her, the pillow-cut stone cloudlessly blue and chunky. Camille had never worn much jewelry, and the ring had seemed foreign and heavy on her finger. She'd told herself she'd get used to it, but it still didn't feel right.

"It's just a ring." She shoved the sapphire into Oscar's palm. "I'm not leaving Australia until we reach my mother and get that stone."

Oscar looked the ring over and then dropped it in his pocket, far from pleased.

Camille handed the postal worker the letter. "Do you know where we could trade something for cash?" she asked him. The man removed the cigar stub from his whiskery mouth.

"I can point ye to the best tradesman in all of Victoria," he answered. "Ye'll find him 'round Alfred Place. Just ask for Ira Beam."

———

Alfred Place didn't have a view of Phillip Bay or the wide, languid Yarra River. It didn't have a view of much at all, except a slew of empty storefronts and residences along a backstreet in the center of Melbourne. Broken whiskey and rum bottles littered the loosely packed dirt road. Camille blew air out of her nose, wanting to expunge the odor of rancid fruit from her nostrils. She stepped around a mound of trash and then a steaming pile of horse manure. A pair of mangy dogs yipped at their heels, pink tongues lolling out the sides of their jaws. Oscar removed his black yarn cap and shoved it into his pocket. Sweat glistened on his temples.

"So this is where we're supposed to find the best tradesman in all of Victoria?" Camille asked. Above them a woman with fleshy arms reached out of a window and reeled in a laundry line.

Oscar took a last look behind them. "At least we've managed to lose the two presents from McGreenery."

"Lost yer way?" the fleshy-armed woman called down to them as she pinned a stained pair of drawers onto a line strung between her house and the next.

"No, we're here on business looking for someone. Perhaps you know him?" Camille replied.

The woman smiled, a tooth missing from her top gums. "Knows lots of people. Who be this?"

She cranked the wheel, little drops of water sprinkling their foreheads as a pair of wet stockings swayed.

"Ira Beam," Oscar answered. The woman stopped the wheel, the laundry snapping to a standstill. Her gummy grin fell.

"What do ye want wif him?"

"So you know him?" Oscar asked. The woman's head disappeared from her window for a moment, then reappeared. She hoisted a bucket onto the windowsill and overturned it. Oscar and Camille leaped out of the way as a gush of brown water splattered at their feet.

"Don't know what business ye have wif that thief, but no friend of his is welcome here." She scowled and drew in the shutters with a smack.

"I think that's our cue to leave," Oscar said, taking Camille's elbow to escort her away. She dug in her heels.

"But what about the ring? We need money."

Not having a single cent to spend made her feel vulnerable. Before, the ability to pay on the spot for a pair of shoes or gloves she fancied had been as natural as grasping for a companion's arm if she happened to trip. Now they were at the mercy of anyone willing to shower them with one form of aid or another. Ugly dresses, odorous turnip mush, shared living quarters with prostitutes, even advice onto whom she should pawn off her engagement ring. What had her life become?

"We'll get the money some other way," Oscar said. "This Beam fellow doesn't sound like someone we want to get involved with."

Camille shook beads of brown water from her newly scrubbed hem.

"Before my father hired you, what did you do for money?" Camille asked as they reached the corner. Oscar slowed down and narrowed his eyes on her.

"Why?" he asked, his suspicion plain.

"I want to know what you'll do to earn money for us," she said slowly, worried that she had touched a sore spot. "You worked the docks, didn't you? What did you do, lading?"

Oscar had given them spare accounts of the first fifteen years of his life: born in Boston, son of Irish immigrants, left home after his parents died of fever. Camille had always wondered if he'd come west with great dreams of wealth from the gold that had just been discovered in the hills surrounding San Francisco. The theory never did quite mesh with Oscar's level demeanor, though.

"I did odds and ends," Oscar answered. *Not exactly enlightening,* she thought as she tried to match the long strides of his legs.

"Maybe I should find a jeweler. They might consider buying my ring," she said.

A whistle rained down on them from the second story of a building. Camille half expected to see the laundress and her wash bucket again. This time it was a man who hung out of a window, the hat in his hands brushing against the exterior brick.

"Just came from the post and I hear you're lookin' for the best tradesman in all of Victoria," he said. Camille groaned, weary of each and every syllable in that sentence.

"We were," Oscar replied. He nudged Camille forward gently, continuing on ahead.

"Whoa, mate, douse the fire at your heels," the man called. "I can introduce you to Ira Beam, long as you ain't lookin' for trouble."

Camille closed her eyes, feeling tired and hot and hungry. She whispered to Oscar, "I think we've already found it."

"Stay put," the man instructed, disappearing from the window. Oscar motioned for Camille to follow him and started again down the street.

"Where are you going?" She grabbed his arm and pulled him to a halt. "Let's just get this over with."

Oscar started to say something in return but sealed his mouth as the man from the window walked out the building's front door. The man popped a hat on his head as his feet hit the dirt, his ankle-length coat originally black but lightened to brown by a layer of street dust.

"So where is he?" Oscar asked, the heat apparently getting to him as well. Or maybe Camille's question about his past had stuck a nerve after all.

"Where's who?" The man took a look up and down the quiet street.

Ira Beam," Oscar answered, his voice loud and deep.

The man clapped his hands, as if getting the point of a joke. His eyes crinkled around the edges when he smiled, and parentheses creased his cheeks.

"Oh, right, right. That was just a cover back there." He stuck out a calloused hand. "Ira Beam."

He was a good deal shorter than Oscar, but Ira looked at least a handful of years older.

"Name's Oscar Kildare. This is Miss Camille Rowen. We need your help."

Ira slid back, palms outward. "Help? Mate, you missed the police by a few blocks."

Camille stepped in front of Oscar, pushing her way into the conversation.

"Are you a tradesman or aren't you?"

Ira's face lit up, his wide grin showing off a set of slightly crooked teeth. At least they were all still there, unlike most of the people Camille had crossed paths with in Melbourne so far.

"Among other professions, Miss Feisty One," Ira Beam answered, pulling at the lapel of his jacket.

"Then you can help," Camille said. Oscar reached into his pocket and brought out the ring.

Ira lit a cigar and chewed it with his molars, taking a moment to inspect the sapphire.

"Beautiful ring, absolutely stunning. A bit small for you, wouldn't you say?" Ira winked at Oscar and took another puff of his cigar. "I'll give you five pounds for it. Tops."

"Five? It's worth more than twenty," Oscar said.

Ira shrugged. "When it was spankin' new, it was, yeah, but now it's all tainted and used. Can't sell it for more than ten, and I need to turn a profit, you know what I'm saying?" Ira stuck his hand into his coat pocket. He eyed Oscar. "What do you need the money for, anyhow? You don't look desperate enough to hawk your woman's ring."

Camille took the ring from Oscar. "I'm not his woman. My fiancé is in America," she said, wondering how Ira knew it was tainted. "Oscar and I need to buy two tickets for the next ship to Port Adelaide."

Ira crossed his arms, the cigar firmly between his teeth.

"You and him are going to Port Adelaide, your fiancé is in America, and I'm guessing that ring's from said fiancé." Ira scratched his temple, raising his sun-bleached eyebrows. "Sorry, love, I'm not catching on."

Camille jammed the ring back onto her finger.

"Listen, my father was on his way to Port Adelaide to get something that belonged to him. Seeing how he went down in a shipwreck that we managed to survive, it's fallen to me to retrieve this thing before a certain someone else can," Camille answered, then refilled her spent lungs.

"Oh, my condolences." Ira fiddled with his wide-brimmed hat. "Who's this *certain someone else*, and what's it you're both racing to get to in Port Adelaide?"

Camille felt queasy as McGreenery entered her mind. She couldn't stand the thought of him reaching her mother first. He'd probably wrench the map from her frail fingers if he had to.

"My mother is in Port Adelaide. She's dying and she sent for my father," she commenced.

"Camille," Oscar warned through clenched teeth.

She ignored him. "There's another man, his business competitor, who she sent for as well. His name is Stuart McGreenery and he just docked in Melbourne's harbor yesterday. He'll be in Port Adelaide in less than a month. We can't let him reach her first."

Ira leaned against the window of the storefront.

"Why not?"

Camille clasped her hands behind her back. The fabric of her honey-brown striped dress, which she'd taken in to make fit right, was damp with sweat. More beads formed on her neck as Ira waited for an answer. She couldn't be too forward, or too trusting, with her information.

"My mother has something he wants, something she took a long time ago," Camille answered.

Ira stroked his chin whiskers. "Money?"

Camille hesitated. McGreenery had said a clever businessman would sell the stone's power to the highest bidder. To beat him she needed to be equally clever.

"A map," she answered.

His eyes twinkled. "To a treasure?"

Camille nodded, and Ira bit the inside of his cheek.

"Well, now you've got me hooked. What's the treasure? Gold? Silver? Jewels?"

Oscar shook his head when Camille looked at him, and she agreed. It wouldn't be clever at all to reveal the bit about Umandu. Ira only laughed and wagged a finger at them.

"I see what you're doing. Keeping things mysterious, are you? Well, it works in your favor, love. All right, I'll cut you two a deal. A good one."

Oscar crossed his arms. "We're more than ready to hear it."

"I take you to Port Adelaide, all primary expenses paid by yours truly." Ira bowed and continued, "When we arrive, I want in on the hunt for the treasure. My friend in Port Adelaide can get us set up with whatever we need. And when we find it, I want half."

Camille gaped at him and laughed. Maybe a bit too haughtily, but who did he think he was?

"There is no need for you to accompany us, Mr. Beam. We're capable of buying our own boarding passes for the trip. All we need is more money for my ring."

Ira mocked her with his own haughty chuckle. "You won't be going anywhere on a ship. The next one for Port Adelaide doesn't leave for a week."

Camille's smug grin crumbled. "Are you sure of that?"

Ira nodded and jammed a thumb into his chest. "Trust me, I know how to get out of a town quickly, and today it wouldn't be by ship."

"Then how will we get there?" Oscar asked. The port city must have been over three hundred miles west.

"Horse and wagon," Ira answered, sounding at ease with his simple plan. Aggravated, Oscar looked away. Ira frowned. "What, you have a better idea?"

Camille touched Oscar's sleeve. "Horse and wagon could work. It might be slower, of course. Mr. Beam, how long should it take?"

He shrugged and kicked at some dirt. "'Bout a month, give or take."

"A month?" she screeched.

Ira whipped off his hat and slapped it against his leg. "You two are extremely picky for having just survived the sinking of a ship." He combed a hand through his tousled brown hair, and Camille noticed how handsome he was. Beneath the dirt and insincerity, anyway.

"Look," Ira said. "There's a place I can go to make a small profit tonight. I'll buy our supplies and we can head out tomorrow morning. It's the fastest way out of here, mates, and it sounds like that's what you're searching for."

Camille knocked her arm into Oscar's, attempting to communicate with him through raised brows and a few nods toward Ira.

Oscar gave a throaty exhale, clearly unenthused. "Fine. But half of the treasure is too much," he replied. "A quarter."

Ira chewed on his cigar another moment. "Let's talk insurance. How do I know you'll pay up?"

Oscar attempted a smile, but it ended up a menacing grin. "You'll just have to trust us."

The Australian huffed a laugh. "Ira Beam doesn't trust no one," he replied.

Oscar startled Camille by grabbing her arm. He pulled her roughly away from Ira, making to leave. They got a good five yards away before they were called back.

"All right, all right!" Ira shouted. "Trust or no trust, I can't resist a new venture, mates. A quarter it is. But you pay for my passage back here. Actually, make it Sydney. Been meaning to visit a lady friend there."

Oscar started to walk back, but Camille held her footing. "Don't you think we should discuss this first?" she asked, wondering where he planned on scrounging up Ira's quarter. A quarter of what? There would be no dividing the stone.

"Either I get a quarter or you find your own way to Port Adelaide," Ira cut in.

"Just hold on a minute," Oscar told Ira. He pulled Camille out of earshot, toward a dark alley wedged between two dilapidated houses.

Turning her back to Ira, Camille whispered, "Why are you promising money we can't pay?"

Oscar leaned close to her ear. "You think he's going to take us there for free?"

Camille's hair fluttered under his breath, and a tremor shivered down her body, all the way to her toes.

"He won't be thrilled when he discovers we've nothing but a stone to taunt him with," she said. They.didn't know this man. He might be dangerous.

"I'd be more than happy to drop this whole plan and head back to California," Oscar said.

"I've already told you, Oscar. You're free to go and do as you please." As soon as she said it, Camille silently pleaded that he wouldn't choose to leave. What would she do without him? Oscar tucked his chin to his chest and fixed his eyes on her.

"If I'm going to help you do this, then you've got to trust me," he said. "I know what I'm doing."

Camille held his stare. "Okay," she said with a nod. "I trust you."

They stepped back to Ira, and Oscar held out his hand. "A quarter and a ticket to Sydney."

Ira took Oscar's hand, raising his brow at the way his hand disappeared in Oscar's. "I'll need a deposit, of course. I think that's where your ring comes in handy." Ira extended his open hand toward Camille. She took off the sapphire and slapped it into his palm.

"And McGreenery?" Oscar asked. Ira nodded and threw his hat back on. He pulled it tight and grinned from ear to ear.

"Leave him to me, mates. I'll meet you at the blacksmith's in town tomorrow morning, eight o'clock sharp."

Oscar took a step closer, towering over Ira. "If you're not there, I'll find you. And you don't want me to have to find you."

Ira cleared his throat and pulled the brim of his hat. "Then I better not oversleep."

He swiveled on his heel with the same light-hearted air Camille had loved about her father and strolled back down the road. The similarity to her father ended there.

"I don't trust that man," she said.

"You shouldn't. I've known plenty like him. He's a card shark and a swindler. He'll probably sell off that ring of yours for gambling money."

Camille expected a pang of guilt, but it didn't come. Her hand felt lighter than before. As beautiful as it was, the ring had been simply too big. Too cumbersome. It got in the way when she dressed, when she brushed her hair, or even when she wrote. She snagged it on the bedsheets, and had even scraped her own skin once while bathing.

"Don't look so grim. When you get home, I'm sure Randall will buy you all the rings you want. One for every day of the week," Oscar said, thick with sarcasm, as they walked back toward the harbor.

"I don't care about the ring!" Camille shouted. She stopped walking and turned to Oscar. "I'm sorry, it's just that . . ."

Oscar patiently waited for her to finish her sentence. Camille looked away, embarrassed. She had scraped Randall's skin with the ring, too. It had been one of their rare moments alone. He'd run his fingers down her back, nibbled on her neck, and she'd waited for her legs to turn to warm butter. She'd waited to feel the desire to kiss him. But the feelings hadn't come. Camille had swept her hand up to stop him, and the ring had left a puffy red scratch on his arm.

Oscar watched her fumble for words, his expression one of concern.

"Never mind," she said quickly and stepped up onto a raised sidewalk, out of the mud.

"Never mind what?"

"It's private."

He continued walking in the street, his head level with hers.

"Private between who?"

"Between me and Randall. You wouldn't understand," she said and lifted her skirt as she descended back down into the muddy street where the sidewalk ran out.

"And why is that?" he asked, sounding put off. Daphne's place came into view. The air smelled of bitter salt water and of wood smoke curling up from the kitchen chimney.

"Oh, Oscar, you're a man of the sea. What could you possibly know about relationships?"

He'd never courted a woman as far as Camille knew. She slowed her pace. Or had he? Oscar stopped in the middle of the cobblestoned walkway leading to Daphne's front door. His eyes blazed with hurt and resentment.

"I do apologize, *Miss Rowen*, I forgot mere sailors aren't worthy of marriage. Isn't that what your father always said?"

Camille's cheeks seared with heat. It was a stance her father had never parted from, but she hadn't known he'd also impressed it upon Oscar. She fidgeted with her hands and fumbled for an apology. "No, that's not what I meant. You're a bachelor, that's all."

Oscar shook his head, unable to meet her eyes. She'd sounded so patronizing. Oscar was handsome, young, and single, and for a man of his class, he made a decent living. Enough to attract an equally decent amount of attention from women, she supposed. Why hadn't she ever thought of that?

He retreated to the street. "I'm going for a walk."

"Oscar, wait —"

He pivoted on his heel. "You know, you're wrong, Camille. And your father was wrong, too."

Oscar turned and disappeared behind the boxwood hedges. Camille clenched two fistfuls of her skirt and stomped up the steps, aggravated over her careless words. She'd been pompous and arrogant, and she hated that she'd hurt him. She cringed at the wounded way he'd looked at her.

She reached for the front door and saw one of McGreenery's men come out from behind the boxwoods. He hovered near the walkway, while the other man continued on, apparently on Oscar's tail. Camille went inside and slammed the door, hoping Ira Beam stuck to his word.

In the middle of the night, Camille leaped to an ear-splitting explosion. Had she dreamed it, she wondered, as she threw off the covers and stumbled out of bed, still submerged in the fog of sleep. On the floor, Oscar peeled off his blankets. Sweat smothered her arms and chest, and dusty air clung to her skin. From behind the curtains came a bright orange flickering. Concerned voices heightened in the parlor below their feet. Pulling the curtain aside, her eyes landed upon a ship in the harbor, ablaze. Shouts rang along the street and darkened figures ran toward the inferno.

They watched a small boy climb to the top of the fire tower two buildings over and swing from the bell's rope. Hollow *clangs* parted the night. Oscar covered his mouth with his hand and let go of the curtain. Camille continued to stare out the window in shock. The fiery ship sitting in the harbor was none other than Stuart McGreenery's.

TEN

The next morning, clouds hung low in the sky and strong winds blew inland from another storm at sea. In Daphne's front room, Oscar sat at a small round table with plates of eggs and toast piled around his elbows.

Camille pulled out a chair across from him. "Celebrating something?" she asked.

A wicked smile formed on his lips, showing off his dimples. "Just a good night's sleep."

She smiled, too, though not without some reservation. Just what kind of person had they partnered with? A thief *and* an arsonist? Camille placed a napkin in her lap and devoured a slice of buttered toast.

Oscar hadn't returned from his walk until well after dark the night before. Camille had already turned down the lamps, pulled the blankets up to her ears, and buried her head in her pillow to avoid having to speak to or see him.

"Oscar." She felt her pulse rise. "What I said to you yesterday was miserable."

He kept his attention on his eggs.

"I didn't mean to be so thoughtless. I was just trying to avoid your question."

Oscar finished chewing. "I'm sorry, too," he whispered. "So what about Randall don't you want to talk about?"

The fork slipped between her damp fingers, and she set it on the rim of the plate.

"It's just . . . I haven't talked about it with anyone. I don't really know how to put it."

She wanted to be desperately in love with Randall and not just fond of him. She didn't want to need to marry Randall; she just wanted to *want* to. It had been her father's greatest hope for her — and for the company. There was no way to explain it all to Oscar, though, without going into her father's poor finances.

As she drew her palm into her lap, it left a handprint of sweat on the lacquered cherry table. Oscar eyed the evaporating mark.

"What are you so nervous about?"

She massaged the healed wound on her temple. It still ached, but she couldn't stop feeling for it each time she thought of her father.

"If you were about to be married, wouldn't you be nervous?" she asked.

He took a sip of his black tea. "Nothing to be nervous about if you're marrying the right person."

Camille dumped a spoonful of sugar into her tea. She knew she shouldn't have bothered asking anyone, especially not a man.

Oscar stopped, his forkful of eggs halfway to his mouth. "Are you rethinking the wedding?"

Camille choked on a bite of toast.

"No!" she said, hammering out a cough. "Of course not."

The front door swung open and a gust of wind rushed inside. Boots scuffled along the floor, and Camille turned to see what pig had shown up at Daphne's so early in the day. Her heart thumped as the door slammed. Stuart McGreenery tucked his arched captain's hat under his arm and pulled off his white gloves.

"A charming establishment," he said. He turned up his nose, and sniffed the air.

"Is that desperation I smell?"

Oscar threw his fork and knife on the table and kicked back his chair. "Did you decide to join us for breakfast?"

McGreenery lunged forward and Oscar rose to his feet.

"I came to see what you know about the hole in the hull of my ship, you insolent whelp," McGreenery said.

Oscar's cheek twitched with pleasure. "Why not just have me escorted down to it with a knife in my back?"

Camille stood and inserted herself between the two men. Daphne sat in the corner of the parlor rolling cigars, her wide eyes darting from McGreenery to Oscar.

"We heard the explosion," Camille said. "What makes you think we had anything to do with it?"

McGreenery retreated one small step and stared down the slope of his nose at her. This time he kept his icy stare level with her eyes. "Because it was not an accident. The explosion was set in a deliberate attempt to keep me from departing for Port Adelaide."

Camille tried to subdue the shake of her knees. "We certainly didn't set it. Oscar and I were in our room."

McGreenery cocked his head.

"I heard you were sharing a room." He glanced at Oscar. "I doubt William would be fond of that."

"You don't have the right to even speak his name," Oscar said, strangling each word.

McGreenery gracefully removed the hat out from under his arm and slipped it back on. "It doesn't matter. Nothing will stop me from reaching the stone, least of all a little girl and her trained monkey."

Camille rushed forward, ready to smack McGreenery across the cheek. Oscar grabbed her around the waist and held her back. McGreenery bowed slightly, grinning with pleasure, and then whisked out the front door.

She shrugged out from Oscar's grasp and watched through the windows as McGreenery sauntered down the street toward the *Stealth*, where she could hear the echo of repairs already under way.

"One day that prick is going to get what he deserves," Oscar muttered. "I just hope I'm the one who gets to give it to him."

"He's an angry one, tha's for sure," Daphne commented from her corner chair. She licked the seam of a paper and then pressed it down, sealing the cigar. "What do those two goons out by the hedges want with you, anyhow? They've been an eyesore the last few days."

The scent of sweet butter and eggs filled her senses, but Camille had lost her appetite.

"He wants to know our every move," she answered Daphne, who sprinkled a clump of tobacco on the next brown paper. Camille turned to Oscar. "How are we going to meet Mr. Beam at eight without McGreenery finding out?"

"There's a back door, you know," Daphne said, jabbing a thumb toward the rear of the house.

"The blacksmith's is within sight of the hedges," Oscar replied. "We show up there, and those two will spot us."

Daphne laughed and stood, heaving her heavy bosom up from the chair. The spots of scurvy had already started to fade from her pale skin.

"Not if they're in the parlor here enjoying some tobacco."

A small mound of cigars lay on a side table. Oscar patted her on the back.

"You're a good woman, Daphne," he said.

"A damn good woman!" she cried as he and Camille rushed from the parlor.

The scent of charred wood traveled heavy on the breeze, and Camille shivered as the wind blew through the thin fabric of her dress. Ira waved at them as they came into view. He sat crouched against the blacksmith's shop, his mud-covered boots tucked underneath him. Three horses swayed their heads nearby, one hitched to a small wagon

filled with sacks and a few crates, and the other two sad-
dled and ready to ride. Ira brushed off his pants and pulled
the cigar from his mouth.

"Imagine my luck last night," Ira said, flashing a clean
smile. "I won all this off the other players *and* that ship
mysteriously burst into flames. I hear it'll take a few
weeks to patch her up. Shame."

Ira and Oscar chuckled together like naughty children;
however, Camille crossed her arms.

"People could have been seriously injured, Mr. Beam."

Oscar sobered, but Ira waved off her concern. "Life's
about risks, love. Can't get anywhere without taking 'em."

Still dubious about their guide, Camille glanced back
toward Daphne's. The front steps were clear.

Ira went over their supplies with them: food, blankets,
canteens of water, and a couple of rifles. He handed
Camille a man's brimmed hat with a warning about the
Australian sun. She placed the timeworn hat, which she
had no intention of wearing, on the wagon bench.

"You know how to drive a wagon?" Ira asked.

"I've sailed a ship." Camille sounded more confident
than she felt. Joseph, their coachman, had done all the
driving around San Francisco when she'd needed to
go out.

Ira helped her up into the driver's bench, then handed
her the leather reins.

"It's simple. You slap the reins to go. If you want to
turn left, you tug on the left rein. Right, you tug on the
right rein. And to stop, you pull back."

Oscar mounted his horse and turned to Ira. "And you're sure you know how to get there?"

Ira waved off the question. "Of course, mate. Got it mapped out right here." He tapped his forehead. Oscar crinkled his brow.

"Do you at least have something we could look at? Like a map and compass?"

"What do you take me for, a blithering idiot? Course I got a map and compass." He patted the breast pocket of his jacket to let them know where he kept them. Camille slapped the reins and the wagon wheels creaked and turned, sinking slightly in the mud as they came out from behind the blacksmith's.

In the harbor, the scorched side of McGreenery's ship, brought up on drydock, had drawn a large crowd of spectators, who graciously blocked the view of the street. By the looks of the *Stealth*'s gutted midsection, it would take more than two weeks to repair.

Platinum clouds blocked the sun, and Camille left the brimmed hat Ira had handed her on the bench. The winds settled once they turned onto a road carved out of the damp, thickly forested landscape. Oscar rode behind the wagon and Ira trotted up front, in the lead. Camille breathed in the fading salt air, savoring it.

Raised bungalows sat nestled in the mountainside, built of bamboo and teetering on tall stilts. Water dripped off massive green leaves. Palm trees bore coconuts, wide fanned-out fronds, and furry critters scuttled away at the sound of their caravan. Some homes had completely leveled yards, the trees having been ripped from the earth for cattle grazing. The soil looked brown and bare in spots and green and lush in others.

As soon as the ocean breeze dissipated, the humidity clung to Camille's arms, neck, and back. Even her hands dripped with sweat. The dense air barely made its way up her nostrils. She parted her lips to breathe and fought to keep her eyes open as they moved through the claustrophobic path. She longed for a cooling breeze, the kind that built over the surface of an ocean and swept onto shore. She had relished them back home whenever she stood on the California Wharf, her toes tipped out over the edge. Mornings were best, the breeze new like the day. One morning, she had hurried down to the wharf, startled by the first clear sunrise in weeks. She'd been eleven or twelve, before Oscar had come to them, and she'd let the wind run invisible fingers through her hair.

Nothing significant occurred that day, no life-altering event. It had been just a morning on the wharf. Her father had tiptoed up behind her, grabbed her by the shoulders, and pretended to thrust her over the edge. He swept her back, away from the peaceful green water, and held her, his arm around her shoulders. Together they had looked out over the bay and agreed there was no sight more spectacular than an ocean waking at dawn.

After hours of traveling through a mix of forest and pastureland, the sun went down, cooling the air. Dusk settled under a quiet sky, excepting a random howl in the distance. They had discovered a clearing in a rocky grazing field, worn with remnants of an old campfire, and had stopped for the night. Camille shivered and pulled a blanket up around her shoulders.

"Was that a wolf?" Camille asked Ira, who was bent over the fire. The echoing howl faded in the crackle of the wood.

"No wolves 'round here. Those are dingoes," he answered. "Wild dogs. Not dangerous, don't worry."

He didn't look at her, spoke too fast, and she didn't believe him. Oscar had helped Ira build the fire, but the kindling was damp from a late-afternoon flash downpour and wouldn't grow past a certain pathetic point.

Ira sat on a patch of wet sod near the fire. "Should reach Bendigo in a day. We'll make camp there, too. Unless I win a hand or two, then maybe we can afford a couple'a rooms."

Oscar sat down, opposite of Ira. "You do anything other than play cards?"

Ira snorted. "What, waste my life tied down to one job, one place?" He stoked a few embers. "Not for me, mate."

"Doesn't it bother you to be moving around all the time?" Camille asked.

Ira shook his head. "Bother? Hell no," he said. "Who could get bothered by fresh scenery every other month?"

Camille shrugged. "I suppose it does sound exciting."

"For a nomad," Oscar grumbled, pulling on his jacket to ward off the chill of the night. "When was the last time you were in Port Adelaide?"

Ira crushed a glowing ember. "'Bout five years ago, right after my mate Monty moved out there."

"When was the last contact you had with him?" Oscar asked.

Ira took a long swig from his canteen, replaced the cap, and scrunched up his nose. "Five years ago," he answered, then let out a wet burp. "'Scuse me, love."

Camille grimaced and sipped water from her own canteen.

"Then you can't be sure he's still in Port Adelaide," Oscar continued.

Ira placed a hunk of salt pork in a pot with a few handfuls of small white beans and water. "Sure I can. Old Monty would've sent word if he packed up." But Ira's face darkened and his hand covered his stubbled beard. "Course, not if Stella went and told him 'bout that time in Sydney."

Camille closed her eyes and knitted her fingers to keep them from forming fists. Oscar sat with his head in his large hands, as though he had an unbearable headache. Looking back at Ira, she figured he probably did.

"Who is Stella and what happened in Sydney?" she asked.

"Monty's wife and an act I can't describe with a lady present," Ira crowed.

"Well, aren't you a gentleman," Oscar said under his breath.

"Don't worry, mate. Stella's conscience is buried so far under her folds of skin, she's bound never to find it."

Ira stoked the small flames and showed them his toothy grin. "She's a lot of woman to love, that Stella."

Camille's eyes watered with shock.

"I don't think you could bluff your way out of that one," Oscar said. Ira jumped into a crouch, bobbing up and down.

"Wait till you see me bluff. It's like an art."

Bluff. The word held on in her mind, and Camille remembered something she'd said to McGreenery that night on the *Stealth*. It had fallen through the cracks as she'd focused on getting to Port Adelaide and the map.

"I bluffed McGreenery," she said. Oscar and Ira stared at her. "I bluffed him into believing I knew why my mother had written to him. I said I knew his secret."

Ira removed the pot from the fire and cursed when the iron burned his fingertips.

"Everyone's got a secret. Hell, some's got loads of secrets. What's so important about his?"

"I don't know. Whatever it is, he didn't seem very happy about me knowing."

Ira sliced the pork into three parts with his knife and handed them each a portion. "Maybe you got a future in poker."

The fire tuckered out in its own good time, and they scrunched down under their blankets. Camille slumbered in the back of the wagon, her head propped on a sack of beans. Looking up at the sky, the blades of the trees seemed to brush the stars and moon. She dreamed of her mother, trying to animate in her mind the beautiful woman in the oil painting in her father's study. How had her lips, the perfect brushstrokes, moved when she spoke? What shape teeth did her smile reveal? How had her laugh sounded? *So many questions,* Camille thought. As she turned onto her side and pulled the blanket up to her chin, a bit of guilt snuck up on her. She wanted the answers, but she wanted the stone and her father more.

ELEVEN

*C*amille pulled the jacket Ira had won in his last Melbourne poker game over her head as rain fell in torrents. They made good time toward Bendigo, but the weather lowered visibility to less than a yard. Her horse struggled to pull the wagon through the muck. Ira came back toward her.

"Let me." He dismounted and helped Camille from the driver's seat. Oscar's horse trotted up to their side.

"A different driver isn't going to make the earth hard again!" Camille shouted above a thunderclap that reverberated like a sheet of ridged metal. She wiped rain from her eyes and trudged to his horse. Ira slapped the reins, and the sunken wheels inched forward. They pressed on, with Oscar riding along their flank. They were on a northwesterly route, Ira had told them before dawn. Highlands lay to the north and south, and a path of densely forested brush right in between would take them west.

The rain cleared quickly, like a spring shower. Nothing more than a light spit speckled their cheeks when there came a cadenced thundering from behind them. One by one they each turned in their seats. Camille searched the green horizon but saw only grass and bush wavering in the heat rising from the earth.

"Keep riding," Ira ordered, sounding uncertain. Camille continued to search the land behind her as the sound of galloping horses' hooves rose and fell.

A rustle of wind, cool and damp, filled her ears. Rogue strands of hair framing her face lifted and tickled her skin as the sound of the wind transformed into something different. It sounded human, like a husky, openmouthed exhale. It tunneled through her ears and into the core of her head. *No, not again.* Camille squeezed her eyes shut as the guttural chanting ripped through. She bowed her head, pressing her chin into her chest as the hollow drums beat through her like the pulse of a throbbing heart. Her own pulse picked up the rhythm, and everything beyond the skin of her eyelids disappeared. Just like in the bath, and in her cabin aboard the *Christina* before that, the chanting abruptly ceased.

She gasped for air, realized she'd been holding her breath, and let in the harsh afternoon light. The sun seared her pupils.

"I said to keep riding," Ira called back to her. He and Oscar had traveled ahead, while Camille's mount had stopped moving. She twisted in her saddle. In the surge of heat coming up off the ground, a most unwelcome shape appeared: two black voids; a narrow, triangular hole denoting a nose; and a pronounced jaw, edged with ghastly teeth. The black skeletal face rippled in the heat, then swirled into a maelstrom and vanished.

"What in hellfire was that?" Ira breathed.

Far back through the trees and overgrowth, where the skeletal face had been, a figure on horseback materialized.

"And who are they?" Oscar asked as a second, and then a third figure, appeared. Ira slapped the reins of his horse, and the wagon rumbled forward.

"Get moving!" he shouted.

Without thinking, Camille dug her heels into the horse's ribs and took off. Wind coursed through her hair, and the horse's jounce threatened to toss her into the brush. The riders came after them, hard and fast. Ira's wagon lurched over mounds and downed tree limbs and teetered onto two wheels around a sharp corner. Camille's whole body shook as she rode, hardly breathing, shins and knees aching from their bowlegged position around the horse's massive chest.

"Here!" Ira shouted. The grunts and snorts of their horses' heavy breathing dwarfed his voice, but Camille followed him as he rolled off the path into a thicket of head-high shrubs. Overgrown limbs flew into her face, scratching her cheeks as Ira led them down a trail that hadn't been touched by hooves or wheels in what looked like years.

Ira veered around another sharp corner, disappearing from sight. Camille took the corner, and her horse barreled through a wooden-frame entrance dug into a hillside. Blackness met her, and her horse reared back.

"Whoa!" Ira whispered, emerging from the dark and taking the reins of her mount. Behind her, Oscar rushed into the dugout. The ceiling and walls had been constructed with roughly cut rocks and packed soil. Ira led them farther in until they were completely hidden. They stood still—still as the dust that had settled back onto the dugout floor—and listened. Blood rushed through Camille's head and ears, but after a few deep breaths, she heard horses' hooves fading in the distance. And then they were gone.

Ira wiped sweat from his brow.

"Who were they?" Oscar asked. He removed the wide-brimmed hat Camille had passed on to him. It was too mannish for her, and her appearance was already suffering enough. It gave Oscar a rugged appearance and blocked the glaring sun better than his sailor's cap, too.

Ira's chest heaved as he stepped back into the sunlight.

"Why did we run from them?" Camille asked. Ira crouched down low and pressed one hand to the ground, raising his other to shush them.

Oscar wiped the sweat from his face with his sleeve and slapped his hat against his thigh. Dust billowed into the air around him.

"They're gone," Ira stated as he stood up and grabbed his horse. He steered the wagon back into the sunlight.

"They being who?" Camille asked as she pulled on her own horse's reins. The mare didn't budge. Camille dug her heels into the earth and heaved. No luck. Ira came back into the dugout, took the reins, and led the stubborn mare out.

"No one," he answered her. "Let's just keep riding. And quick."

Oscar jumped into his saddle and rode in front of Ira's path. "Not until you tell us what just happened. Do you have people after you?"

Ira tried to move around Oscar's horse, but Oscar blocked him again.

"I don't have people after me, got it? But finding a gang of riders comin' up fast on your tail ain't a good omen. And speaking of bad omens, what was that thing back there? Am I the only bloody person who saw a skeleton's face in the air?"

Camille shot a look at Oscar, whose eyes had cut to her. She couldn't explain it without bringing up Umandu, and she didn't want Ira running out on them yet.

"What are you going on about?" she asked.

"Ira, have you been drinking?" Oscar made a swipe for Ira's canteen. "What's really in there?"

Ira jerked away. "I'm not drunk! Never mind, then. Must have been a trick on the eyes," he said, but a faraway look told Camille he didn't quite believe it. "Lucky for us, I recognized where we were and made a swift turn."

Camille looked back into the dugout. "Is this a mine?"

Ira shrugged and finally made his way around Oscar's horse. "From my gold-diggin' days. Never made a go of it. Lost more money than I made."

Camille mounted her horse, her dress clinging to the sweat on her back and arms. The chanting had again preceded a stroke of bad luck. She didn't believe for an instant those riders were nothing to worry about. They had something to do with the stone, but she didn't know what.

They kept a swift pace the rest of the day, stopping to rest only twice. Ira refused to say anything about the three riders.

Oscar and Camille abandoned the subject as they shuffled into the mining town of Bendigo at dusk. People filled the rambling street, and laughter echoed out of busy taverns. Oil lamps lit the walkways at sparse intervals, illuminating communities of white tents adorned with hand-chiseled signs like BATH and FOOD and one that even advertised a reading of one's fortune inside for only a sixpence. Camille searched the limited number of buildings for hotel establishment signs, her head splitting from tension and exhaustion.

Ira eyed one of the bawdy taverns as they rode by. "How 'bout I win a few rounds and get us a hotel room?"

"How about you take the money you'd put in the center of the poker table and use it to get us that hotel room?" Camille replied. He swiveled in his seat.

"My skills are gonna turn rusty with you around," he muttered, then pulled in front of a two-story sandstone hotel called the Kismet.

They loaded up their backs with the rifles, canteens, and food — nothing safe left unattended — and entered the lobby. The first floor was a plush gathering spot for what looked to be successful miners. Forest-green silk curtains, embroidered with gold thread, shielded the entrance to the saloon. Oscar pulled Camille close to the drapes as Ira went to the desk to talk to the clerk.

"What happened earlier?" he asked. Camille dropped a sack of kidney beans on the rug. Never in her life would she have imagined she'd enter a hotel carrying a sack of beans.

"You mean about the riders? I think Ira's not telling us the whole truth," she said.

Oscar shifted the weight of the two rifles on his back. "No, I meant with you, when you went all rigid in the saddle."

Camille kneaded her shoulder to work out a tight knot.

"It was that awful chanting again. It came right before those riders appeared." *Like a warning.* A curse wouldn't warn her, would it? Perhaps the legend of Umandu was all wrong. But if it was wrong about the curse, what else could it be wrong about? McGreenery had accused her of knowing nothing about the stone. She hated that he'd been right.

"And the skeleton face we lied to Ira about not seeing?" Oscar went on. Camille scratched the bridge of her nose and avoided his glare.

"That, uh, could be something to do with the curse," she answered hastily. Oscar groaned and jangled the rifles again.

"This is only the third day. The rate we're going, we won't make it to Port Adelaide in one piece," he said.

Camille hushed him. "We've already cheated death once, Oscar. For some reason we were meant to live. I believe it was to go to Port Adelaide and find my mother and the stone, not to die trying to get there."

Oscar peeled back the green drape an inch. Inside, men smoked and laughed while admiring three large golden nuggets in the center of a table.

"I believe in what I can see. What I can touch and smell and taste. That's what's real to me." He let the drape fall. "I don't know what that mirage was back there on the trail. I don't know if two stones were ever really stolen from the Underworld or if just saying a name curses you, but I'm having a hard time putting stock in a magic stone that's never been seen outside the imagination. It's just not reasonable."

So Oscar didn't believe in Umandu. And he probably saw her as nothing but a silly little girl who did.

"Why does it have to be reasonable? I'm tired of being reasonable. What reason was there for the *Christina* to go down? For my father to die? I said the stone's name for the first time that night, just before the storm returned. I sent my father and his ship to the bottom of the sea, and I can't make any sense out of it. It isn't logical, it isn't anything

I can touch or smell or taste," she said, struggling not to break down into sobs. "But I believe in what the stone might be able to do. I have to believe in it."

Oscar softened his pursed lips and shifted his weight from one leg to the other.

"After everything that's happened," Camille continued, "I'm ready to throw reason overboard. Something inside me says what we're doing is right. And that even he's right." Camille nodded toward Ira, who had stopped to flirt with a waitress.

"Are you telling me you actually trust him?" Oscar asked.

Camille inspected their guide as he propped an elbow on the clerk's desk and shoved up the brim of his hat. He leaned toward the waitress and murmured something in her ear. The waitress gasped and smacked Ira across the cheek.

"That might be going too far," Camille replied. The waitress swiveled on her high heel and rushed through the drapes, into the smoky saloon.

Camille turned to Oscar and lowered her voice. "Since we're being honest with each other, I wish you'd quit being such a crab. You seem irritated by everything. I don't remember you ever being this way before."

Quiet and serious, yes. But not angry.

Oscar gripped a rifle and a pack of provisions and leaned closer.

"That was before the wreck. Before everyone on the *Christina* died but us."

Camille shrank away from him. "You do blame me, then. You think it's my fault because I said the stone's name."

Oscar looked as stunned as Camille. "Blame you? Of course not. None of this is your fault."

Camille's first instinct was to argue with Oscar, insist she was to blame, remind him that *she* had said Umandu's name and *she* had let go of her father's hand. The words stopped up behind her tongue as she stared at the green drapes, remembering the waves, the lashing rain and lightning, and the engorging fear the moment she realized her father's hand had left hers.

Ira walked over, rubbing his cheek.

"Women," he said, then winked at Camille. "All but you of course."

He held out two keys in his palm.

"Two?" Camille asked, overjoyed at the thought of having her very own room. She imagined peeling off her dirty dress and stockings, washing the dust and sweat from her body, snuggling under warm blankets and letting the feath ers of a goose-down mattress cradle her. Pure heaven.

"Last stop in civilization, love. Thought I'd treat you."

Camille took her key and headed for the stairwell, its walls swathed in old paintings, sketches, and yellowed maps. *Curse of Umandu.* What curse? Tonight she'd be sleeping in a real bed, without Oscar on the floor beside her to make her worry about snoring or talking in her sleep, without the starry sky for a ceiling, without hearing men and women doing unthinkable things in the next room over.

"Guess this means I'm stuck warming your backside tonight," Ira said to Oscar as they reached their rooms, directly across the hall from one another. Oscar unlocked the door.

"Let me give you some advice. Warming my backside will get you killed."

Ira bobbed his head. "Good advice." He tipped his hat to Camille. "If you need anyone to warm your backside, love, I'd be honored."

Oscar shoved Ira into their room.

"Good night, Camille," he said. Camille laughed and unlocked her door.

"Good night, Oscar."

———

Camille hovered over a deep ditch the next morning, her nose pinched closed against the privy's stale stench. Four walls of thatch concealed her from the bustle of Bendigo as she hurried through what had to be the worst element of traveling through such a rudimentary settlement. She stood up and let her skirt fall back around her ankles. Outside, the sun had baked the mud dry in the streets. A man sat outside a walled tent, cheeks, chin, and neck lathered with white shave cream; the barber skillfully skimmed the blade up the man's throat, over his Adam's apple and the curve of his chin. The next tent glittered with tin and pewter pans, mugs, plates, and kettles. The pure entrepreneurial flavor of Bendigo seemed so much like home.

She'd used the inn's back door to run to the outhouse, but on her way back she wanted to round the building and enter through the front door. She wondered what the place looked like in daylight and what the rest of the street had to offer.

Women scrubbed dirty britches and long underwear in tubs of soapy water, slapping the wet rags onto already laden clotheslines. The scent of strong coffee, ground with chicory, drifted under her nose from a nearby camp. The streets and sidewalks were packed to the brim, every person busy with a task or destination.

Camille climbed the first step to the inn's porch, but faltered on the second. A whistling wind in her ears caught her off guard, and that's when she heard it again. The chanting. The drumming. Indecipherable words beat in her ears, harsh and urgent and solely in her own head. She squeezed her eyes shut and gripped the banister, certain she was going insane. And then silence.

When Camille opened her eyes, they focused on three men up the street. Camille darted behind one of the wide porch posts, thankful she at least hadn't seen the hideous skull again. Peering out, she watched the three men, mounted on their steeds, as they spoke to a few miners.

The three riders from the day before, she was certain of it. Their thick black beards and broad, beefy shoulders were impossible to forget. She watched the miners scratch their cheeks and shake their heads. Then, out from behind the three giants, another horse and rider appeared. He removed his hat, a brimmed one like all the others, and wiped his forehead with a white handkerchief.

"Lucius," Camille whispered, her cheek pressed against the post. Her whisper seemed to travel the length of the long, dirt-packed road, for as soon as he replaced his hat, Lucius flicked his eyes toward her.

He saw her, sat straighter in his saddle, and reached out his arm, pointing. Camille saw his lips move. *"There!"* he told his companions, and all three of the beefy black-bearded men noticed her hiding behind the post and cracked their reins on their mounts.

Camille fled around the back of the building, in through the rear door, and up the narrow set of stairs to the second-story hallway. She banged on the door to room six.

"Oscar!" she cried. "Oscar, wake up!"

The door whipped open. Oscar stood before her, his shirt half buttoned.

"It's them. The three riders from yesterday. Lucius is with them, and they saw me." Her voice trembled from the run upstairs. Oscar hooked the last button on his shirt, and Ira appeared behind him, wiping a streak of shave cream from his cheeks.

"Bloody hell, I knew it," Ira said. He swung a bag and a rifle over his shoulder.

Oscar took up the second rifle. "Knew what?"

"I knew I recognized those blokes."

Oscar thrust a hand into Ira's chest as he attempted to barrel through the open door. "Who are they?"

"Listen, there'll be a time for me to sit down and spill my guts, but now ain't it. Those are the Hesky brothers on our tail. If you want to live to see Port Adelaide, grab your things and let's fly."

Oscar relented and piled his back with their supplies.

"Which way'd you come back in?" Ira asked Camille as she heaved one of the sacks of beans over her shoulder.

"Through the back," she answered.

"Then that'll be where they'll go. You two head down to the front door. I'll take the back way and try and stall them."

Camille caught Ira's sleeve as he entered the hallway "No! What if they recognize you?"

There came a burst of noise from the bottom of the back stairs as the door was thrown wide.

"I love a game of chance," Ira said with a wild grin. "Now go, and get under the tarp in the back of the wagon. Go!"

Oscar and Camille ran down the hallway as the back stairs shook under heavy feet. Oscar held out a hand to slow her as they descended the main stairs, their sacks of supplies bouncing off the walls and sending the framed pictures awry. He peered around the corner, then continued into the front room, where he tossed the two keys toward the clerk without even stopping to look at the startled man.

"I hope everything is fine," the clerk said. "Was your stay —"

The front door flew open. Lucius Drake stepped inside. Camille rammed into Oscar's back as he stopped, he and Lucius locked in a motionless, wordless duel. They stared at each other, waiting for the slightest twitch of the other to indicate who would make the first move. Lucius went first, taking a swift step back through the front door.

Oscar dove toward him, grabbed him around the collar, and hurled him inside, slamming the door with a kick of his leg. He shoved Lucius against a wall, knocking a table aside and rattling the hurricane lamp on it.

"Why are you following us with those men?" Oscar asked, his fists curled into the collar of Lucius's jacket. Lucius struggled to free himself, but Oscar lifted him and smacked him against the wall again.

"Answer me! Who are they?"

"I-I dunno, I swear! Cap-Captain McGreenery wanted me to help them find you, s-something about how you were trying to steal something from him," Lucius answered as doors upstairs started to crash open. People screamed as the Hesky brothers entered the wrong rooms. Camille ran to the window, saw Ira running toward their wagon.

"Oscar, we have to go!" she said in a low hiss. Camille searched the stairwell as more shouts and banging doors sounded. The clerk pressed his back against the wall of hooks holding room keys and stared wide-eyed at Oscar and Lucius.

"Downstairs!" one of the men bellowed from the top of the stairwell.

Oscar turned to Camille. "Get behind the curtains!"

She hurried through the green drapes that had hidden the gold miners the night before. The parlor still smelled of cigar and pipe smoke, though now only two men sat by the hearth. They looked up from their conversation, annoyed as Oscar flew through the drapes. He firmly grasped the back seam of Lucius's jacket with one hand. The other held a rifle, the barrel poking Lucius between his shoulder blades.

"Get them out of here or you'll be the first one I shoot," he whispered to Lucius. Camille slid up against the wall as Oscar let the drapes drop around the barrel of the rifle, obscuring it from view.

"Where are they?" one of the brothers asked Lucius. His gruff, coarse voice was almost as frightening as his size. Oscar nudged the rifle into Lucius's back.

"Uh, they're not here," Lucius said, then cleared his voice. "Didn't have a room, clerk says."

"But we saw her run behind this one," a near-matching voice said.

"Th-there's another establishment next door" came the trembling voice of the clerk.

A few loud slashes of a whip and commotion outside stole Camille's attention. Their wagon hurtled past the windows, Ira in the driver's bench, his arm raised to slash at the horse again. He was leaving without them! And going in the wrong direction, too, back the way they'd come the night before.

"Go!" a scraping voice shouted. The front door smacked open. The porch rattled as the Hesky brothers stomped down the steps. Oscar let the rifle fall, and a moment later as she peered out the parlor window, careful not to be seen, Camille saw Lucius mounting. All four of them raced after the speeding wagon, Lucius chancing a short glance back at the hotel windows.

Oscar took Camille by the arm and pulled her out of the parlor. "Come on."

"But he left without us! I can't believe him!" she yelled. Their guide was gone; Ira had abandoned them.

"What are we going to do, Oscar?" she asked as they stepped onto the porch and looked up the street. Dust from the wagon, and the horses in pursuit of it, clouded the air.

"We'll find a place to hide first, make sure they don't get to us again, and then I'll —"

A shrill whistle pierced Oscar's next word. The two of them spun around to find Ira sitting on one of their two remaining horses beside the porch.

"You didn't leave us!" Camille cried.

"What kind of con do you think I am?" Ira asked, smiling. "Let's go, we got about five seconds before they realize I paid some bloke a couple shillings to tear outta here with our wagon."

Oscar mounted the second horse from the porch and pulled Camille in front of him, the bag of beans landing heavily on her lap. They galloped down the street in the opposite direction the Hesky brothers had taken, the rifle Oscar had slung across his chest slamming into her back.

Ira turned off the main road, onto a path similar to the one they'd diverged onto when running from the Heskys the first time. The trees grew thick and the path darkened under the canopy of tangled branches and leaves. Roots, rocks, and divots riddled the way. They rode fast, the over-grown limbs and shrubbery whizzing past their heads and raking their legs and arms as they followed Ira up a steep incline, deeper into the wooded path.

Camille's head started to throb near her wound. The bruise surrounding her scar had yellowed and then faded to light violet, but now with every jounce and plunge of the horse, she imagined it growing red and swollen again.

"Who the hell are the Hesky brothers?" Oscar yelled to Ira as the incline leveled off.

Ira shouted back over his shoulder, "Who the hell is Lucius?"

Camille longed for the galloping to stop, for the sack of beans to quit punching her in the gut and giving her the urge to vomit. Yet she didn't want to stop putting distance between them and the Hesky brothers, whoever they were, either.

"Lucius Drake. He's a traitorous sailor who survived the wreck with us," Camille answered as the rifle clacked into her spine once more.

"He signed on with the *Stealth* after we arrived in Melbourne," Oscar added, his voice dipping and breathless from the ride. The path in front of them was hardly a path at all, just a thin lane of trees and a coating of leaves and pine needles over little-used dual ruts.

Ira held up a hand and pulled back on his horse's reins.

"Whoa, whoa." He turned his horse to face them. "The *Stealth*? The ship I made a crater out of?" Ira caressed his half-shaven cheek. "Well, that's not good. Not good at all."

Camille swiveled around and looked up at Oscar. The spiced scent of his skin distracted her again, clouding her focus. He dropped his eyes to her, held her gaze a moment, and then looked at Ira again.

"Why is that not good?" he asked. Ira motioned for them to keep riding.

"The Hesky brothers are hired bushrangers," he answered. "Baddest lot in all of Victoria. Shipped here from England after doing time in Newgate gaol for murder."

"And now they're free?" Camille asked. Ira rolled his shoulders, looking back at her briefly.

"It's not my fault the Crown chose to colonize Australia with convicts. The Hesky brothers make a living here on the things that'd get them cuffed and chained back in England."

A stray band of sunlight broke through the overgrowth, blinding Camille for a moment. The tall trees creaked and swayed in a gusty wind. The leaves turned, showing their silvery backsides. Rain. That would be just her luck.

"Lucius told me McGreenery hired them to come after us," Oscar said as their horse abruptly stopped. It dipped its head, thrusting Camille forward as it munched on some wild ferns curling up from the damp forest floor.

Ira pinched up his face, as though watching a rabbit being skinned.

"If he hired the Hesky brothers, this McGreenery fella doesn't want you ever reaching Port Adelaide or any other corner of the world again."

A flash of ice streaked up Camille's arms.

"McGreenery wouldn't kill us," she said, but then doubted herself. He'd been adamant about getting to the map and stone. And she'd tricked him about knowing his secret. Did he not want that secret, the one she didn't *really* know, let loose?

"As long as the blood isn't left on his hands, I think he'd do anything to keep us from getting to that map." Oscar tightened his hat around his ears. He focused on Ira. "What now?"

Ira waved in front of them, toward the muddle of a path ahead.

"Got us on a different trail. We can't keep on the lowland route to Port Adelaide now that those blokes are trailing us. This route's shorter, but it takes us right through the highlands. Dangerous riding. Testy weather."

Camille shifted in their shared saddle, the beans again jabbing her in the belly. Sticks and leaves crunched to the right of her, and a furry red creature scuttled up a tree trunk and into a cavernous knot.

"What if we just let the Hesky brothers and Lucius pass us? Then get back on the lowland trail?" she asked.

Ira shook his head as Oscar tossed him one of the burlap sacks. "It'll take them a day at the most to realize the trail's gone cold. Then they'll turn around. If we follow them —"

"They'll bump right into us," Camille finished his sentence. She rubbed down the prickles on her arms. "So the highlands?"

Ira nodded and tugged the reins, moving up the trail. Oscar swung his rifle to the back, away from Camille. She slid down the dip in the saddle; the press of her body against Oscar's was unladylike, even for her. She imagined Randall's rigid glare if he saw her right then, cradled in Oscar's protective arms. Could this be all it would take for him to call off the wedding? To pull out his investments?

"You might have more room if you rode with Ira," Oscar said softly, his chest vibrating as he spoke. Surely, Randall would agree. But the enfold of Oscar's arms and chest was as comforting and reassuring as it was improper. She pushed the image of Randall aside.

"If it's all right with you, I'd rather stay here," Camille replied. She hung on to the horn of the saddle as they started to wind through the woods once more. Oscar leveled his lips with her ear.

"I'd rather you stay here, too." He closed his arms around her a little bit tighter. She blushed, knowing she should reprimand him for being so bold. But his boldness exhilarated her more than it bothered her. In fact, it didn't bother her at all.

Ira glanced over his shoulder. She half expected one of his coy grins as he regarded the closeness of Oscar's arms, but instead she received only an intent stare and a question.

"Just what the devil does that map lead to?"

TWELVE

*I*ra squatted in a pool of knee-deep water and plunged his head under the surface. He craned his neck and whipped his hair from side to side, sending streams of water down his shoulders and back.

"Cover your eyes, love, I'm going for a swim." Ira winked and pulled his shirt over his head. Camille laughed and averted her attention as he finished undressing. A great slap of water told her it was safe to look again, and when she did, Ira filled up his cheeks and spouted water from his lips like a fountain.

"We've been on the go for nearly a week now, mate, and the heat's not doing you any favors. Jump in," he said to Oscar, who sat fully clothed on a sun-bleached rock.

The three of them had followed a mere trickle of a stream since dawn, watching it widen and deepen, until they came upon a rocky crevasse filled by clear blue waterfall runoff. The constant pounding of water not far in the distance was enough to soothe Camille's spirits. There was something uneasy about the forested hills they'd been traveling through. Perhaps it was the dappled light, or the chilly shadows that set in with dusk.

"Come on now, take a dip, and we'll leave our lady for a swim of her own." Ira winked at her again and she worked to hide her amusement.

Camille did want a swim, a chance to freshen herself after spending the last week growing sweaty and filthy in front of Oscar on their shared horse. She had been discreetly sniffing the sleeves of her arms as they climbed through the forest, and soon she hadn't been able to tell the difference between her sleeves, Oscar's shirt, or the horse. They'd turned into one big heap of stink.

Oscar kicked off his boots. He pulled up his shirt and before she could turn away, Camille saw a series of long, thin scars on his ribs and torso running vertically and diagonally along his back. Not from the wreck or anything recent. The wounds had healed completely, and the gnarled marks were whiter than the rest of his skin. They looked like marks of a whip. Who could have done this to him?

Oscar had never removed his shirt and tucked it into his trouser pocket like some other sailors while working on the *Christina*. He was probably self-conscious about the scars. Unlike some of the other sailors who kept their shirts on to cover flabby stomachs, Oscar's was smooth, lean with muscle, and, other than his old wounds, flawless. Camille caught herself staring at him as he unbuckled his trousers. She bowed her head toward the trees and listened as he splashed through the water to the ledge, joining Ira.

"I think I just spotted supper." Oscar pointed toward a school of shimmering fish beneath the surface.

"Now, there's a winner," Ira crowed, and the two men swam for the line of trees with great plans to sharpen a stick and spear the fish swimming in between their legs. Camille lay back on her own bleached rock to wait for her turn to soak in the mountain pool. The tremendous heat had left her sweaty and dusty, and every time she licked her lips the salty grit also made her thirsty for her canteen. She listened to them slap the water like two boys, cursing one another every time the fish obviously made a stealthy getaway.

Stealth. McGreenery managed to work his way into more and more of her thoughts with each passing day. The repairs on his ship would be well under way, and if Ira had been correct, the Hesky brothers and Lucius had already felt the lowland trail go cold. Perhaps they'd turned around, back toward Bendigo, and ventured onto the highland trail.

Camille, Oscar, and Ira could only continue on into the Grampians, toward the western coast of Victoria where Port Adelaide lay. When they arrived, what would come next remained a matter of speculation. Would her mother already be dead? Would McGreenery have somehow reached her and the map first? Camille's throat closed off and her stomach churned. What if her mother had already found the stone? What if Umandu had been sucked of its powers? She almost laughed at herself. *Powers*. Oscar had been right; it sounded preposterous.

The branches of the trees around the mountain pool rustled with birds, twittering among themselves. *Their own little bird language,* Camille thought as she closed her eyes. She welcomed the chance to doze and didn't mind the sun bronzing her bare forearms, sleeves rolled up to the elbow. But would her mother? Camille wondered what kind of woman she was. The kind who brushed seashell dust on her cheeks and nose for a porcelain complexion, or the kind who liked to walk barefoot and free of crinolines and corsets?

She thought to roll down her sleeves in case her mother fell into the category of seashell dust and fine manners but stopped short of doing so. It was hot and sticky, and if her mother didn't approve of Camille's rugged complexion, what did she care? Camille couldn't fool herself, though. She would care. Most definitely, she would care.

A grating squawk of a lorikeet roused Camille from her dozing. Oscar's and Ira's voices had traveled away without her noticing. As she scanned the pool, she saw no one. A steady undercurrent rippled the surface like desert sand. They had rounded the corner of the stream up ahead, she figured. Probably chasing fish.

Perhaps it would be a good time for that swim. She peeled off her boots, but didn't strip down completely in case the two men decided to come splashing back before she had time to get out and dry off. She removed her dress and, in her drawers and corset, slid into the water, freezing compared to the warmth of the sun. The small hairs on her arms stiffened. She dipped below, craning her neck and letting the water comb her hair as she broke the surface. She dipped again and again, staying below as long as her lungs would allow. Camille wondered if she'd ever be able to submerge herself in water again without thinking of the way her father had died.

The final time she broke for air, she heard a snap of a branch behind her. She twisted around, but the rocks and bank were bare. Camille emerged from the water and searched the trees, running a hand down her slicked hair. Her pulse rose in anticipation of the dreaded chanting or the image of a skeleton's visage somewhere in the trees. A new sweat broke out on the nape of her neck as she saw a pair of wide, brown eyes peering at her from behind the limbs of the trees. But these eyes were real, as were the pointed ears, flaring nostrils, and a white muzzle. Camille let out a sigh of relief and her shoulders relaxed.

"Are you spying on me?" she asked a butterscotch doe that stood as immobile as the trees around it. Camille took a small step forward; the deer's hind legs bent, and the animal pranced back, fleeing into the woods.

Camille chided herself for being so jumpy. The Hesky brothers were a few days behind, at the least. But what if they had been the ones in the forest watching her instead of the doe? She shivered as it dawned on her that she might not have been able to protect herself.

"Forget the beans tonight!" Ira shouted from around the river bend. "Caught us some nice-lookin' pike for supper."

Aware her appearance was nothing short of scandalous, Camille bounded over branches and fallen pine needles to the shield of her horse. Ira's whistle pierced the air.

"You should'a warned us you weren't dressed, love. Though I'm not entirely sorry to see you in your unwhisperables."

She grabbed the blanket from the back of her horse and wrapped herself in it. Oscar appeared from around the bend, four pike speared on a stick. She watched him stride through the water just behind Ira. The muscle of his pale chest, stomach, and arms was enough to make her forget her clothing was still yards away near the water's edge. Camille faced the forest as he and Ira approached the shallows. She listened to them slosh out of the water and counted off a minute as they pulled on their trousers and shirts.

"Finished. Your innocence won't be spoiled if you look now," Ira called.

She turned and saw Oscar had come up to the other side of her horse. He didn't seem to know what to do with his eyes; they met hers, lowered to the blanket she held tight around her chest, and then focused on the horse's stringy black mane. He held her dress over the saddle, half looking at her, half trying to be gentlemanly. But when she thanked him and tried to take it, he held on.

"What is it?" he asked, then released the dress. Camille tightened the blanket around her chest. "You look frightened. Did something happen?"

She hadn't realized she'd looked upset.

"It's nothing. A deer just startled me, that's all." She nodded toward the woods.

He backed up from the horse, his eyes lifting to her bare shoulders and then away.

Ira grabbed the rifle from his horse and sprang for the trees. "When? Which way did it go?"

"Ira Beam, you are not going to shoot an innocent animal," she said, shaking out her dress.

The Australian leaped into the forest. "I'll meet you upriver!" he shouted, and then he was gone, his noisy tear into the woods enough to scatter tree ants, let alone any remaining game. Camille turned to Oscar.

"What's upriver?" she asked, dressing behind her horse. The cotton stuck to her wet skin as she pulled on the dress.

He buttoned up his shirt and strapped the spear of pike to his saddle. "A clearing we spotted. We'll make camp there tonight. Are you okay?"

She tugged on her boots. "I'm fine. Like I said, I was just startled."

They started walking, the soles of Camille's feet still coated with pine needles and dirt. She'd been too distracted to brush them off before dressing.

Oscar turned to her as they rounded a bend and came upon the flat clearing. "You were afraid it was Lucius and the Hesky brothers."

"I wasn't afraid," Camille said quickly, embarrassed he could read her so well.

"It's okay to be afraid. You've been through a lot the last few weeks."

He halted his horse and took down his pack and canteen.

"You have, too," she said. Camille didn't want to be handled like a fragile eggshell.

"I didn't lose my father." He unscrewed the canteen cap and plunged it into the water. "I didn't get abducted at knifepoint."

She grabbed her canteen and followed him. "I can take care of myself." But the doubts that had just swarmed through her stayed firmly planted.

"I can see that," Oscar replied with just enough lilt in his voice to irk her.

"Well, are you so untouchable? Did my father's death have no impact on you at all?"

He screwed the cap back onto his canteen with extra force. "Of course it did."

"You'd never know it the way you're acting. He gave you everything, and you don't even seem eager to find the stone," she said, but immediately regretted it.

Oscar crossed his arms, his jaw set. "I'm well aware of what William did for me. Trust me, Camille. And I'm sorry if I don't seem as eager as you are to be cursed by an ancient stone. I'm just trying to keep you alive out here on this warpath of yours."

Camille stepped around a fallen log and climbed onto a mossy boulder, rising up to Oscar's height.

"No one charged you with being my savior." Camille's voice shook, the confrontation not something she really wanted.

"No one had to charge me with it. I made the decision on my own the night the *Christina* went down." Oscar sealed his lips as if he'd let something slip he hadn't intended.

"What are you talking about?" she asked, her boots slipping once on the moss. He avoided her by looking out at the stream. He took a few moments to answer, and when he did he still didn't meet her stare.

"Do you remember when you woke up on the *Londoner*? When you asked me if I'd seen your father?"

Camille nodded, and hoped their argument was over. "You said you didn't see him."

He shook his head. "I lied. I did see him in the water. He was trying to stay above the surface after I got ahold of the dory."

It was as though freezing shocks of ocean water were striking Camille in the face all over again. She jumped from the rock, the hem of her skirt nearly tripping her.

"Did you row to him? Did you try and save him?"

He shook his head again. "No."

"Why not?" she screeched. "Oscar, how could you not help him?" She couldn't blink. She couldn't do anything but stare at him in disbelief. He'd abandoned her father, the man who had given him everything.

"Because I spotted you," he answered, hardly loud

enough for her to hear. "I saw you in the waves and I chose to row to you."

She loosened her fists, stunned.

Oscar sat down on the rock, the toes of his scuffed leather boots buried in the dry layer of pine needles.

"I tried to go back for him," he said, kicking at the needles, "but by the time I pulled you out of the water and looked back, he was gone."

She couldn't move, could barely breathe. If she'd only held on to her father's hand. Oscar would have been able to save them both.

"If there had just been a way to get to the both of you," he said.

Camille sat on the rock beside him, laying a tentative hand on his arm. "You're the most capable man I know, Oscar. If there had been a way, you'd have found it."

She pressed her hand against his solid arm, the flaxen hairs covering his skin coarse against her fingertips. She wanted to soothe him more, reassure him like he always did her. But the image of her father struggling to stay above the waves, and how he must have felt when he watched his first mate row away from him, his last hope fading, wouldn't allow Camille to say a single word.

A gunshot punctured the air and spooked the birds on tree limbs above. She drew her hand back as the flutter of wings beat out the echoing shot.

"Let's hope he didn't shoot himself in the foot," Oscar said, his darkened expression brightening. The humor relieved her, and she got up to gather sticks for the campfire. She crouched and scooped a few dry limbs into the cradle of her arms.

"Why me?" She said it before she could stop herself.

"What?" Oscar asked.

"My father and you were like father and son. Your loyalty's always been to him first. Why would you row to me?"

All the times she'd felt the rise of her skin under the palm of his hand, the rapid pace of her heart, the breath lost from her lungs. She'd hoped her touch had left warmth lingering in him, too. She'd imagined her scent intoxicated him, drew him to her, even though it was selfish and senseless.

Ira broke into the clearing before Oscar could answer.

"I was this close!" he shouted, holding his thumb and index finger an inch apart. "Nicked her with that shot, I did."

Oscar smirked and shook his head, visibly relieved to move away from Camille's question.

"Doesn't matter none. We got pike. See this one?" Ira made sure Camille was looking. "Caught this one with my bare hands."

"He's lying," Oscar said, building the fire. "He's got fingers made of sweet butter."

Ira shrugged. "All right, I'll let her think you caught 'em all if that's what your ego needs."

Dry kindling sizzled in the campfire by the time the crown of the moon rose above the treetops. Camille kept picturing what Oscar saw the night of the storm. How would she have decided if she'd been in the dory, faced with the option of saving her father or saving Oscar? She couldn't imagine letting either of them drown. She ate a whole fillet of pike in silence, chewing on the tender, flaky fish and picking flimsy bones off her tongue as she stared into the flames.

"You two could drown a whale with all your sulking," Ira groaned from his stretched-out position against a felled tree trunk. He toasted his stocking feet by the fire and rubbed his expanded belly. "What's the matter with the both of you, anyway?"

Camille looked to Oscar and saw his furrowed brow. She still longed to ease his worry, but didn't know how. Did he regret his choice? She sat back with the thought of it. All this time she'd been placing the blame on herself. Oscar must have been doing the same thing and maybe wishing he'd rowed in the other direction.

"All right, you two need some cheering up. How 'bout a nice ol' ballad to raise your spirits?" Ira sat forward and rubbed his palms together.

Camille brought the blanket around her shoulders. "What is it?"

"It's called 'Bold Jack Donohue.' You like to sing, yeah?"

She shrugged and admitted she'd sometimes sung sea chanteys with the sailors.

"All right, then, it starts like this:

"Come all you gallant bushrangers
    who gallop o'er the plains,
Refuse to live in slavery,
    or wear the convict chains.
Attention pay to what I say,
    and value if I do,
For I will relate the matchless tale
    of bold Jack Donohue."

"See, it's a good tune."

Camille laughed as Ira sang and transformed himself into an actor, eating up the attention.

"Sing the rest of it," she said. Ira complied and taught Camille the next verse.

"Come all you sons of liberty
    and everyone besides,
I'll sing to you a story
    that will fill you with surprise
Concerning of a bold bushranger,
    Jack Donohue was his name,
And he scorned to humble to the crown,
    bound down with iron chain."

Their voices echoed over the stream and along the edge of the trees. She saw the tail end of a smile on Oscar's lips.

"I thought you didn't like to sing," she said. He'd always remained silent while the crew sang their sea chanteys.

"I don't," Oscar said. "But you have a pretty voice."

His compliment shaped a bashful smile onto her lips. She was glad for the firelight, already casting a reddish glow to her skin.

"And what 'bout me, mate?" Ira asked.

"Couldn't say. I was trying to block it out," Oscar replied.

Camille, and even Ira, laughed.

"So, who was Jack Donohue?" she asked as the echo of their laughter faded.

"One of the first bushrangers," Ira answered.

"But I thought the Hesky brothers were bushrangers," she said. Ira nodded and took a swig of his canteen.

"They are, but they're the bad kind. Good ones want to live their own way, without the Crown telling them what to do. They're bushmen, farmers, and hunters. The bad ones rob settlers, steal, and kill."

Ira continued to whistle the tune, but doubt had already settled back under Camille's skin. What were they doing way out here in the forest, climbing into dangerous territory? Perhaps Oscar had been right after all. Sydney would have been a safer bet.

She glanced at Oscar, settled back against the same log as Ira. He caught her stare, and it was as though he could hear her thoughts. His full lips curved into a small slanted grin to reassure her. It worked. Camille lay back on the sack of beans she'd untied from her horse and brought the blanket up to her chin. She closed her eyes and listened to Ira's voice as he mumbled the rest of the ballad.

"Nine rounds he fired and nine men down
    before that fated ball,
which pierced his heart
    and caused him for to fall.
And as he closed his mournful eyes,
    he bid the world adieu,
Saying, 'Convicts all, pray for the soul
    of bold Jack Donohue.'"

THIRTEEN

hey pushed on through the highland trail, into the Grampians along paths that wound up steep hills, then plunged into roughly cut gorges. A tamed stretch of wildflower-studded fields was a welcome treat one afternoon.

Camille shifted uncomfortably in the saddle she shared with Ira, his legs pressed too closely against her own. He meant nothing by it, she was certain, but she still preferred riding with Oscar. Unlike Ira, Oscar was attentive to the proximity of their bodies and at least attempted to hold his legs as far back as possible. They'd been taking turns riding double in order to keep the horses motivated. It had been nearly three weeks since they'd left Bendigo, and Camille had to admit her own motivation had started to taper.

That morning, they'd packed up camp at dawn, another night spent under the stars—another night Camille had spent in silent prayer that Umandu did exist, that her father really would return to her. She missed him more than words could describe. *Miss* seemed too inadequate a word. His absence made her feel vacant. At least Oscar didn't speak of her father and didn't expect her to, either. He must have been thinking of him, though. She was. Always.

Camille heard their horse slogging onward, nostrils flaring, throat grunting as they trod through the wildflower field. The sun appeared to have reached its zenith. Whether it was noon or two or still morning, Camille didn't care. The importance of time had begun to drip away as the air thinned out high in the peaks. The air was different, and it became difficult to take a deep breath. Even Ira wasn't talking. Camille didn't know if she liked the breathless silence. At least when Ira sang, or when he and Oscar threw sarcastic remarks at each other, there were words to fill up her mind. Without them, she retreated to what Oscar had revealed earlier. *I chose to row to you.*

Oscar suddenly pulled in the reins of his mount and jumped from the saddle.

"What is it?" Camille asked, concerned he'd seen a bobcat or some other flesh-eating animal she'd been worrying would attack them. He only stretched his arms above his head, the grasses brushing against his waist.

"Need a break from the saddle. Look at this grass." He ran his palm over the tips of it. "Too good not to lie down in."

Ira immediately hopped down and fell to the ground. "Thought I was the only one thinkin' that."

Camille slid off her horse. A slender breeze bent the field's tall blades, and she breathed in the fresh scent of grass. With a deep sigh, Camille let herself fall back. She flopped her arms above her head and closed her eyes, a rest well deserved. The weather had been dry, but riding and walking twelve hours every day had left her body sore. Camille wiggled her toes. Her stockings were squishy from sweat, and she smelled atrocious. The forest clung to her, the silt, leaves, and dirt. Above everything else, she was in dire need of a bath.

Camille heard the rustle of grass. She opened one eye and saw Oscar settling down beside her.

"We can spare a few minutes," he said. She sat up and cradled her knees in her arms. He plucked a blade of grass and commenced peeling it down the center. They heard the Australian snoring from his spot a few yards away, completely hidden in a blanket of green.

"I guess we can spare more than a few minutes." Oscar smiled and met her gaze, holding it a moment. She suddenly realized how horrible she must look — her hair, her clothes, her skin.

"Do you miss him?" he asked, not seeming to notice any of those things.

Camille uprooted a purple flower and a white daisy near it. "Of course I do. But I'm hoping with the stone I won't have to very long."

"Not your father, Camille. Randall."

She took a deep breath, shocked she hadn't thought of

her fiancé for so long. How many days had it been? A full week, maybe more.

"Oh. Well . . . I suppose I do."

Oscar raised an eyebrow and laughed at her clear lack of conviction.

Camille shrugged. "What? A lot has happened and right now getting back to San Francisco isn't something I'm concerned about."

Oscar nodded and chewed on the tip of his blade of grass.

"It's not that Randall isn't a perfectly good man," she said, fiddling with the flowers in her hands. The roots crumbled dirt onto her lap. "He's kind and caring and handsome and an excellent businessman."

Oscar continued to nod.

"And he'll make a fine husband, I'm sure," she added, knowing he really was all those things. If only all of them combined could make up for what she didn't feel while with him.

"I'm sure," Oscar repeated. Had he been mocking her? She thought she had caught a trace of sarcasm. All this talk about Randall had her itching.

"Why do you ask?"

"Just wondered if you missed home," Oscar answered and threw the mangled blade of grass behind him.

"Do you?" she asked, ashamed to let Oscar know how little she desired to return. He thought for a moment, tugging up another switch of grass and rolling it between his fingers.

"No," he answered with stark certainty. "I have everything I'd miss right here."

Every inch of Camille's body smoldered under Oscar's gentle, and so very forward, gaze. He'd miss her. She looked into his gray-blue eyes, rimmed by thick, honey-colored lashes — had they always been so full? The bridge of his nose crooked to the left slightly, perhaps broken in a fight after he'd moved from her father's carriage house to a small apartment along the San Francisco harbor front. She'd never noticed the charming imperfection before.

She watched as his eyes traveled over her own features, touching on the wound by her temple and settling on the heart-shaped fullness of her lips.

Oscar held his piercing stare. "We probably won't arrive home in time for your wedding."

She pictured the wedding gown hanging in her closet. The veil. The shoes. Even the strands of pearls, all laid out awaiting her return. *Return.* The heavy word weighed on her as Ira continued to snore and Oscar continued to study her in a way that made her feel captivating and beautiful.

Camille stood up, not sure if she'd been inching toward him. His lips had certainly seemed to be getting closer.

"Randall will understand, I'm sure. He's a very reasonable person," she said, her voice rapid.

Oscar started to stand. "Where are you going?"

"No, please, sit," she said. "I . . . I just need to, um, use the trees." Camille jiggled her nearly empty canteen to strengthen her excuse. She turned in a circle until she spotted a copse of trees. She had to be somewhere other than hidden in the flowers with Oscar, somewhere she could try and convince herself that Randall might one day be able to look at her with the same intensity Oscar had just displayed.

Oscar sat back down, and Camille trampled the grass on the way to the safety of the trees. Another attack of guilt snuck up on her as she glanced back at Oscar, who was watching her walk away. Camille would miss her own wedding — and she didn't care one bit.

FOURTEEN

t first sight, Port Adelaide disheartened Camille. It was not at all what she'd envisioned. The port was not situated on the ocean but on a broad tidal river, across from which lay nothing but marshy swampland and the thinnest horizon of ocean. They'd passed through the city of Adelaide a little under an hour before, its homes and streets and farms quaint and established. Being so near to their destination had inspired them into a canter, excitement and anxiety stirring Camille's nerves as they rode faster than they had the last handful of days. The port, however, was far from the city's equal. The rectangular grid of streets held homes by the dozen, but wharves, warehouses, and harbor stores were the dominant features.

"Used to call this place Port Misery," Ira said as they slowed down to pass a long string of yoked bullocks. The cattle train pulled carts of lumber along the connecting road toward Adelaide city.

"That's fitting," Oscar said. It was early morning and their mare well rested, so he shared the saddle with Camille.

She crinkled her nose as they entered the port town. The smell of a tidal river was deeper, more pungent than the scent of open water. For the first time, Camille wondered how her mother had lived. The fishy, stagnant air made her worry the past sixteen years of her mother's life had been spent in squalor. The pity brewing inside Camille surprised her. She had expected to feel angry or resentful, even superior to her mother, not sorry for her.

Ira led them toward the wharves, all of which bustled with activity. So this was the place her mother had chosen to call home, all the while knowing her daughter was alive and growing up thousands of miles away. How had she lived with her choice? In her letter she'd said she'd never stopped loving Camille. That didn't necessarily mean she regretted abandoning her. She could still meet Camille and decide she wasn't the daughter she'd imagined all these years. What if she was disappointed in the way Camille had turned out?

She filled her lungs and held the air in her chest. She was being absurd. If anyone had a right to be disappointed, it was her, not her mother. But her nerves seemed to think differently.

"Follow me, mates," Ira called back to them. Camille shifted in the saddle to look at Oscar.

"Who do we find first? Ira's friend or my mother?"

He glanced down at her, looking as if he sensed her desire to stall. Had he always been able to read her so well?

"Whichever comes first, I suppose," he answered.

"Monty'll be easy to find," Ira said. "Never wanders far from the action."

Ira had been telling them about his friend Monty over the last few days, and the way he made it sound, they were close as kin. Camille was positive his talent for stretching the truth had been at play, but she still looked forward to meeting another human being. She'd had enough of lizards and snakes and birds and possums to last the rest of her days.

A light drizzle fell from the low gray clouds. Coldness seeped through her, and a hot bath and feather pillow grew just as tantalizing as the map to Umandu itself. They followed Ira as he guided them down narrow streets. Crushed seashells kept the road dust down, and they glittered with the rising sunlight. People throbbed around a harbor marketplace set in the middle of the street. Vegetables, fish, fabrics, fruits, and livestock were displayed in a mishmash of carts and crates and under tents. All of a sudden, Ira held up a hand and waved. He swiped his hat off and waved that, too.

"Hey there!" he called out to a stocky man atop a horse fifty feet away, surrounded by other market shoppers. The floppy brim of the man's hat shadowed his eyes, but not his lips, which had twisted into a scowl.

"What'd I tell ya, eh? Close to the action. Hey there, Monty!" Ira called out again. Monty halted his horse and stared a long moment as Ira continued to shout, "Bet you didn't expect a visit from me, right?"

Camille leaned back and whispered to Oscar, "That's Monty?"

"He doesn't look happy to see an old friend," he replied. Monty slapped the reins, and his horse barreled toward Ira. Teeth bared, Ira's old friend heaved a great scream before throwing himself from his saddle and knocking Ira from his. The two tumbled to the street, horses bucking and scurrying.

"You bastard!" Monty spit, pummeling Ira's stomach. Ira tried to free himself, but with no luck.

"Monty! Whata'ya doin', mate!" Shoppers dropped their vegetables and fruits and encircled them. Oscar released the reins of their horse.

"Should I go help him out?" he asked.

Camille grinned. "Who? Ira or Monty?"

Monty barreled another fist into Ira's gut and lifted him by his jacket collar.

"You got a lot of pluck coming here, Ira Beam." Monty dropped him and then hoisted himself up. Sullied, Ira stayed on the ground a few moments, clutching his middle.

"What's with the warm welcome?" he gasped, rolling to his knees.

Monty swiped off his hat to clean it and let loose a torrent of black, curly hair. "Last time I heard your name, it was coming from my ol' lady and how the two of you shacked up in Sydney."

Ira regained his posture and attempted to give a reassuring smile to Camille and Oscar.

"I can't believe this," Oscar sighed as onlookers slowly went back to their market goods.

"I can," Camille said. Monty inspected Ira's companions, then shoved a thumb toward them.

"Them with you?" he asked Ira.

"Monty, listen, mate. We can make peace, can't we?"

Monty shoved Ira back and walked to his horse. "Go reconcile with some other woman's fool husband."

Ira practically trod on Monty's heels as he followed. "We need help, Monty."

Monty shoved him back again. "Help! You want help after beddin' Stella? My arse'll be blowin' you out help 'fore I do!"

Camille's mouth opened in shock, and Ira looked as bowled over as she.

"Now there's no call to speak like that in front of a lady," Ira said. Monty looked at Camille bashfully, but only for a moment.

"Get on with it, Beam. What the hell do you want?"

"Remember that favor you owe me? From that time we were in Melbourne?"

Monty cinched the rope on a few packages strung to his saddle. "Don't press your luck."

"All right, all right. Forget the favor. I'm asking you as a friend." Ira ignored Monty's rigid glare. "We just need some help getting set up for a journey, is all. Maybe a place to lay low the next couple days."

"You've got the nerve to invite yourself into my home?

What makes you think I'd give you anything more than a swift kick in the—"

"Mr. Monty . . . sir," Camille interrupted to halt the man's next verbal storm. "Please. It's important. We have people following us. People we don't *want* following us."

Monty scratched his bearded chin. "Ira, what trouble have you dragged these people into?"

"Whoa, whoa!" Ira waved his hands in front of him. "For once, it's not me the bad guys are after. It's them. One hundred percent them."

Monty looked doubtful. "What kind of danger are you in?"

Ira's arrogance softened. He stuck his hands in his pockets. "If they find us? The kind that won't leave us breathing."

Ira's friend chuckled.

"I'm serious, Monty. It's the Hesky brothers."

Monty's eyes darkened. "Hesky brothers?"

"Seen 'em myself in Bendigo," Ira said.

Monty looked at Camille and Oscar. "What do they want with you?"

It was too long of a story to tell standing in the middle of the street. Ira introduced them and then Monty led them to his home, a small beach hut just beyond the last wharf. Oscar relayed their story, leaving out the part about Umandu of course, before they came upon Monty's house. It teetered on a pile of massive rocks, most likely dredged from the riverbed. Camille could almost feel the two-room abode sway as she stepped inside.

Sea salt had whitened the floors and glass windows. Food-caked dishes and rust-stained pots lay scattered along the kitchen table. Clutter filled every corner, and cooking lard had yellowed the stovetop and wall behind it.

"Stella's eased up on the housework," Ira said as he shut the door. "Can I at least say hello to her?"

Monty yanked off his boots and tossed them aside.

"Good luck finding her. It seems she had an affinity for home wreckers and thieves."

Camille hovered near the door. Monty eyed her. "The place won't jump out and bite you, woman. Sit down."

She took enough of a step forward to ease their host. "Mr. Monty, I appreciate your help."

Monty threw a log into the stove and slammed the cast-iron door shut.

"Ira ain't even told me yet what kind of help he plans to wiggle outta me. So what do you want? Money?"

Ira tossed his hat onto the table. It landed atop a half-drained bottle of rum.

"Not exactly," he answered. "Once we get that map Oscar here was tellin' you about, we'll need to move fast. Either by land or water. Not sure which yet."

"Then why don't you go get the bloody map already?" Monty asked.

Camille closed her eyes against a burgeoning headache.

"Do you know a Caroline Rowen?" she asked. They hadn't thought of a way to track her mother down once they arrived in Port Adelaide, a settlement large enough to make finding her complicated. Camille had unreasonably pictured herself coming upon her mother's house as if it were the only one in the city. *So naïve,* she chided herself, and the disappointment of it made her question if she was being naïve about other things, too. McGreenery had certainly sounded amused at her plans to resurrect her father, as if it wouldn't work the way she expected.

Monty scratched his dark hair. "Rowen? Name ain't familiar."

"Maybe she changed it," Oscar suggested.

"What about Greer?" she asked, recalling her mother's maiden name. But again Monty shook his head.

"We'll find her," Oscar assured her as Monty picked up Ira's hat and tossed it back to him. Monty uncorked the bottle of rum and drew a big gulp.

"Without a name? Good luck," he said, then croaked a wet burp.

Camille's headache intensified. Oscar ducked to avoid the ceiling beams as he peered out a cloudy window.

"We should go, then," he said. Ira, seated in one of the rickety chairs, leaned back on the two rear legs.

"Happy trails, mate," he said, crossing his arms behind his head and closing his eyes. Oscar shoved the back of Ira's chair as he passed, and the front two legs slammed onto the floor. Ira's hat flew from his lap. Oscar scooped it up and handed it back to him.

"That means you too, *mate.*"

The center of Port Adelaide bulged with chaos. People demanded lower prices at each market tent, chickens and hens clucked at their fate, more bullock carts were in the process of loading, children laughed and tossed rocks at one another. Camille could hardly concentrate on her task.

The three of them wandered by rows of warehouses near the water, just as salt-stained as Monty's. The stench of urine, manure, body odor, and rotting fruit told of too many people living in one place. With every step, Camille wanted to turn and run back to Monty's shack. What if they couldn't find her mother? What if she had already died? Or what if McGreenery had already gotten to her? And if they did find her, what would Camille actually say? They continued walking aimlessly, not knowing where to stop or whom to ask. None of them were willing to admit it, either. So they wove through the street, looking at ships bobbing in the harbor, at lading cranes lifting cargo, and at fish vendors gutting and filleting their bug-eyed catch.

"This is ridiculous," Camille finally exclaimed, coming to a stop in the middle of the street. "Look at us. We're wandering like fools."

A great thrust from behind knocked her forward. A pair of feet tangled themselves between her boots and trod on her ankles. Ira caught her before she hit the shell-strewn street, but the man who had rammed into her fell to his side. A small crate crashed ahead of him.

The man grunted as he crawled to his knees. "What in hellfire are you doing standing in the middle of the street like that?"

Camille's ankles ached from where his boots had trampled her. "What are you doing not looking where you're going?"

He reached over, still on his knees, and inspected the crate. The sides had splintered but not snapped.

"I've got twenty bone china plates inside this crate, and if any are damaged, you'll be paying for them." He got to his feet and tried to lift the crate again. Oscar stepped forward, hoisted it up, and then shoved it back into the man's arms.

"You'll just have to be more careful next time," Oscar said. The man glared at him but reacted as most people did when faced with a formidable threat from Oscar: He bit his tongue. Camille's eyes fell to the crate, to a blue emblem emblazoned on the side. CAROLINE'S CHINA. The man turned to be on his way.

"Wait!" Camille cried. He looked back, puzzled. She gestured to the crate. "What is Caroline's China?"

The man glanced at the emblem, as if he himself needed to see it to know the answer. "A china shop. Why?"

"Does a woman named Caroline own it?"

"That would make the most sense, don't you think?" the man answered.

"What is her last name? Rowen?"

"No. McGinty," he answered. "Who's asking?"

"Can you take us there?" Oscar replied instead. He shrugged when Camille looked at him. What's the harm in trying, she guessed. The man hooked his chin ahead of them.

"Hurry up, this load's getting heavy."

They followed him as he shuffled along the street. The man stepped quickly, not looking back to see if he'd lost them in the crowds. Camille's head swam with both hope and the possibility of a dead end. The stranger stopped in front of the store, an oval wood-framed sign hanging above the door. CAROLINE'S CHINA. Camille's pulse gained momentum.

"I'm off," the man said, and disappeared into the side alley.

Camille hesitated in front of the shop, staring at her wavy reflection in the door's glass. Oscar placed his hands on the slopes of her shoulders. She covered his hands with her own.

"I don't think I could do this without you, Oscar," she said. His fingers flexed, his touch light enough to comfort but strong enough to encourage. Camille opened the door, and the three of them filed inside.

A brass bell chimed sweetly, but there was no one at the counter to greet them. The shop was small, its narrow shelves displaying rows of ivory plates, hand-painted teacups and saucers, blown-glass decanters, porcelain salt-cellars, and silver tableware. Crates were stacked on a counter near the door to a back room, lids off and packing paper spewing out.

"Hello?" Oscar called when they heard muffled conversation in the back room. The stranger must have been delivering the crate, Camille figured as she picked up a wineglass. Its stem was so delicate a slight squeeze might shatter it.

"Careful," said a voice from the back room. Camille looked up and saw a man coming through the doorway, his back to her as he pulled a tall crate to the counter.

"Those are more for show than actual use," he said, talking to her over his shoulder. Camille carefully placed the glass back on the shelf. He turned around and grabbed a crowbar from the counter.

"How can I help you?" he asked. Camille started to speak but, when she saw his face full on, went mute.

He was a boy, not a man, though tall and broad-shouldered. He met her eyes as he started to pry the top off the crate but immediately stilled his hands. He dropped the crowbar and stared at Camille. The hair on her neck perked as she took in his dark almond-shaped eyes, his cascade of shiny black hair. And his mouth. Those lips. She'd seen them thousands of times before.

"Who are you?" she whispered, her voice so soft she wondered if the boy heard her. Oscar and Ira and the rest of the shop faded away. Camille looked at his nose, the way it humped slightly in the center. She touched her own nose with the tips of her fingers, felt her own subtle bump.

"Samuel," he answered, his voice catching in his throat. "You're her. You're Camille."

He came around the side of the counter, wiping his hands on his shop smock. She forced herself to speak. "How do you know my name?"

"You don't know? She sent a letter to your father months ago."

Samuel then turned to Ira. "Are you William Rowen?"

Ira checked the space behind him, over each shoulder, then snorted. "Me? Her father? I'm gonna pretend you never said that."

"William's dead," Oscar explained, staring at this boy with disbelief. He saw the resemblance, too, Camille realized.

Samuel parted his lips and looked back at Camille. "I'm sorry. I didn't know."

"We've come to find Caroline Rowen," she said, her pulse still racing. "She's my mother. *She* sent my father the letter."

He nodded and flexed his jaw. "Her name isn't Rowen any longer. It's McGinty. Caroline McGinty."

"How do you know her?" Camille asked, though she was afraid to hear the answer.

He clasped his hands in front of him and rocked onto his heels.

"I didn't expect to have to tell you. I thought for sure your father would have," he said. Camille continued to stare at him. He sighed softly. "She's my mother, too."

Tears welled up in Camille's eyes, and her head spun. And that's when she saw it. His chin. The deep, dark cleft that she had seen on only one other man, a man her father despised. *What I carried with me in shame to Australia.* The words her mother had written in the letter. Words Camille had completely misunderstood. Not the map to Umandu. Nothing she could carry in her hands. She'd carried her shame inside her. A baby. Stuart McGreenery's baby.

FIFTEEN

*O*scar's hands caught Camille by the shoulders just in time. He steadied her, kept her from falling. Samuel watched her with unease. The cleft and his eyes, black as pupils, were both mirror images of McGreenery's.

"You're sixteen," she whispered. Samuel nodded. Sixteen years ago her mother had left San Francisco. The timing, the reason, the letters. It all couldn't have been clearer now. It all made sense. But how could her mother have done something so awful? How could she have been unfaithful to Camille's father with a rodent like Stuart McGreenery?

"Do you know who your father is?" Camille asked Samuel before she could stop and think. Did he know the truth, or had her mother withheld information from Samuel just as Camille's father had from her? Oscar stepped up beside her.

"Why don't you take us to see her," Oscar said. "Your mother."

Samuel looked from Camille to Oscar, then nodded, removing his shop smock. Perhaps he knew to be quiet.

Perhaps he was too uncomfortable to say anything at all. Camille didn't want to believe it — the man who led them out of the china shop and up the street was her brother. Her half brother. And he had Stuart McGreenery's blood running through him.

The house Samuel led them to sat on the rise of a small hill about five minutes away from the docks and the china shop. The air still hung heavy with the cloying scent of fish and seaweed. Camille walked in a blur of motion. The brown sea grass beneath her feet changed into a brick path as Samuel swung open a battered front gate. Everyone was stony and silent as they made their way up the path toward the front door. Camille couldn't grasp the fact that her mother was inside. In a few moments she would set eyes on the woman who had always been lost to Camille. Lost and buried under seventeen years of lies. She ground her teeth in an effort to keep tears from spilling.

"Mother is upstairs," Samuel said as they all stepped inside. The low ceilings left only an inch or two between the crown of Oscar's head and roughly hewn wooden beams. The wavy, white plaster walls were patched in spots and decorated with shell-framed portraits, green sea glass bottles, and paintings of the ocean. All of these things reminded Camille of her father, and she wondered if they had reminded her mother of him as well.

"She hasn't even been able to go into town," Samuel said to Camille. He spoke to her as though she was the only one with him. "I don't know how she made it this long. The doctor says the consumption should have claimed her months ago."

Had Caroline Rowen been waiting for her? Her father maybe? Or had she been holding on for someone else? For Stuart McGreenery? Camille turned her head to the set of narrow stairs, the steps scuffed and steep. The house was far from the grand townhouse in San Francisco. Her mother would have lived a much more affluent life had she stayed. Though her father never would have accepted a baby that wasn't his own, would he?

"I'll tell her you've arrived," Samuel said and climbed the steps. As his muscular form disappeared behind the turn in the stairwell, Oscar's shoulders dropped. He let out a sigh and turned to Camille.

"Do you think he even knows?" Oscar whispered.

Ira sat with a plunk on the couch. "Knows what?"

"You've obviously never had the privilege of meeting Stuart McGreenery," Camille said.

Ira snorted. "I'd certainly like to meet the bastard now, that's for sure."

The ceiling above their heads creaked with the weight of Samuel's steps. A door opened and closed lightly.

"From the looks of it" — Camille searched Oscar's face for affirmation — "you've just met his son."

Ira scooted to the edge of the couch cushion. "Holy gallnipper! You mean that McGreenery bloke and your mum pulled the wool over your father's eyes a time or two way back?"

Camille couldn't look at Ira, or Oscar. She'd been completely duped, and she felt like a fool. She moved to the blackened hearth, where a small fire was fading. The door upstairs clicked open, and footsteps creaked along the ceiling once again. Samuel came down the stairwell and stopped on the last step.

"She's ready to see you," he said.

Camille's knees turned soft. She caught a glimpse of herself in an oval mirror hanging near the door. Her tousled hair was dirty and peppered with snarls. It needed a good wash and brushing. And her dress! Not only was it horrid and out of fashion, it also needed scrubbing and mending.

"I can't," she said. "I can't let her see me like this. I'm not presentable."

Ira harrumphed from the couch, his feet now on the table before him. "Presentable be damned. She's your mum."

Samuel placed a foot on the next step, obviously anxious to lead Camille up. *My mum,* she thought, pressing her skirt with her hands and trying to smooth back her hair. All the more reason for her to want to look her best. Camille wanted her *mum* to see what she'd left behind and all the years she'd lost. She wanted her to see that, despite never having had a mother, she got along just fine. That she'd survived and was strong and able, even if she didn't feel it at the moment.

"Do you want me to come with you?" Oscar asked. Camille almost said yes, but shook her head. She had to do this on her own.

Samuel led Camille up the steep stairs. Her feet hardly fit on the steps, the boards were so narrow, and the cramped upstairs had even lower ceilings than the sitting room. Two windows, one at each end of the hallway, lit the painted canvas floorcloth.

Newly sprayed rose musk hung heavily in the air along with something unsavory, which clung to the back of Camille's throat. Her mother should be dead by now, Samuel had said. Camille sensed Caroline Rowen's body had faded faster than her will.

Samuel stopped at a door and rapped his fist on it twice.

"Come in," a soft voice answered. Camille's heart leaped, then slowed. Samuel pushed the door ajar and stepped aside. Camille met his eyes, saw their uncertainty, and then he turned and walked back toward the stairs. He wasn't coming in with her.

"Come in," the soft voice said again. Camille opened the door the rest of the way.

A woman rocked slowly in a wicker chair by the window, a purple-and-emerald quilt covering her legs and feet. Her long, ebony hair, pulled back into a loose bun, was streaked with white. Caroline Rowen didn't look at her daughter but kept her eyes on her hands clasped in her lap. Camille wondered if she had heard her walk in. But then her mother's shoulders began to shake, her chin quivered, and her lips drew into a thin line. She was sobbing when she finally lifted her head and looked at Camille.

"Oh," her mother gasped, pressing a handkerchief to her mouth. Camille stared at the woman who had always sat perfectly still and lifeless in the portrait hanging in her father's study. Without a second thought, Camille crossed the room and opened her arms. Her mother took her in an embrace and squeezed her, quaking some more as a fresh batch of tears fell.

"Oh, my darling," she whispered into Camille's straggly, travel-filthy hair. "I'm so sorry. So sorry."

Camille marveled in the feeling of being locked in her mother's arms. She didn't want to move, she never wanted to stop hugging her mother. Right then, she would have forgiven her everything. Her mother's grip loosened, and Camille sensed it was time to step back, to finally talk. She wiped away her tears while Caroline cleared her throat and sniffled.

"Isn't it odd?" her mother began. "I've been waiting for so long to set eyes on you again. Dreamed nearly every day of what you might look like. What I'd say if I got the chance to come face-to-face with you. And here you stand and I've no idea how to begin."

Her mother took a labored breath. The lips that had been so full and red in the portrait were now thin, ashen, and cracked.

"My father is dead," Camille blurted, without thinking. "He went down with the *Christina* on our way here."

The frail muscles in her mother's neck tightened, and the yellowed whites of her eyes showed her sickness.

It was as though life drained out of her, even as they spoke.

"Samuel told me he'd died. I had so wanted the chance to say —" She shook her head. "I don't know what I would have said. But to see him once more and end things the right way, once and for all. . . . I wish I could have."

Caroline turned her head toward the window. Afternoon light cast shadows across her cheeks and hair, revealing how badly the consumption had laid waste to her beauty.

"Samuel. He's McGreenery's son, isn't he?" Camille asked, shocked by her boldness but not willing to waste another moment. Her mother kept her eyes locked on the harbor.

"He is. William didn't share my letter with you?"

"Not exactly."

Her mother's shoulders sagged. "What did your father tell you about me while you were growing up?"

The question fell sideways from the topic of Samuel. Camille guessed this had been one of the questions her mother had pondered for years.

"That you died giving birth to me," Camille answered. She didn't want to answer any more of her mother's questions. Too many of her own cluttered up her mind. "Did you leave us because you were pregnant with McGreenery's child?"

Her mother sighed and looked to her lap. "Camille, I made the greatest mistake of my life with Stuart McGreenery." She placed a bony hand over her chest. "I love Samuel with all my heart, but I had everything with your father, and with you. I threw it away because I imagined being with Stuart would be exciting. I was so very, very *stupid*." She nearly spit the word into her lap. "Stuart had asked me to consider running away with him. I thought nothing could be more romantic." She leaned back into the chair and stared out the window once more. "I said yes."

Camille took a deep breath and bit the inside of her lip, hard. "How could you?" she asked.

"I was young, not yet eighteen. I wanted romance and excitement, not marriage." She glanced, watery-eyed, at Camille. "And as much as I loved you, I didn't know if being a mother was right for me. If I'd be any good at it."

Camille's feelings of utter forgiveness from just moments ago waned. She herself wasn't yet eighteen but knew with every last ounce of her soul that she would never have abandoned her family.

"So you planned to run off with Stuart McGreenery. You wanted to be his wife? The mother of his child? We weren't enough for you? My father was a good man. He was a good father, and you left him."

All of Camille's reservations about whether or not her mother would like her or approve of her took flight. Who cared what a selfish woman like her mother might think?

"I knew he was a good man, that he'd be a good father. I couldn't take you away from him. The way he coddled you, sang to you, took you into the cupola to point out the moon and stars." The corner of her mouth twitched into a smile. "He and Stuart were fighting over the business. Their friendship — if you could even call it that — turned after William came back from Sydney with . . . well, I suppose you know . . . that map, and they agreed to dissolve the company."

So the map had been the catalyst for her father and McGreenery's rivalry. The map and her mother, of course. Camille felt so rushed, so on the rampage to have her questions answered. Part of her demanded to slow down and let her mother speak, but she quashed the voice.

"So you took it? The map, you took it with you when you left?"

"Please listen, Camille." She strained her voice and leaned her head back. "Please just hear me out."

Camille clasped her hands behind her, squeezed her fingers together, and nodded.

"When I discovered Stuart's true intention was only to get to the map, everything I thought I loved about him spoiled. I saw that all he wanted in life were the things other people had — money, power, even me. He planned to sell the stone to —"

"The highest bidder," Camille finished for her. "He told me as much in Melbourne."

Her mother sat up straighter. "Melbourne? He is here? In Australia?"

Was that excitement that brightened her eyes? A blade of resentment pierced Camille's chest when she thought of her mother anticipating Stuart McGreenery's arrival as much as her own.

"Wasn't that your plan when you wrote to him?" Camille asked.

"I didn't write to Stuart! I only wrote to your father. I had Samuel scribe the letter."

The quilt covering her mother's legs slipped as she sat forward. She seemed to wilt in the chair as she tucked the quilt back around her legs. "Samuel must have taken it upon himself to write to Stuart."

Samuel had also told William that a letter had been sent to McGreenery. But why? Had Samuel wanted to rub in his existence like salt on a wound? Or had he just wanted to lay all the cards faceup on the table?

"I don't want Stuart to have the map, Camille. That stone is too powerful for the likes of him."

Caroline kept her eyes locked on to Camille's, trying to burrow her point in. She took a shallow breath before continuing.

"I tried to destroy the map, but it wouldn't burn when I held it over flames. It wouldn't tear, either. Even the sharpest blade was unable to cut it. It had a power, Camille. I found I couldn't bring myself to toss it into the rubbish or bury it in the ground, and I realized it had a power over me as well. I couldn't forsake it."

"But you could forsake us, your family," Camille said, beginning to lose her composure.

"I had no other choice. I—" Her mother cast her eyes to her lap. "Just after Stuart told me his plans for the map, I discovered I was pregnant. And your father had been away for months."

Sickness edged into her throat with the image of her mother pregnant with Stuart McGreenery's baby.

"I made hasty arrangements and left you with your nursemaid before William could return from sea," Caroline said, still unable to look at her daughter.

"Why didn't you just tell my father about McGreenery's plan? Why didn't you simply confess to everything you'd done? Instead, you abandoned your life to protect a map, to protect yourself. You chose to go into hiding because you didn't have the courage to face your mistakes!"

Her mother reached her frail hands out to her. She started to cough, a hoarse, grating cough. She brought her hand to her mouth and spread a handkerchief over her lips. Camille went to her and gripped her shoulder. On the side table were a glass and a pitcher of water. Camille lifted the pitcher with shaking hands as her mother continued to hack and fight for air.

The bedroom door flew open and Samuel rushed to their mother's side. He grabbed the glass from Camille's hand and tilted it to his mother's lips. Oscar and Ira hovered in the doorway as the coughing fit abated. Caroline took the handkerchief away from her mouth. Spots of bright red blood coated the linen. Samuel slammed the glass on the side table.

"She needs to rest. Whatever you two were arguing about can wait."

Ashamed they'd heard their raised voices downstairs, Camille started for the door.

"No, Samuel," Caroline said hoarsely. Camille stopped

and turned to her mother. She sat up in her chair, pushing back her emaciated shoulders. "You're right, Camille. I was a coward. I was afraid of everything."

Beads of sweat dripped from her cheeks and her neck, soaking the collar of her blouse. "I've never made excuses for what I did. I won't start now."

"Just tell me why you took the map," Camille said. "Tell me why running away was the only answer."

Samuel stormed up to Camille. "That's enough!"

And this time her mother didn't protest.

SIXTEEN

*C*amille made it halfway down the staircase before the door to her mother's room opened and then slammed again. At the bottom of the stairwell, Oscar and Ira turned as if expecting Caroline herself to be running after them. But it was Samuel, his face red and eyes nearly popping out of their sockets.

"I hope you're pleased with yourself," he roared. "She could have choked to death on her own blood. Is that what you want?"

Camille gaped at him, her jaw dropped. "Of course not! Why would I have come all this way to *want* something like that?"

Samuel gripped the banister. "Why *did* you come? To badger her with questions? To throw the mistakes she made in her face?"

"You're acting as if I'm some sort of intruder. I didn't show up here uninvited," Camille said, her voice shaking.

"I won't have you troubling my mother anymore," Samuel said through clenched teeth. He shoved past her.

"She's my mother, too," Camille whispered.

Samuel whipped around. "She's no more your mother than I am your brother. She left you, remember? She's a stranger to you, and you're a stranger to her. Do you really think you have a place here?"

Tears sprang to Camille's eyes.

"I never wanted her to send that letter to invite you both here," he said. "She was already sick, and I knew facing you would kill her."

Samuel rummaged through his vest, his hands fighting with the fabric of the pocket. He wrestled free a brown, rolled-up piece of leather and hurled it at Camille, striking her leg.

"Here! This is what you came for, isn't it?" he seethed. "Take it, then." Samuel rushed down the stairs. Camille, Oscar, and Ira remained silent as the front door swooshed open, then slammed.

"He's right," Camille said, her voice barely a whisper as she bent to pick up the map. It was about the length of her forearm, ruddy, ancient-looking, and tied off with a frayed red string. Not exactly the ceremonial passing she had predicted.

"Don't listen to him, love," Ira said.

"But he is right. I shouldn't have come." A sob blocked her throat.

"She wanted you here. She asked for you," Oscar said. Camille continued down the stairs, into the sitting room.

"I thought I wanted to come. I thought I wanted to know the truth about everything. I'm not so sure anymore."

Her mother's reasons for leaving, and for loving McGreenery, were piteously inept and naïve. Caroline Rowen had discarded her duties to her husband and baby in favor of lust. In favor of a worn leather map. Camille couldn't begin to grasp it. She opened the front door to a freshening wind. The port's bell tower chimed as if to indicate her visit was indeed at an end.

Outside, free of the musk rose–infused air masking the presence of death, Camille headed for a white-picket-fenced garden. Knee-high weeds tangled the brown grass and sprouted from the cracks of a nearly hidden slate path. Shrubbery hung over the fence, and brittle, unkempt limbs poked out from in between each time-withered stake. Camille saw a stone bench near a bed of weeds, the plot probably once providing her mother and Samuel with herbs. She brushed off a few shriveled leaves and sat down.

A hollow pit. That is what her stomach felt like as she looked up at the lace curtain shrouding the upstairs window where her mother lay recuperating. A hollow pit, endless and impossible to fill. She ran her fingertips along the soft leather of the map. The absurdity of it all struck her. She'd wanted this map more than she'd wanted to meet her mother. She was as selfish and single-minded as McGreenery, and now with the map in her possession, she couldn't even bring herself to open it. Disgusted with herself, Camille set it on the bench beside her.

A small wisp of smoke spiraled from the chimney, taken on the breeze, the beginnings of a storm gathering over the ocean. Oscar swung open the creaky garden gate.

In the grassy meadow in the Grampians, where he'd bared his soul to her, Oscar had said he would miss her. More than he missed her father? How could Oscar feel that way about someone as selfish as herself?

Oscar sat beside her and picked up the map.

"Nothing spectacular, is it?" she said. "I nearly expected it to be made of gold."

He laughed quietly. "Have you looked at it?"

She shook her head. Oscar grasped the red string and pulled it loose. The leather unrolled and Camille gasped. The map shimmered with what did look like gold dust, and in the center a long and twisting vein of silver sparkled like the Pacific Ocean at sunset. Camille moved closer to Oscar and peered over his arm at the map.

"How can this be?" she asked. The silver line ran from the harbor of a crescent-shaped cove labeled TALLADAY, through green forest, then a stretch of amber land that looked crackled and burned, and then through more forest, this one hilly with sharper bends and curves. Along the silver line were drawings. Stamped into the stretch of crackled amber was a series of wide-topped cylinders. They coiled around and around, like tight springs, each one connecting at the base to a flat, black disc. Camille had no idea what they meant. The drawings stamped into the emerald forest were more straightforward: arched entrances, and in the center of each a pair of sharp, black fangs.

Carefully, Camille touched the map with a single fingertip. She ran it along the silver line, which ended at an etching that looked like a great stone tomb. A dark, stamped triangle hovered over the tomb's summit. Camille drew her hand away. A dusting of silver glittered on the pad of her fingertip. The surface of the map now undulated the way a glassine lake, disturbed by a skipping rock, might. The impression of Camille's fingertip along the silver path rippled away. Awestruck, she brushed her finger through the emerald forest. The tops of the trees swayed as if bent by a heavy gale.

"I've never seen anything like it," Oscar said. "It really *is* magic."

Camille took the map from him and flipped it over. On the reverse side was an odd-looking symbol: two triangles, one right side up, the other turned on its crown. Their bases were nearly joined, forming a diamond. Nothing special compared to the front of the map. She turned it back over and ran her hand across the body of sparkling blue water labeled SPENCER'S BAY, which was just north of Port Adelaide. The water churned under her touch, the glitter left on her fingertip cool and damp.

A sudden beam of amber light rolled across the surface. Camille held the map away from her as the amber beam surged over the upper right corner, illuminating letters that hadn't been there a moment ago. They sparked and smoked anew, burning into the leather.

"What is it?" Oscar asked, staring at her with concern.

"Those letters," she breathed, trying to read the tight calligraphy. "Did you see that? They just appeared!"

He bent his head toward the map.

"I don't see anything. What letters?"

She watched his eyes roam aimlessly over the map, searching for the words she could so plainly see. How could he not see them? The flash of amber had nearly blinded her.

She pointed to the words without touching them, afraid they might scald her skin.

"Right here. You really can't see them?"

Oscar shook his head, glancing quickly at her, then back to where her finger pointed.

"So, what do they say?" he asked.

Camille squinted her eyes and read out loud. *"Be not fooled by the first that you see, the stone is made plain to only the worthy. Close your eyes, conjure your thoughts, speak not a word, for it reads your heart."*

Camille read the words again, this time to herself. The riddle was instruction on how to use the stone. Umandu had the power to see deep into her heart, to know the person she most wanted to bring back to life. But why couldn't Oscar see the inscription?

The words on the map threw off more sparks and then burst into flames. Camille chucked the map to the ground as the flames ate at the words, burning them into oblivion. And then, with a final puff of black smoke, the flames disappeared.

Camille leaned over and snatched up the map. The leather was unharmed, the upper corner empty, just as it had been before the amber flash had revealed the inscription. She recalled what her mother had said, how nothing, not even fire, had been able to harm the map.

She turned to Oscar, who stared at her with caution.

"I take it you didn't see the flames, either?" she asked. He shook his head slowly. "Oh. Splendid."

Camille carefully rolled the map and tied it with the string, then placed it in her skirt pocket. She rubbed her glittering silver fingertip on her skirt, thinking again of how Umandu actually worked. It would read her heart.

Her mind retreated to her mother. "She's not going to make it much longer. You don't think my heart might choose to bring *her* back instead of my father, do you?" She covered her mouth with her hand. "I'm sorry. That's horrible for me to even say."

The wind kicked up, blowing Camille's hair across her cheek. The locks tickled her nose and whipped into her eyes.

Oscar tucked the wild strands of hair behind her ear. Like the time he'd touched her cheek on the *Christina*, his hand left a trail of fire. He rested his hand against her neck, and pressed his fingers into her skin just enough to make the blood inside her veins throb. She had the sudden urge to melt right into him, to just let him absorb her and keep her safe and snug. She'd wanted this moment for so long, though she'd tried desperately to ignore that she did. She had a duty. A duty to her father, to Randall.

"Don't doubt what you want, Camille," Oscar whispered as the space between them closed. His eyes, as gray and brooding as the incoming storm, didn't waver from hers. His lips were full and inviting, the warmth of his body, alluring.

"My, my, isn't this an enchanting picture."

Oscar dropped his hand, ripping Camille from her trance. McGreenery stood at the garden gate, Samuel by his side. Camille and Oscar leaped to their feet.

"I have to say, I did not see this one coming," McGreenery said with a smirk. "What will you do once you return to San Francisco, Camille? Move to the wharves and tie bait bags for a living?"

A flush crept up her neck, a mixture of fury and embarrassment. Oscar's body went rigid, his jaw and shoulders tightened. McGreenery must have just barely pulled into port.

"I see you've arrived on our heels once again," Camille said, trying to deflect the humiliation burning her ears.

McGreenery slipped off his flawless white gloves and sneered at her. "I would never have guessed a silly girl and her pet monkey could outrun three bushrangers and a Jack-tar."

Oscar moved to charge toward him, but Camille grabbed his arm. McGreenery roared with laughter.

"Still roped in by the Rowens, Kildare? Even with William in a watery grave. Will wonders never cease?"

Camille released Oscar's arm and started for McGreenery herself. Just then a cry pierced the air. She searched the yard and her eyes fell on the front door, where Ira stood, frantically waving his hand.

"It's your mum!" he called, cupping his mouth to prevent the wind from taking his words up and away. "You better get in, quick!"

Samuel broke into a sprint, followed by Camille and Oscar. McGreenery stayed put by the garden gate. Sweat beaded on Camille's back as she raced up the last step leading to the cramped upstairs. She heard her mother coughing and gasping as Samuel threw open the door. Caroline lay crumpled on the floor beside her rocking chair, Ira already at her side and trying to lift her.

"Mother!" Samuel cried. He took one of her arms and helped Ira bring her to the brass-frame bed. Camille scooped up the lap quilt that had fallen to the floor and covered her mother's legs.

Blood coated the handkerchief in Caroline's hand, sweat dotted her nose and chin and forehead. She rolled to her side, still coughing.

"Camille," she gasped.

"I'm here," Camille answered, bringing the covers up around her mother's neck. Camille's heart beat madly, her legs felt weak. She'd never seen anyone so ill and it frightened her.

She thought of the story Juanita had helped weave for her father, about how her mother had struggled through labor and collapsed after delivery. The sweating, the arching of her back, the gasping for air. It all mirrored what Camille had always envisioned her mother's death to have been.

Caroline started to settle. Her coughing quieted, and

she reached out her hand. Camille hesitantly took it. Her mother's fingers were cold, her palms sweaty.

"Forgive me," her mother whispered. Her eyes glistened as she stared at Camille. "Please. Forgive me."

Samuel watched Camille with such intensity she could nearly hear his unspoken plea for her to answer their mother's request.

"I do," Camille said. With unexpected wonder, she realized it was true, even after all the betrayal and secrecy. Caroline Rowen had made a mistake large enough to alter all their lives, and somehow Camille still felt an innate need to forgive her. She was still her mother, still once the woman in the portrait in her father's study. Camille had always dreamed of knowing what her mother had been like in life, instead of that one, flat dimension. Now that she had been given that chance, even fleetingly, she didn't want it to end, let alone on a note of resentment.

"I do forgive you," Camille repeated. Her mother's lips turned up into a half smile, the one captured in the portrait. Camille knew that look. She squeezed her mother's hand, feeling closer to her. Not like a stranger at all.

SEVENTEEN

*L*oosely turned soil lay heaped beside a burial site as the soft morning sun hardened into afternoon light. Her mother had stopped breathing an hour past midnight. Camille had held her hand as her gasping settled and eyes fell vacant. She hadn't realized how firmly she gripped her mother's frail fingers until Samuel pried her hand loose. Now, less than twelve hours later, the burial was nearly over.

Winds whipped the preacher's long, thinning hair across his spectacles, and the pages of his Bible flipped and fluttered as he spoke. A decent-sized crowd dressed in muted colors gathered around the grave site. Camille's dress had been washed and wrung out, her hair and skin scrubbed clean in a hot, soapy bath. And though Samuel had bid her take whatever dress she wanted from their mother's closet, Camille hadn't been able to do it. She'd put back on the unfashionable homespun, still slightly damp.

Camille stood with her arm entwined in Oscar's, their fingers laced. His hand was the firm grounding she sorely needed that morning. Always dependable, always constant. Camille leaned against him, and he gave her hand a slight squeeze.

Ira was on her other side with his hat in hand, his messy hair blowing about. They were outsiders, strangers. People had sent them curious glances as they'd descended upon the cemetery; Camille wondered if any of them noticed her resemblance to the woman they came to pay respects to.

Samuel, however, shook hands, received somber pats on his shoulder, kisses on the cheek, and stood beside the preacher, the spot reserved for the closest kin. Jealousy nibbled at Camille, but she pushed it away. It wasn't the time, and it didn't matter, anyway.

"We commit to the ground the body of Caroline Camille McGinty," the preacher said. Camille tightened her fingers around Oscar's hand. She'd never known her mother's middle name. Had it always been Camille, or had she changed that, too, after she'd come to Port Adelaide? She tried to make eye contact with Samuel, but he didn't oblige. He had been avoiding her all morning.

The night before, after Caroline had died, Samuel had sat on the edge of their mother's mattress and wept. Camille didn't have the memories of her, or the bond with her that Samuel did, to do the same. Her own tears had spilled, but they weren't for her mother. They were for her father, for the memories of him and their unbreakable bond. Camille had tried so doggedly to be strong and unwavering that she hadn't yet cried for him the way she should have.

Her father had been the one to soothe her after nightmares, never Juanita or another house servant. He had read to her each evening before bed, and when Camille had discovered Shakespeare, they'd acted out the parts, each of them taking on such preposterous English accents they would end up in hysterics. Each time she wore a new dress, he would insist she never looked lovelier. And at every dinner party to which they'd been invited, Camille would straighten his tie in the seconds before their driver helped them from the carriage. All these weeks Camille hadn't been able to let go. Why should she if she could find the stone and bring him back?

How it would actually work still eluded her. His body, wherever it may be, was no doubt bloated beyond recognition. Perhaps picked apart by sea creatures. The thoughts were vile, but it was a fact. If the stone brought him back to life, how would he be? Where would he turn up? Doubt trickled into her mind.

Finally, Samuel's eyes traveled over to her, but they drifted by and latched on to something else. Looking over her shoulder she saw Stuart McGreenery at the rear of the gathering. The sight of him deepened her grief.

"May she rest in peace. Ashes to ashes. Dust to dust." The preacher threw a chunk of earth onto her mother's simple casket. People moved forward and followed the same ritual, and soon the plopping of dirt on wood seemed louder than the wind. Camille unlaced her fingers from Oscar's. Instead of dirt, Camille tossed in a white rose she'd been holding in her free hand.

"Come now, love," Ira whispered in her ear, gripping her shoulder. Saying good-bye to her mother hadn't been as difficult as she'd imagined it would be. After all, she'd only known her — really known her — for a day.

Ira's hand slipped away, replaced by a heavier grip. Oscar. She let him lead her toward the wrought-iron cemetery gate. With McGreenery in Port Adelaide, they'd decided not to stay another night. Oscar and Camille had unraveled the map the evening before, away from Ira. The enchanted etchings had left them in utter awe again, but the amber flash and the sparking letters had not returned as Oscar held the map for both of them to see. When they'd heard Ira come in the front door, Oscar had spirited it away. He simply told Ira they needed to head up toward a place called Talladay.

"We've got a ship ready to take us up Spencer's Bay," Ira said as they walked toward the cemetery gate. Monty had grudgingly decided to aid their cause, nudged along by a few bottles of whiskey, compliments of Ira.

"The *Juggernaut* leaves tonight on the high tide," Ira said as McGreenery slid in front of them.

"Camille," McGreenery greeted her, as cold as the dirt surrounding her mother's coffin.

"I'm not in the mood to listen to anything you have to say." Camille walked around him. Oscar and Ira passed by, close enough to resonate a threat. He ignored them.

"I should think you'd be eager to speak with me," McGreenery said.

She peered back at him.

"Eager to speak with you about what?"

"About the copy of the map my son was clever enough to make."

Camille searched for Samuel and found him still speaking with the preacher. He met her fiery gaze but didn't flinch. Why would Samuel even bother to give her the map if he'd planned on giving a copy to McGreenery all along? Camille's mind tumbled in all directions. It was as though Samuel couldn't decide whether to help her or compete with her.

"It looks as if the race for the stone continues." McGreenery sneered.

Camille winced.

Ira's cheeks blanched and his pupils dilated.

"Bloody hell," he whispered. He slowly twisted around, toward Oscar. "Not *that* stone?"

Oscar nodded uncomfortably. "We, uh, had a feeling you wouldn't be so keen on helping us if you knew."

Ira's mouth formed an O.

"You deceived your guide, did you? To what level will you stoop, Camille?" McGreenery asked.

She stepped toward him. "Who are you to talk? You deceived your partner and stole his wife! You planned to rob him and you used my mother to do it."

"You could have bloody told me," Ira mumbled under his breath.

Camille ignored him, her body shaking as she continued to stare McGreenery down. "My mother saw through your lies. She saw right down to your shallow, black soul. It doesn't even matter that you never loved her. *She* left *you*. At least she had some sense of principle. You've never cared for anything but power and money. You'd trade anything for it. Even Samuel, I'd wager."

"Trade me for what?" Samuel asked, stepping up behind them without warning. "Am I nothing more than a card to be played?"

"That's not what I meant," Camille said.

"I'd hoped you'd at least have the decency to remain civil until we'd left the cemetery," Samuel said. "But you couldn't manage even that, could you?"

Ira snorted, still trapped in his own conversation. "Treasure. Bah! Bloody treasure . . . it's a rock people get murdered trying to find!"

Camille glared at her brother. "You copied the map and gave it to him. Why would you betray our mother like that?"

Samuel tugged on the collar of his jacket and adjusted his tie. "We've discussed things, and he's agreed to help me find the stone."

Samuel glanced back at the grave, the earth in a pile around it. "I've instructed them to leave the nails out of the coffin and let the grave be for a week."

Camille stared at the coffin in horror, battling the revolting image of her mother pushing aside the lid and climbing out. Even without a single crease in his flinty expression, McGreenery exuded satisfaction.

"He's lying to you," Camille pleaded. "He has his own plans for the stone. You don't know him like I do."

Ira stopped pacing back and forth and pointed at Camille. "You can forget my help, just forget it. I'm not riskin' my neck for a stone I can't profit from."

Oscar stepped in front of Ira and shoved him out of the conversation once and for all.

Samuel turned back to Camille. "Just because you were robbed of your father doesn't mean you have the right to rob me of mine."

Camille laughed out of frustration. "Open your ears! He used our mother to get to the map. He isn't going to help you!"

People started to stop and stare.

"I've heard quite enough," McGreenery said, the pleasure of hearing them argue clear. "Samuel, get your things. We're leaving on the high tide."

"No!" Camille cried.

Samuel straightened his shoulders and lifted his chin. "I'm sorry you won't be able to bring your father back. I truly am. But I'm going with him. He is my blood. My family," Samuel said, though a flicker of doubt lit his eyes.

"So are we. I'm your sister," she whispered.

"Half sister," he corrected, as if *half* sliced their tie to one another into something less worthwhile.

"No need to further humiliate yourself, Camille," McGreenery said, taking Samuel gently by the arm. "I imagine you'll do plenty of that when you arrive back in San Francisco as this ape's wench."

Oscar growled and lunged for him. He hurled McGreenery against the iron gate. McGreenery staggered to the side, but then rushed Oscar. Both men tumbled to the dirt in fisticuffs before Ira and Samuel and a few others pulled them apart.

"Stop this!" Samuel shouted. McGreenery dusted off his jacket, his nose and lip bleeding. A part of Camille reveled in the sight of his blood. Oscar looked as if he'd pounce again if it weren't for Ira's firm grip on his arm.

Samuel took a step toward Camille. His eyes were as black as McGreenery's, but they held something deeper. Samuel hesitated. Camille sensed he wanted to say something, but he shook his head and walked away. McGreenery wiped the blood from his face with a handkerchief and then followed his son.

Oscar swiped a trickle of blood from his nose with his sleeve. Ira slapped him on the back.

"How'd it feel, mate? The bloke deserved worse'n that, but you got your fist in there pretty good."

She'd have loved the chance to knock McGreenery to his knees herself. But as Camille took Oscar's arm and they started walking away, he stayed silent. Drawing McGreenery's blood hadn't made anything better. Her father was still dead. Her mother was still laid out in a casket only a few feet away. Samuel had still chosen McGreenery over her.

And the most difficult part of their journey had only begun.

EIGHTEEN

*W*hiskey?" Camille cried as she stood on a wharf in Port Adelaide harbor. "You brought us onto a whiskey cargo ship?"

Ira spread out his arms. "And rum, love. Don't forget the rum."

The high tide slowly swallowed the wharf pilings, and the *Juggernaut*, a whiskey runner, was in the final process of loading.

"Listen," Ira said to both Oscar and Camille, who looked at their escort with doubt. "There couldn't be a better cargo to ride with than whiskey and rum. You think if there were pots and pans and spoons in there, the captain would take her full chisel to Talladay? People pay a pretty price for liquor, mates, and the ones delivering it make out like bandits."

The *Juggernaut* wasn't worth the ten crowns it cost Monty to secure a spot aboard. The schooner didn't look seaworthy with its chipped paint, barnacle-covered hull, sloppy lines, and patched canvas sail. It was hardly the

Stealth's equal, and Camille worried over the schooner's efficiency as Ira greeted the captain.

"Captain Mulligan, this here's Miss Camille Rowen and Mr. Oscar Kildare," he said, and stepped back to let the stout, barrel-chested captain inspect his passengers.

Captain Mulligan cleared his throat. "I'll thank ye to stay below most hours of the day and out of the way of me crew. Otherwise, it's good to have ye aboard. If ye need anything, miss, ask me first mate, Harrington. Sir." He nodded to Oscar and then returned to his ship.

"Charming," Camille whispered.

"It isn't high class, but it'll do the trick, yeah?" Ira said, coming back to face them. "Well, I guess this is it. You two should get aboard."

Camille sighed. "You're really not coming?"

"I told you. There ain't no profit in that hexed rock for me, now is there? Only one person can benefit from it." Ira twitched his nose. "And I'm still ticked you bloody lied to me about not seeing that bony face in the air back before Bendigo. Thought my brain had gone soft."

Oscar lifted a heavy bag of provisions Monty had set them up with after the funeral. Food, water, blankets, phosphorus matches, a rifle, and plenty of bullets.

"I meant what I said earlier," Oscar said. "We'll get the money we owe you from William's insurance holders in Sydney."

Camille remained quiet, hoping they still had insurance money to send.

Ira waved his hat at them. "Yeah, yeah. It's a good thing I like you two. Well, I'm not one for mushy good-byes, so off you go now, love. I've got to go see if I can con Monty into letting me stay on with him a while longer."

Ira kissed Camille on the cheek, and Camille hugged him. The Australian squeezed her in return, locking his arms around her.

"Ira," she said, her lungs not able to take a full gulp of air. He nestled his chin in the crevice of her neck. "Ira!"

He released her and hooted, "Well, if I can't have any bloody treasure. . . ." Ira smiled and tipped his hat to her. She shook her head, smoothing her dress down. Oscar laughed and extended his hand. Ira looked at it twice before taking it.

"You actually thanking me, Kildare?"

"I'm actually shaking your hand, Beam," he answered with a grin.

"All right, get on with it, then." Ira sent them one last wave before walking off toward Monty's shack.

Camille and Oscar met Harrington in the galley. The second level sported low ceilings and dirty floors, and as the dour first mate escorted them down the narrow corridor, Camille already traced the biting odor of liquor from the hold.

Harrington shoved open a door. "Here it is."

The room was little more than a pantry with a bunk built into the wall, and a strip of floor as wide as Oscar's shoulders.

"Is this my cabin?" Camille asked, stepping inside.

"Belongs to both of you," Harrington replied.

"Both of us?" she gasped. "That's impossible, Mr. Harrington."

"Take it or leave it, miss." His callous look flouted his polite tone.

Oscar took the door and walked in behind Camille. "Thank you, we're fine here," he said. The first mate grimaced before moving away. Oscar closed the door lightly.

Camille balled her hands into fists. "Ira said nothing about one piteously small room!"

The sheets on the bunk were messed and the pillow flat as a griddle cake. There was no porthole, either. The only light, a miniature hurricane lamp already lit, was set inside a crevice in the wall. Without it, the cabin would be pitch-black.

"Looks like he paid us back in advance for lying to him," he said.

"I can't believe you're not upset. How are we supposed to live for the next two weeks? Captain Mulligan wants us to stay below. In this room, with no light, no space."

All cramped and close and with only one bunk. She didn't add that. It was obvious enough.

"I'll sleep on the floor," Oscar offered, as though reading her mind. She looked at the wooden planks, covered in droppings. Mouse droppings at best, rat droppings at worst. Rats bit, and if a wound got infected the infection would be unstoppable.

"You can't sleep on the floor," she said, though he couldn't sleep in the bunk with her, either. "Let's not think of it right now. The only important thing is getting up Spencer's Bay. And then to the stone before McGreenery and Samuel."

If McGreenery and her brother got there first, everything would be lost. She'd lose her father all over again.

A sudden explosion of sound sent Camille doubling over. The incomprehensible chanting hurtled back into her head, battering her eardrums. The drumming and grunting was so thunderous she could barely hear Oscar shouting her name. He gripped her arm to steady her as the pitch and pace of the mantra intensified. It hadn't happened since Bendigo, and she'd hoped it had gone for good. Camille covered her ears and grated her teeth, burying her head in Oscar's chest. Then just as quickly as it had come on, the chanting vanished. Her ears rang, but the noises had stopped.

"Camille? Camille!" Oscar shouted.

"I can hear you now," she said, breathless. "It was the chanting. That god-awful chanting!"

Oscar stared at her in bewilderment.

"I'm not crazy, Oscar."

"I didn't say you were," he replied. "Are you okay?"

She shook her head. No, she was far from okay. The chanting hadn't been so loud before. It nearly deafened her this time.

"It seems like every time I hear it, something horrible follows. Like a signal that something bad is about to happen."

Oscar opened the door to their cabin. "I'll go up top and make sure everything's okay. Are you going to be all right in here alone?"

The ringing in her ears subsided. "Just don't take too long," she said, certain something was wrong.

"I'll be right back. And since it looks as if we're going to be spending some time alone together" — he looked around the cramped cabin, his eyes catching on the bunk before shifting uncomfortably to her — "I think we should talk."

Camille pushed back her shoulders, forgetting the chanting for the moment. She nodded, and Oscar quickly closed the door, leaving her alone in their prison.

She paced the strip of floor. Were they going to talk about their sleeping situation or about the way he'd nearly kissed her in her mother's broken-down garden? Camille had almost been able to feel Oscar's lips on her own. She picked up the worn blanket on the bunk and shook it out. *Ridiculous.* He probably hadn't given the attempt a second thought and, if he had, was probably wishing he hadn't done it.

She sat heavily on the hay pallet. Perhaps she was just spending too much time with Oscar, and her head and heart were being tricked into thinking it was acceptable to have these romantic thoughts about him. Before, in San

Francisco, she'd easily been able to push them aside whenever they came. She'd had her father, Randall, and the eyes of society to think about. None of those things were with her now.

In the corner, the oil lamp hissed and sputtered. Camille looked up from the pallet and saw a puff of black smoke rise from the lamp's glass chimney. But instead of dissolving, the cloud of smoke expanded. It eddied and shifted, and Camille instantly knew what shape it would take. The teeth of the lately absent skeletal face grinned maliciously at her, its jaws open wide.

Camille backed up on the pallet as the billow of smoke doubled in width and height, looming like the chartreuse wave had in the Tasman Sea. The cloud lunged toward her, its jaws snapping shut so close to her face she felt the rush of air against her eyelashes. She stumbled off the bunk as the door to her room swung open and smacked against the wall. Camille wheeled around.

"Oscar, we have to leave right—"

The man standing in her door wasn't Oscar. His massive girth blocked the exit, and his long black beard reached the center of his chest. One of the Hesky brothers moved toward her. Camille screamed and tried to bolt past him, but he reached out a thick, grimy arm and thrust her into the wall. She felt a sharp blow to the back of her head. Pain crackled through her, and everything else blacked out.

———

It was damp and dark when she came to. Her arms ached and her head throbbed. Before she even opened her eyes, she smelled the heady scent of whiskey — and something else. Something overpowering. *Smoke.* Her eyes instantly focused. Her wrists, bound with rope, had been slung over a ceiling hook in the *Juggernaut*'s hold and she hung suspended in the air. The toes of her boots dangled at least a foot from the floor. Beside her were two other limp figures also suspended from hooks, and beyond a stack of barrels, she saw a flickering orange glow.

"Oscar!" she tried to shout to the larger of the two figures. Her gagged mouth let nothing more than a grunt escape. She looked again to what seemed to be a pile of burning sailcloth.

"Oscar!" she cried again, and thrashed on her hook. All around her, barrels of liquor were stacked vertically and mostly lashed with ropes and netting. As Camille swung from side to side, she noticed a few freestanding barrels, one close behind her. With ungainly thrusts back and forth, Camille managed to lock her toes onto the rim of the barrel. If she could just slip the rope up over the lip of the hook, she'd be free. She strained, stretching her arms until the muscles burned, and teetered on the barrel. She fell forward, free from the hook, and crashed to the floor.

Camille ripped the gag from her mouth and hurried to Oscar, who was still unconscious. The growing firelight illuminated welts around his eyes and lips. She shook him hard but he only groaned.

"Oscar, wake up. We have to get out of here!" She looked around for another barrel, but when she tried to push one over toward his legs, her wrists still bound, it didn't budge an inch. It was too heavy, and so was Oscar.

"I can't get you down!" she cried, looking back at the flames. They ate at the ribs in the hold and were inching closer to the dozens of netted whiskey barrels.

A muffled grunt from behind Oscar caused her to turn. The other figure whipped his legs back and forth, dangling from his hook.

"Lucius!" Camille ran to Lucius Drake and grabbed his legs. With a little lift, he toppled to the floor. She tore the gag from his mouth.

"You!" she said, but knew she didn't have time to be angry with him. "Help me get Oscar!"

Lucius stood up and held out his wrists. "Untie me first. This place is going to blow when the flames reach the barrels!"

"Just grab his legs. Now!"

Lucius huffed and did as he was told. Together they lifted Oscar enough to release him from the hook. Their muscles gave way and all three tumbled to the planks.

"Oscar!" Camille slapped his cheek. "Wake up!"

Lucius got to his feet and ran for the ladder.

"You have to help me with him!" Camille yelled, but Lucius only continued climbing. "You coward!"

She shook Oscar's shoulders and slapped his cheeks. Finally, his swollen eyes fluttered.

"Get up!" The heat from the expanding flames drenched Camille's face with sweat. She noticed the dry sailcloth had been laid out in a long path to the whiskey barrels. The Hesky brothers must have wanted to give themselves plenty of time to flee the *Juggernaut*.

"We're going to explode!" she cried, and Oscar finally came to. In a moment he was on his feet, pulling her up with him. They reached the ladder as a sailor started to climb down.

"Get off the ship!" Oscar shouted to him. "Get out, she's about to blow!"

They ran down the corridor, past their minuscule room, and to the galley, where more sailors had converged on the companionway. They all struggled up the narrow ladder, sailors overrunning one another. Oscar wrapped his fingers around Camille's arm, dragging her as he climbed. They raced to the portal, but the gangway had been detached. The *Juggernaut* already floated a good hundred yards from the wharf.

"Jump!" a sailor behind them cried before leaping over the railing. He landed with a splash, followed by another sailor and yet another. Camille stepped onto the railing, Oscar's bound hand still in hers. An earth-shattering explosion ripped through the hold and the second level, splintering the deck. A fireball mushroomed in the air, and the force of the blast propelled Camille from the railing.

She landed in the water, felt it rush up her nose and fill her mouth. The shock from the blast wore off quickly as she realized her wrists were still tied. No matter how she struggled to free them, the rope wouldn't budge. Lungs screaming for air, Camille kicked her legs and broke the surface. She gasped for breath and slapped the water with her bound arms. The river shimmered with the blazing fireball that had once been the *Juggernaut*. Bobbing heads of sailors swam for shore, where a crowd had massed. The one sailor Camille searched for, though, was nowhere in sight.

"Oscar!" Camille screamed, before dipping underwater and choking. Kicking hard, she kept above the surface, but her muscles ached. Her nose stung from the salt water, and she knew she had to swim for shore or else she would go under for good. Swimming on her back seemed to work best, and within minutes her shoulders bumped into a wharf piling. Wrapping her legs around the piling, she found the knot on the rope and gnashed at it with her teeth. Her lips and wrists bled by the time the rope dropped into the water. She clung to the wharf piling and looked out to the ship, the flames dying down.

"Oscar." Salt water stung her eyes. On the beach, people helped sailors ashore, but she didn't see him there.

The Hesky brothers were probably among the onlooking crowd, waiting to see if she or Oscar or even Lucius crawled out of the water. Oscar would have thought of this and avoided the crowd. If he had made it off the ship.

"No," she said, refusing to believe he hadn't. She swam even farther under the wharf, where slime covered the pilings and the wood stank of rot, though the shadows shielded her well. How long could she stay in the frigid water, bleeding and aching and afraid? Until the crowd dispersed, until she knew for sure the Heskys wouldn't see her when she ran for Monty's shack.

"Hey!"

Camille startled, and then saw a figure clinging to one of the pilings. Lucius.

"You coward! You snake!" Camille swam toward him and jabbed her fist into his chest. Lucius blocked her next blow and shoved her back under the wharf.

"Quiet down," he hissed. "You want the Hesky brothers to hear you?"

"You led them to us," she said, quieter. "How could you?"

Lucius wiped water from his face and splashed to the shallow end of the wharf. Camille followed and her feet hit the sand. Her head throbbed and her stomach rolled. She thought she might vomit but swallowed it back.

"Listen, I swear I didn't know they were planning to kill you. Or me, obviously," he said. "McGreenery didn't say anything like that when he asked me to go with them. I was the only one who knew what you and Kildare looked like, and well . . ."

Camille slapped him across the cheek. "If Oscar's dead, I'll feed you to the Hesky brothers myself."

Lucius shut his mouth and rubbed his cheek. Camille waded out of the water and crouched behind the lowest piling that propped up the wharf.

"Do you think they're out there?" she asked, searching the crowd for the three burly monsters. The skies were massing into an inky blue, dusk quickly fading.

"I don't see them," he answered. "Damn McGreenery."

Camille wrung out the hem of her skirt, shivering. She couldn't stay out much longer without catching ill.

"I'm leaving," she said, and ducked out from under the wharf.

"And going where?"

She looked back briefly. "Somewhere safe."

Camille took off down the harbor, sneaking behind people who still watched the *Juggernaut* burn in the bay. They didn't notice her as she swished by, soaking wet. When she looked, she saw Lucius had followed her. She ran in the direction of Monty's shack, praying Ira and Monty were there. Maybe they'd heard the explosion, though, and run for the shore. It didn't matter. She'd be there when they returned.

Everything blurred as she ran, the urge to vomit creeping back. Light filled Monty's shack when it finally came into view. A flash of heat tore through her and, as when she'd collapsed in the dory after the *Christina* went down, pops of orange and magenta lights burst before her eyes. She reached the steps and tumbled up them, shoving the door wide. Down a whirling center of narrowing vision, Camille saw the shadowed figure of a man.

The silhouetted man stood in front of Monty's stove. He sprinted toward Camille as her knees buckled. And then the lights in the room pinched out.

NINETEEN

*S*trong arms wrapped themselves around Camille, drawing her close. She smelled salt and sweat and wood, and the scents reminded her of the comfort of every childhood embrace. The rapid beating of his heart filled her ear, and for a brief moment everything was right and just. Her own heart swelled with joy. Her father was alive. He had survived the wreck of the *Christina* and he'd found her at last.

"Of course I'm alive." Her father soothed her as she cried, his raspy voice so real and so near. Camille dug her fingers into his shoulders, clinging to him as he helped her lie back down.

"It's all right, I got off the ship okay. I'm alive," he said again. But his voice sounded different now. "I said I'm alive, Camille. Open your eyes and look at me."

Camille's heart shriveled as her eyelids fluttered open and she saw the ceiling of Monty's shack.

"Camille?" Oscar leaned over her, his calloused hand on her cheek. "Thank God. You've been delirious for nearly an hour."

Tears slipped down her cheeks as the truth stung her with renewed vigor. Her father wasn't alive. He was truly gone. It had been nothing but a hallucination.

"Why are you crying? Does something hurt?" Oscar asked, lightly prodding her arms and then checking her head. She was lying on a cot in front of the blazing stove, blankets covering her. They were scratchy and too heavy. She tried to push them away.

"No." Oscar blocked her arms. "Don't do that."

"Why?" she asked, her throat dry and sore.

Oscar looked apprehensive as he tucked the blankets tightly around her arms and neck. "Your clothes were soaked. You were shivering and flush with fever."

"Had to take 'em off, love," Ira said, coming to the foot of the cot. "You gave us quite a scare. That lump on the back of your head worked you over something nasty."

Camille stared at Ira, then Oscar. The crushed hope of her father being alive withered under the heat of embarrassment.

"You . . . you removed my dress?" she whispered. Oscar backed away from her, as if he'd just slid his hand over an open flame.

"No, no, I didn't."

She looked to Ira.

"Much as I'd been honored, the Irish bastard wouldn't hear of it. Quite the prude."

Frustrated and head still piercing with pain, Camille felt the blood rush to her cheeks. "Well, then, who?"

"Nothin' I ain't seen before, woman," Monty grumbled from his seat at the table as he sprinkled tobacco into a pipe.

Camille gasped and pressed her lips together. She caught sight of her dress hanging on a rack by the fire.

"W-what happened?" she asked, trembling. "I mean, on the *Juggernaut*. How did the Hesky brothers get aboard?"

"The captain hired them this morning to load the barrels into the hold," answered a voice that Camille didn't immediately recognize. But then she tilted her head in the direction of the front door and saw Lucius Drake.

He sat in a chair, arms tied behind him and ankles bound to the chair legs. A fresh bruise blackened the skin beneath his left eye. Compliments of Oscar's fist, no doubt. She wished she could have seen the fight.

"You let him in here?" she asked, then winced. God, how her head throbbed. She wasn't sure if the hammers chiseling away at her skull were from the blow from that Hesky brother or the explosion.

"We couldn't risk sending him out to be seen by the Hesky brothers. He'd trade us in to save his own skin in a flash," Oscar answered.

"They rode faster than we thought," Ira said. "Got here and found the only ship heading up Spencer's Bay. After talking with McGreenery, Drake-o figured you'd be on it. Smart little donkey's rear."

Camille shut her eyes and tried to focus on anything but the pain shooting between her temples. The wound from the fall against her bureau on the *Christina* had given her a splitting headache for days. The scar had just barely started to fade to white. It was about an inch long, horseshoe shaped, and by her brow. She didn't hate it as much as she thought she would. Having it made her feel strong, proof that she was a survivor. She would survive this, too.

"What now?" she asked.

"We could find another ship heading to Talladay," Oscar suggested.

Monty looked up from his pipe.

"Ain't one. The *Juggernaut* was it, and for quite a time, too."

"We can't stay holed up in this house," Camille said. "We need to get to the stone before McGreenery. He's already left!"

She wished her dress would hurry up and dry so she could get out from underneath the blankets.

"Buggers think you're dead. Go out into town, and they'll take another shot at it," Ira said, and he was right.

They were trapped.

"Listen, your chances at getting to this rock are looking pretty grim, mates," he said. "You still got San Francisco. You got a wedding to get to don't you, love? Why don't you two just come with me back to Sydney. You can get home from there, right?"

Camille kept her palm on her forehead, nausea starting to build again.

"Sydney is twice as far as Melbourne and we haven't any money, Ira."

Besides, she'd come this far. She couldn't face giving in now.

"Doesn't matter. Monty here's got a rig that'll take us there," Ira said.

Both Camille and Oscar snapped their heads toward the gloomy-faced Monty.

"You have a ship?" they asked in near unison.

Monty grimaced.

"Ain't the kind of ship you're lookin' for. I already told Ira the *Lady Kate*'s not seaworthy." Monty pulled the pipe from his lips and leaned forward. "She needs caulking, barnacles scraped, canvas repaired. There're four of us, and we'd need at least two more to cover all watches. You couldn't ask for a more difficult voyage."

Camille rose up onto her elbows, trying to keep the blanket as high on her neck as possible.

"But it's just up Spencer's Bay," she said.

Ira groaned from where he leaned against one of the walls, his arms crossed. "You're not giving up on that cursed rock, are you?"

Giving up on the rock meant giving up on her father. Camille again turned to Monty.

"Please, Mr. Monty," she said, preparing to offer him compensation for his help, though how much and how to pay gave her a moment's pause.

Monty eyed each of them, even Lucius, and then sat

back in his chair. "Oh, bloody hell." He popped his pipe into his mouth. "I'll think about it."

Caroline Rowen's house lay quiet, the windows dark and vacant. Camille and Oscar rushed up the brick walk, the gate creaking so loudly that the Hesky brothers, wherever they were, had probably heard it. Monty's shack hadn't enough floor space to accommodate all of them, and Camille had started to feel the squeeze of its filthy walls around her. When Ira suggested she and Oscar sneak back to her mother's empty house to search for supplies and money, and to sleep, she'd dressed fast, never minding the dampness of her skirts.

Oscar opened the unlocked door and they stepped into the shadowy sitting room.

"Do you recall where the lamps were?" Camille whispered. In the dark, in someone else's home, whispering seemed more appropriate. A clunk off to her right and the screech of table legs skittering across the floor made her cringe.

"I don't remember that being there," Oscar said.

"I'm glad we don't break into houses for a living. We're appalling at it," Camille said, laughing as the room brightened. Oscar had found an oil lamp and lit the wick.

"One light's enough," he said. They didn't need to draw too much attention to her mother's house.

Camille felt like an intruder. If her brother had been home, instead of having sailed off with McGreenery, she still would have felt like an intruder. Oscar yawned and gestured to the stairwell.

"Let's get some sleep," he whispered. "Before dawn we'll see what we can gather up."

His eyes rested on her forehead, on the new bruises and gashes from the *Juggernaut* blast.

"You look awful," he said.

Camille narrowed her eyes to slits. She grabbed the lamp from his hands. "Thank you very much."

"I didn't mean it like that," he said, following her as she climbed the narrow stairwell.

"You look just as whipped," she said over her shoulder. Camille already felt like a load of dung — her head throbbed, her limbs ached, and the rope marks around her wrists burned. She didn't need to be told she looked dreadful, too.

"The bruises, Camille. Your injuries look awful, not you," he said. She walked down the hallway in self-conscious silence. Blackness smothered the space outside the lamplight. It seemed the only things that were real were in the limited sphere of light and everything else was nothingness.

She opened the door to the room in which she'd already spent one sleepless night. The room was truly Samuel's, but he'd given her the use of it. She'd mostly just lain on the bed and wept as her mother struggled out of the world the next door down. Camille set the lamp on the dresser. The blue-and-silver fleur-de-lis wallpaper glowed a uniform gray.

"I hope you don't mind sleeping in her room. I can't do it," she said. Her mother's bed had been stripped, the linens burned, the quilt washed and wrung out. Still the ghosts lingered, too fresh. Camille walked to the window and pulled back the curtain. The *Juggernaut* continued to burn in the harbor, the flames now low and weak. Smoke blocked the starlight like dense San Francisco fog.

She buried her face in her palms. "What am I thinking, to be going after this stone? You were right. It can't be real. How can it possibly work?"

Oscar stepped up behind her, close enough for her back to feel his warmth. Close enough to sense the moment his hands would touch her. They traveled down her neck and rested on her shoulders.

"You saw the map," he said softly. "There has to be something powerful about the stone. I don't know if it'll bring William back, but what else do we have to lose?"

His warm hands slipped down her arms, thoughtfully, as if anticipating her flinching away. She was too stunned to breathe, let alone move. He'd never touched her so brazenly before. He took her hips in his palms and leaned her back, against him. She went willingly. His chest and stomach felt solid and sure, yet comfortable, too. Camille took a shallow breath, remembering how before the wreck, she'd wondered what Oscar was to her. Not a friend, not an acquaintance, but somewhere in between. Like two people just waiting for the right circumstances, the right moment, to begin. This moment, these circumstances, felt right.

Oscar's breath warmed the back of her head, his lips brushing against her hair, loosened from a braid. He drew a lock away from her neck and kissed the skin just beneath her earlobe, against the throb of her quickening pulse. Like the blackness outside the dome of lamplight, there seemed to be nothing more in the world than his lips, his touch, and the flood of heat consuming her.

With a gentle nudge, Oscar turned her toward him. He looked at her the way he had in the Grampians meadow — as if she was the most fascinating woman he'd ever seen. Under his gaze she felt fascinating, too. Captivating . . . wanted. He traced her jaw with his lips, kissing the angle of her neck ever so tenderly, as though he weren't certain she wanted him, too. Camille closed the inch of space left between them, her body pressing against his. The muscles in his chest and arms tightened. He *was* wanted, and she needed to show him how much. No one was there to watch, no one to judge, or tell her the lips caressing her were unworthy of tasting her skin.

With those very thoughts, Oscar's grip loosened. His lips retreated.

"This isn't right," he whispered, catching his breath.

Camille stared at him, her hurt and disappointment plain on her face.

"You're engaged, Camille." He looked around the room. His eyes rested on the bed. "I shouldn't be in here."

All of a sudden, Camille completely and fully detested Randall. Good, sweet, well-meaning Randall infuriated her with his mere existence, with his big sapphire ring and his marriage proposal and his bright, wealthy future as the savior of Rowen & Company. She didn't want any of it if it meant she couldn't have Oscar's kisses, the return of his hands, and his body pressed close to her own.

"I want you here," she said, the words unable to express the desires stampeding her mind.

Oscar licked his lips but stepped toward the doorway. "I can't. If you're going to marry Randall—"

Camille hushed him. "No, don't. Please, don't." She didn't want to hear Randall's name coming from Oscar's lips, not when she so desperately wanted to kiss them.

"He's not here. And you are, and . . . what if you stayed?" she asked, unable to believe the words had come from her mouth. He lost the tense hold of his shoulders and stared at her with disbelief.

"Nothing improper, of course," she added quickly. "What if you just stayed until . . . until I fell asleep?"

Citrus and cloves charged through her senses with their dizzying effect as Oscar stepped back inside the room.

He tilted his head and looked sideways at her. "Just until you fall asleep?"

She nodded, her throat too tight with nerves to speak.

Oscar hung his jacket on the back of a chair and undid the first few buttons of his checked shirt. Camille's fingers trembled as she reached for the lamp on the dresser and twisted the knob, lowering the wick until the light it gave off was that of a small candle's flame. She sat on the bed, and the other side of the hand-rolled mattress dipped with Oscar's weight. She didn't know how to look at him, if she should lie down or just come to her senses and ask him to leave. God, she wasn't doing any of this right.

"You sleep sitting up?" he asked.

Camille smiled, thankful he'd lightened the moment enough for her to lean back onto one of the pillows. Turning on her side, she saw he'd already taken the same position. They lay without touching, without talking, only looking. His eyes grazed her body, slowly absorbing the pink skin of her neck, the slight curves of her breasts, and the arc of her hip. He didn't need to lay a finger on her for the breath to stall in her lungs.

He breeched the few inches between them by sliding his hand atop hers, his skin warm and dry while beads of nervous sweat formed hot on her back. Camille reached out and let her fingertip travel along the fullness of his lower lip and down the curve of his chin. With one sweeping movement, Oscar pulled her tight against his chest and kissed her. A sensation kindled between her hips, spreading to every nerve ending in her body. This was it, the fire and heat she'd always yearned for. All these years, and Oscar had been right in front of her the whole time.

TWENTY

~~~~~~~

*M*onty's dire warning about the *Lady Kate* had been more than accurate. Just two days into their mission, all five crew members conceded the sloop's condition was just as terrible as he'd described.

"She's leakin' like a teat!" Monty howled from the hold. Ira rolled with laughter, as did Lucius, whose hands and legs had been cut free with the stipulation that he work aboard the *Lady Kate* as their fifth crew member. Even Camille was considered a sailor aboard the ratty sloop, and she had worked with renewed verve since setting sail the morning after the *Juggernaut* explosion.

Oscar had roused her before dawn after just a handful of hours of sleeping side by side in her mother's house. As she'd hoped, he hadn't left for her mother's room after she drifted off. She'd cherished the feel of him next to her, his rhythmic breathing no longer a distraction but a comfort in a world where comforts had become so scarce. They had kissed more, too, but he had remained as gentlemanly as possible, restraining his hands to her thighs, hips, and waist.

Being there with him had felt right — like it had always been that way. But as soon as they'd made their way back to Monty's cove, out in the open once more, an awkward silence crept in between them. The kind they would suffer at home, whenever they'd found themselves unexpectedly alone. Camille didn't know what to say without sounding like a lovesick fool. And too many questions bubbled up inside. Did he want something more? In the reality of day, everything they'd done was unbelievably irresponsible. They'd kissed and touched and held each other as though they were the ones to be married. But he didn't have the resources to save her father's company, to save her from ruin. Besides, when they brought her father back, their being together would be impossible.

Instead, she had focused on escaping Port Adelaide without catching the Hesky brothers' attentions. It turned out to be quite simple. Camille and Oscar and Lucius had slipped aboard the sloop before the sun rose and stayed belowdecks until they were far from shore.

Now they were moving up Spencer's Bay with no land in sight. Camille was growing weary of Monty's foul language, too.

"Is she in danger?" she called down into the hold. Monty sloshed through the dingy green bilgewater and clambered up the slick metal rungs, breathing more obscenities.

"No danger, just damned annoying," he answered. "The ol' girl's got plenty of years on you, woman. Worry 'bout scrubbin' the supper pots, why don't you?"

Camille bit her tongue and turned her back to him. Monty had made no exceptions for her; in his opinion she was still just a girl and shouldn't be allowed on deck. Thankfully, Oscar and Ira had convinced him otherwise. There may have been just two sails on the small sloop, but there were plenty of chores to tend to. More leaks had to be caulked, ripped and worn sails repaired and oiled, knotted ropes smoothed out and braided again. And then there was the food. Three meals, plus coffee or tea at all hours of the day and night, and most of that was left to Camille. So she found sleep in scattered patches whenever she could, slung in a hammock in the galley.

Oscar kept his distance, though she caught him staring at her a few times while they were on watch together or during a meal. Each time she met his penetrating gaze, she looked away with a shy grin.

Two more days into the sail, Camille was on her hands and knees scrubbing the filthy galley floors when a bell clanged on deck, signaling the change in watch. Watch consisted of two men, or one man and one woman when it was her turn. Oscar descended the companionway into the galley and sat on a bench at the table. Dried blood covered the sleeve of his shirt, shorn from elbow to shoulder.

"What happened to you?" Camille exclaimed, hurrying over to inspect the wound.

"Pulley came loose off the rigging," he said, his eyes sleepy and bloodshot.

"Let me clean it," she said.

He inspected his shredded shirtsleeve. "It's all right."

"Until you develop gangrene," she replied and picked up a clean cloth. Laundering everything from towels to socks had also fallen to Camille. She felt as if she did everything aboard the *Lady Kate*, and only now saw just how slack her time had been on the *Christina*.

A bowl of cold seawater sat on the tabletop, ready for polishing the galley dishes. She dipped in the towel and pointed to Oscar's shirt. He grimaced, unbuttoned it, and tossed it aside.

The gash was long and deep, and Camille's stomach turned over when she touched the towel to it. Oscar winced as sea salt entered his wound, the pink-and-white flesh no longer bleeding. She wiped dried blood from his skin, wishing a doctor could clean and stitch it properly.

Gooseflesh freckled his chest and arms. Her eyes rested on his back, on the lines of lighter-pigmented skin she'd first seen on the forest trail in the mountains. A dozen or so scars overlapped one another and had healed crudely. Now, seeing them up close, she was positive they were from a whip or belt. Camille ran her finger gently over the rough contours of his back.

"Who did this to you?" she asked. She thought he might shrug away, but he sat still.

"Uncle." The single word held a ton of bitter weight. Camille dropped her hand.

"After your parents died?" she asked.

He moved from the bench. "Can we talk about this another time?"

Camille dropped the cloth back into the bowl of cold water and excused herself into the small pantry off the galley, cordoned off by a heavy calico drape. She had no need for anything inside. She'd pushed too fast, too hard. For four years Oscar had hardly spoken a full sentence about his life in Boston. She shouldn't have expected him to reveal everything after one night spent in each other's arms.

The floor creaked under the doorframe to the pantry as Oscar followed her. She tried to hide her flushed cheeks.

"He drove a buggy around Boston and used the same whip on me that he did on his horse," Oscar said slowly. "I got myself into trouble a lot after my parents died, and I guess he thought it was the best way to keep me in line."

A stormy draft shivered in by way of the galley hatch. He let the calico drape fall into place and took a few steps closer to her.

"One night, I wised up and didn't go home."

Camille blew out the match she had used to light the oil lamp. The lamp's flame sputtered, lighting the shelves and sacks of meal and flour.

"I'm sorry," she said, wishing she could say something more meaningful.

"I'm not. If he'd been a good uncle, I'd have stayed in Boston. Never would have found my way to San Francisco," he said.

Camille knew where the rest of his story led and grinned.

"And you never would have rescued my father from a pickpocket," she added.

He started to laugh, a quiet, almost personal chuckle, like he was thinking about some funny memory. Camille caught the bug of laughter and wanted to join in.

"What is it?" she asked.

"Your father didn't need a rescuer. He caught the pickpocket himself," Oscar answered, a hand on his abdomen from all his laughter. "And then he invited him inside for dinner."

Her smile fell flat. She stared at him, trying to comprehend what he'd just said.

"You?" she asked, dumbfounded. "You were the pickpocket?"

Oscar nodded, scratching the back of his head. "Yeah. I wasn't very good at it."

Her father could have had him arrested or shooed him away without thinking twice. But he'd invited Oscar inside. He gave him work, food . . . a real chance.

"Why didn't he tell me?" she asked, feeling like she'd been duped once again. All the lies her father had woven to cover up his secrets had become so frayed, Camille wondered if she had truly known him at all.

"To give me a clean slate with everyone. Even you." Oscar moved toward her in cautious, deliberate steps. "We're alone. We should talk."

The pantry was cramped and dismal despite the oil lamp, and Camille had a sudden urge to flee.

"About what?" she asked, her ears burning. She still reeled with the knowledge that the pickpocket story hadn't been real, just like her mother's story hadn't been real. Oscar stopped within a few inches from her and reached a hand around her waist.

"About our night together, Camille," he answered, his dimples forming. "There's a lot to say."

She heard McGreenery's voice in her head. *No need to humiliate yourself. You'll do plenty of that back in San Francisco as this ape's wench.* "Maybe too much," she said, and drew up her shoulders to slide out of his hold. "We need to stay focused on reaching Talladay. On the stone."

He took a step back. "What's the matter?"

"Nothing," she answered too quickly, grabbing a bottle of molasses. She didn't need it, but she couldn't look at him. What if she'd made a horrible mistake? She'd led him on and couldn't follow through. This was *Oscar*, for heaven's sake. As much as her father had adored him, he never would have condoned a romance. He'd always made it clear no daughter of his would marry a man of the sea. Besides, if she were to admit her feelings for Oscar, Rowen & Company would be finished. She'd have no holdings, no money, no leverage in San Francisco.

"Is it Randall?" Oscar sounded out the name with care,

as if testing dangerous waters. Camille closed her eyes and turned her face away from him, not wanting to have to see him when she said what she needed to say.

"I have a duty, Oscar, just like my mother did. She failed at hers and look what happened; she destroyed so much. My father asked me not to say anything, but if I don't marry Randall . . . I'm sorry, Oscar, I just have to."

Camille tried to edge by him, but Oscar held her back with his arm.

"Do you think I'm a fool, Camille? Don't try to blame marrying Randall on some duty you think you have."

She parted her lips to insist he was wrong. He cut her off.

"If this is how you really feel, then you had no right to ask me to stay with you that night. You gave me a taste of what being with you might be like, and now you're asking me to walk away. Who do you think you are?"

Camille shook her head. He wasn't listening. He had no idea how difficult it was for her, too, to have that one taste, that single moment of pure bliss to feed off of for the rest of her life.

"I don't have a choice —"

He slammed his fist against the pantry shelf behind her.

"I don't have a bank vault filled with money, or ten suits hanging in my closet to choose from each morning. I know I couldn't give you all the things he could, but I *can* give you something he'll never be able to. I love you, Camille," he said, his mouth so close to hers his breath moistened her lips. "I love *you*. Not your last name or your pretty face or all the business opportunities you could bring me." He laid his palm just beneath her neck, his thumb caressing the skin above where her heart lay. "Just you."

She stared at him, unblinking, unable to breathe, let alone speak. Oscar's arm fell away.

"You do have a choice, Camille. Or should I already be calling you Mrs. Jackson?"

He stormed from the pantry, Camille on his heels. Promise or no promise to her father, she had to tell Oscar everything.

"Please, Oscar, wait, if you'll just listen —"

The companionway steps rattled, and Ira bounded into the galley. Oscar scooped up his shirt and shoved his arms inside the sleeves as Ira kicked out a bench at the table and sat down.

"I've never been so friggin' tired in my life," Ira said, grabbing a mug for coffee. "And I once played a game of poker that lasted two days."

Camille ignored him, Oscar's anger still stinging. She'd created a massive mess. Ira peered at her, then at Oscar.

"Why're you two all red in the face?" he asked. Then his cheeks drew up and his teeth glistened. Oscar caught him before he could speak.

"Save it, Ira," he said, quickly glancing at Camille. She couldn't plead with him to listen to her explain with Ira there. Oscar buttoned his shirt and left the galley. Ira directed his wily grin toward her.

"Save it, Ira," she echoed, and resumed scrubbing the floor.

A few days later, a single gull flapped its way through the clouds of white fog surrounding the *Lady Kate* and circled the headsail. Camille had brought a bucket of wash water up on deck to toss overboard.

"A seagull!" Camille called out to Oscar, who was standing at the helm. She craned her neck and sheltered her eyes from the bright haze with the plane of her hand. She'd pushed her curls from her face with a bandanna, tying her hair back with no thought for fashion at all. The gull cawed and swept around the sloop a few times, before continuing on.

"Land's near," Oscar replied. The blithe comment couldn't hide his hope. He was as eager to be free of the *Lady Kate* as Camille was. Since their argument in the pantry, it had been impossible to concentrate on anything, and he still wasn't looking at her or saying more than four words at a time to her. Whenever she tried to speak to him, to explain why Randall could be her only choice, he either made up an excuse to part her company, or someone butted in, ruining her chance.

The day after spotting the seagull, a port city appeared on the horizon. *At last,* she thought as she and Oscar and Ira took turns peering through the spyglass. They had made it!

Oscar put down the spyglass and unrolled the map. It shimmered again, leaving gold dust on his fingers, but again, no amber flash. Even without the flash and spark-ing letters, each time Camille saw the map, it erased any doubt she harbored about whether or not Umandu was real. How it would exactly bring her father to the surface of the Tasman Sea was another quandary.

"See this inlet?" Oscar pointed to the map. Everyone but Monty, at the helm, leaned over to see. The inlet lay slightly south of Talladay.

"What about it?" Lucius asked. He bit his nails, unin-terested. He'd already expressed his view that the whole magic rock business was insane. The second time Lucius had started to mock Umandu, Ira had purposefully tripped him, sending him straight into an open grease barrel.

"Look how much closer it is to the stone's trail than the harbor is," Oscar said. He ran his finger from the inlet, through a drawn clump of forest, to the shimmering silver vein. The map seemed ancient and Talladay was an infant harbor, so why it was even marked plainly on the map Camille couldn't figure. It must have been some kind of magic. The iridescent silver line started at Talladay's har-bor, but cutting through from the inlet would be a significant shortcut.

"You think that McGreenery bloke anchored there?" Ira asked.

"No, he's too proud for that. He would have moored in the harbor. Besides, he doesn't think his competition is still breathing," Camille answered. For the first time since the pantry, she and Oscar met each other's eyes. "We might be able to make up for lost time."

He nodded and shouted to Monty, "Make for the inlet!"

Monty spun the wheel. The boom swept the deck, over their heads as they ducked. The *Lady Kate* recharted its course and headed toward the smaller inlet. As they sailed closer, the forest seemed to darken: each trunk only a foot or two from the next. A boulder the size of Camille's San Francisco townhouse made it impossible to get closer than two hundred yards to the inlet's thin beach. They heaved and lashed sails, and once the anchor sunk to the inlet floor, the *Lady Kate* came to a standstill.

"The stone mound looks far inland," Oscar said as Ira and Lucius lowered the single dory into the calm water.

"We have enough water to last us three days," Camille said, grabbing the bag with the canteens, a rifle, a box each of ammunition and phosphorus matches, dried cod, beans, and a single pot and spoon. Only she and Oscar were leaving the *Lady Kate*. Monty refused to leave his ship, and even if Lucius had offered to come, which he hadn't, Camille would have declined.

"Ira, we could use you out there." Oscar tried one last time.

Ira shook his head.

"Like I said before, mate. Ain't no profit in riskin' my neck."

Oscar climbed down the ladder and rocked the dory. Camille threw him the bag of supplies and then followed.

Oscar untied the dory and took up the oars. "If we're not back in five days," he said, glancing at Camille quickly, "weigh anchor."

He thrust the oars under the surface and sliced the water. Camille paid attention to the shore. If she glimpsed Ira or Monty, or even Lucius, watching them row away, she was afraid she'd see their skepticism, carving room for some of her own to breed.

On Oscar's fifth solid row toward the beach, Ira pierced the air with a whistle.

"Oh, bloody hell!" he shouted. "All right, all right, just don't expect me to do this for nothin'!"

TWENTY-ONE

*T*he belly of the dory, now beset by three people, scratched sand as it hit the shallows. Ira and Oscar leaped over the side, splashing and pulling it the rest of the way ashore. Oscar reached into the dory and hoisted Camille. His fleeting touch spoiled her concentration, and she pictured him lying beside her, their legs braided together, his lips brushing the edge of her chin, moving toward her mouth . . . she hissed to herself to think only of the trail. The opportunity to mend their quarrel could wait until they were on the other side of Umandu.

"I won't fiddle around with you," Ira said, watching the forest. "I don't know the territory. So I ain't your guide. You lead the way, and I've got your back."

Camille grabbed the bag and moved first, swiftly departing the sun-drenched beach and entering the shadowy forest. It was nothing like the highlands they'd traversed on the way to Port Adelaide. Sand and seaweed, exposed roots, and downed trunks riddled the ground. When she stepped, the floor sunk with her weight. The soft, marshy feel stretched into the air, except the humidity was cold, instead of warm.

Oscar quickly took the lead, compass in hand, with Ira in the rear. Camille pretended the bag's rope, slung diagonally across her chest, wasn't cutting into her neck. She didn't want them to think she couldn't handle a bag, albeit a heavy one. Oscar didn't even offer to take it from her, she noticed. He would have — that was, before she'd treated him like a used handkerchief.

Sheets of dewy white webs extended from one tree trunk to the next. Oscar stripped them away with his bare hands. The sound of the surf fell off, and the croak of bullfrogs and shrieks of lime green birds set in. Every now and again Ira cursed, slapped at his skin, and then cursed again. The insects buzzing around her head never touched her skin, but came close enough to her eyes and nostrils and mouth to be a nuisance.

"Holy gallnipper, how long till we hit the magic trail? It's gloomier than my own funeral in here."

Camille adjusted the bag's rope and looked at Ira. "Don't even joke about that."

Since the moment they'd entered the forest, she'd felt like something was listening. Like they'd woken some sleeping creature, and now it followed them with silent cunning. The deafening chants had not returned to pierce her eardrums, but danger still felt close.

A few paces ahead of her, Oscar peeled away another cobweb, the octagonal spinning so massive Camille didn't even want to imagine the size of the spider that had created it.

"Mate, you got a stomach made of iron," Ira said.

A flash of orange and black swept in front of Camille's eyes and she felt an odd tug on her dress. She looked down and froze. A spider with a body the size of her fist flexed its hairy legs on her skirt. It started to scuttle up. Her scream echoed through the forest as she swiped the spider off. It hit the marshy ground and scampered under a log. Oscar grabbed her arm and pulled her toward him.

"Did it bite you?"

She shook her head, arms and legs stiff with fear.

"I've never seen one so bloody big," Ira said, running past the log as though the spider would leap out at him. Oscar started walking again, his hand on the small of her back. She exhaled with more than one kind of relief. He was at least still concerned for her.

As they started to pick up their pace, another black critter swung down from a nearby tree. Camille saw it flying toward them, but her warning shout was too slow. The spider landed on Oscar's shoulder, fat and furry and swift as its legs darted up his neck.

Oscar shouted an obscenity as he whacked the giant from his skin. Camille heard it *thud* against the leafy forest floor. Unfazed, the spider quickly sprang to its finger-length legs and darted toward her boot. Her shrieks echoed again as it leaped onto her hem. With his foot, Ira knocked the spider back to the ground, and before it could bounce back up, Oscar smashed it with a stick. The squashed giant oozed yellow-and-green blood onto the marshy ground. Camille gagged and tasted her breakfast oats in the back of her mouth.

"What in all wrath are those monsters?" Ira panted as he twisted around, looking for more.

Camille looked up to the trees to try and spot any others that might be descending from glossy webbing. Terror paralyzed her as her eyes landed on a colony of glistening webs in the treetops. An endless number of black dots massed above their heads, dangling from tree limbs. Oscar and Ira followed her horrified stare.

"Run," Oscar whispered. Camille sprinted forward, her skin and scalp tingling with imaginary spider legs. The bag of provisions slammed against her back, tugging at her neck, but she didn't care. They didn't slow down until the gigantic spiderwebs grew sparse and the squawk of birds took over.

Camille huffed for air, her chest tight. Sweat had formed a dark V on the back of Oscar's shirt. Her legs, neck, and shoulders ached as she walked to keep up with him and not hold Ira back. Shorter trees, scrub pines, and gnarled shrubs signaled an end to the forest, and then it ceased as abruptly as it had began. Camille stepped out onto hard, dry land. Not sand or even soil, but a rock-hard surface, crackled like a shattered vase poorly pieced back together.

Ira rolled up his sleeves. "Salt flats," he said.

"You mean this used to be a lake?" Camille asked.

Ira nodded. There seemed to be no end to it. The white, barren wasteland nearly blinded them in the sunlight.

"Do you figure we'll cross it 'fore nightfall?" Ira asked.

"There's a chance," Oscar answered, but stooped to gather sticks and a few thicker logs just in case. Camille slid off the bag and opened it up. It would be a pitiful fire, she thought as Oscar dumped in the wood.

"I'll carry the bag now," he said, and she gratefully handed it over. Within the first few minutes, Camille couldn't even remember the cool of the forest. The sun, unencumbered by clouds, started to burn her forehead and nose. Not once did Oscar glance her way to check on her; not once did he ask her how she was faring. He'd always cared before. She stared at the back of his head, expecting him to turn. He didn't. She simmered with resentment as they tromped onward across the dried-out lake bed.

He hadn't even tried to listen to her side of things during their fight in the pantry. Needing to marry Randall and wanting to love Oscar were two entirely separate things. Oscar might understand that if he knew the whole truth about her father's business. He might even find a way for them to be together secretly after she took her wedding vows with Randall. Why couldn't she have them both? As soon as the notion formed, she tossed it aside. She knew Oscar too well. He'd never settle for being second best, when in all honesty, he wasn't. She should have never asked him to stay with her that night. If anyone knew, if Randall ever found out . . . and then to have Oscar himself not even speaking to her . . . she'd been such a fool.

"Do either of you need water?" Oscar reached into the bag and rummaged around. Camille walked right ahead, not wanting one thing from him, even if she was dying of thirst.

"The only thing we need is to keep—" A shock of air engulfed her as the lake floor disappeared from beneath her feet. Camille let out a brief scream, her voice drowned by a rush of air as she fell through a hole she had not seen as she'd stormed away from Oscar. Blackness encircled her, the blinding light from the salt flats gone in an instant, along with the sound of Oscar hoarsely crying her name.

She scrunched up her eyes and ground her teeth, preparing to hit bottom. She was going too fast, picking up too much speed—she'd break her legs. Maybe worse. Camille's fingernails raked the sides of the shaft, floundering to grasp anything to stop her fall. Too much air rushed up her nostrils, she couldn't breathe, couldn't scream. Her backside brushed against the shaft, her skirts billowing around her face, and then she was sliding along the shaft's surface, smooth and cold. The endless downward slope leveled off slightly, but she still slid with ever-building momentum, catapulting around sharp corners. It wouldn't stop; it wouldn't end.

Icy water suddenly besieged her, filling her mouth and throat as her skirt flattened against her face. The momentum she'd gained didn't release her but pushed her down, her arms and legs powerless to start kicking for the surface, wherever it may be. The darkness, the water, the fall, they all disoriented her beyond any simple recovery. Panic seized her as her lungs deflated by the second. She was going to drown, just like her father had.

But then her body started to rise. Resisting the urge to gulp in a mouthful of air and be met with a rush of deadly water, Camille held on, waited, knew she couldn't do it, and then at last broke the surface.

Her gasp for air echoed in her ears, her coughs and heaves burned her throat and chest. More air — she couldn't take in enough of it. Rubbing water from her eyes, feeling light-headed and weak, Camille tried to see through the darkness. Water filled her boots, weighing her down. She tugged them off and let them sink. She needed her feet as buoyant as possible and her hands free. Her legs and arms parted the water to keep afloat. The water on her tongue tasted ripe with minerals, but was fresh, not salt.

"Hello?" she called. Her voice ricocheted above her head. Somewhere, water dripped. It sounded like a trickle of water onto rock. With one arm still in the water to help with treading, she reached the other above her head. Her fingers hit a coarse ceiling of lichen-slimed rock. She lowered her arm, holding it horizontally as she swam to one side, then the next, feeling for the edge of whatever underground pool the shaft had dropped her into.

Arms aching, her gasps for air coming hard and uneven, Camille finally touched a cool, wet wall of rock. The blackness was so thick her eyes bulged as she tried to see something. Anything. What had happened? There had been no hole that she had seen. It was as if the dried-out lake bed had opened up and swallowed her. There had been no chanting or drumming or snapping skeletal jaws to warn her this time.

She listened for Oscar's screams, knowing he would be shouting for her. Would he leap in the hole to come after her? No, she prayed not as she clung to the jagged rock, resting her body against it. There were no screams, no calls of concern. She'd fallen too far, and her own shouts would be futile, too. What was this place?

The path to it is said to be riddled with traps, endless holes in the earth where you fall forever. McGreenery's warning to her that night in Melbourne's harbor. She scraped her forehead along the rock as she pictured the map in her mind. Along the silver line there had been dark, stamped cylinders. Holes in the earth! She could have throttled herself for being so mindless.

After a few moments, her breathing became regular. Her thinking started to pick up its normal rhythm, and rationality kicked in. There had to be a way out, but without the ability to see where she was or what was around her, she'd have to rely on other senses. *Sound?* She listened. *Drip, drip, drip.* Water, of course. Nothing new there. *Taste?* She'd already determined the water was fresh. *Smell?* Her nose sniffed the musty, pungent air. Using her sense of touch, Camille ran her fingers along the rock, felt more slimy lichen and patches of moss. The water must have covered the rocky wall for a long time, but now the surface had lowered

How many men had been swallowed by the salt flats and plunged into water, only to find no surface to break? Camille shivered, the water freezing and the idea of human bodies or bones around her unnerving. Other things may also be around her, she realized. Creatures could be gliding near her legs, searching for food. *Stop! Use your wits,* she demanded of herself. *Don't let fear take over.* Umandu still waited somewhere, and McGreenery was still on his way to it. With a deep breath, Camille glided along the rock wall. Perhaps there was an opening, perhaps another watery chamber with an exit. Simple logic told her the water had come from somewhere.

She slid along, hoping she didn't hit a wall or, worse, tread upon another object in the water. Oscar probably thought she was dead. God, how miserably she'd treated him, too, when back on the *Christina* he'd been the one willing to risk everything to just talk to her, to just look at her. He'd saved her life. He'd gone with her on this insane quest to find a stone that might not even exist. And she'd led him to believe that she was brave enough to disobey her father's wishes and choose him instead of Randall. The only things stopping her were money and social standing. In the pitch black of the underground pool, the insignificance of them stood out with undeniable clarity.

The only thing Camille really wanted, the only thing that really mattered, was Oscar. She *was* brave, wasn't she? Look what she'd done. She hadn't run back to the safety of San Francisco, but toward something dangerous and unknown. And Oscar had gone with her. He was it, the man she wanted to be with, and not just in sporadic or imagined trysts. Camille slowed her crawling as it dawned on her. She loved him. She loved Oscar Kildare. She loved him enough to give up everything she'd ever known.

She glided along faster, scraping her knees and hips along the rock. Her scalp banged into the ceiling. Camille swore under her breath and gripped her head. The water had either risen, or she'd reached the edge of some kind of dome.

"Damn it," she hissed again, the tips of her toes numb. She closed her eyes and realized it was darker with them shut. She opened them, and sure enough the space around her had a slight yellow tinge. She peered into the water and saw a glimmer of light so feeble she thought her eyes were playing tricks on her. But no, there it was again. It was real. The ripple of the water's surface distorted the light. She could actually see the water's surface.

This was it, her way out! Camille dipped below the surface and opened her eyes. The fresh water didn't sting as salt might have, and she saw the light was far beneath her feet. She watched it to see if it moved. . . . She'd heard deep-sea creatures sometimes glowed to lure their prey. But this orb of light stayed still.

Breaking the surface, she took in air and wiped her nose and eyes. It would be a long way to swim, a long time to hold her breath, and with no promise of escape, either. Anything could be looming in the water, too, waiting for her to dive under. What else could she do but cling to the rock, waiting for her whole body to go numb and send her into a state of shock? Oscar was out there, most likely thinking her dead, believing she died loving Randall Jackson. She had to try and get to him, even if it meant drowning in the process. One way or another, if Camille stayed put, she'd be dead.

She readied her lungs by taking deep gulps of air. She had to stretch her lungs in order to hold as much oxygen as possible. Camille stared at the water, at the slender light radiating her only hope in the world.

"Father," she whispered. "If you're listening, I'm almost there. I've nearly made it. I can't do this alone, though. Please, I need you to guide me."

Terrified the next few moments might very well be her last on earth, Camille filled her lungs to capacity and dove beneath the surface. Eyelids wide, she kicked and parted the water with her arms, slanting down toward the light. *One, two, three,* she heard herself counting each stroke in her mind. Ticking off the seconds since her last breath dredged up a feeling of panic, and so she instead thought of what lay beyond that light. It was so far beneath the surface. Swimming down suddenly made no sense.

Stop and turn back, or continue on? She couldn't decide, but her legs kept kicking, the orb of light spreading in width. *No turning back.* The pressure at the back of her throat burned, and every survival instinct ordered her to exhale to take in more oxygen. *Focus on the light.* If only she could have just a small bit of air, just a half breath to rejuvenate her lungs. The light . . . it was so close, just an arm's length away.

"My Camille." His water-muted voice broke through the blackness. *Father?* In front of her, a perfect, involuntary vision of him materialized, his flushed cheeks and wide smile, his windswept hair pushed high off his forehead.

"I'll always be here to guide you," he said, his lips moving in time with the voice in her ears. *"For as long as you need my guidance."*

It *was* him! His face shone in the center of the orb of light. Camille reached out her hand, but touched the edge of a grainy rock instead of the weathered skin of his face. His image wavered and dissolved, and in its place, Camille saw a shoulder-width hole carved into the coarse rock. She darted through and immediately started rising. Up, up, she shot, her pulse throbbing through her throat and ears.

Camille guzzled air into her lungs as she broke the surface. Hacking on water, weeping with relief and misery, she soaked in the sun's warm rays on her face. Out. She'd made it out! And her father . . . she'd seen him, nearly touched him he'd been so real. Not a figment of her mind, no. He'd been real. He'd come to guide her.

She bobbed in a gleaming blue pool of water, surrounded by forest trees, boulders, and a flat mossy patch of sod. Camille kicked her tremulous legs toward the shore. Her whole body quaked with fatigue as she crawled out of the water, drenched to the bone. The mossy sod cushioned her as she fell, cheek pressed against the earth, eyes dry and burning.

This place was the complete opposite of the barren salt flats. She pushed herself up, her body protesting as she stood. Woozy from lack of air to her brain, Camille leaned against a thick tree trunk. Its branches sprouted low and were thick and tangled. Perfect for climbing. The only way to see where she'd come out was to go have a look. Her muscles ached as she pulled herself onto the first tree limb. Pitch stuck to her fingers and hands as she continued up, branches stabbing her in the ear and catching in her hair. Her wet dress hung like heavy sailcloth.

Finally, through the thin upper branches, she looked out beyond a treetop horizon. Not far in the distance lay the sun-bleached salt flats. The fall in the shaft had seemed endless, and for good reason. It had taken her unbelievably far. Oscar and Ira were probably still out there, perhaps still in danger of falling into another hole. She'd been lucky the water level in the underground pool had been down. The curse of Umandu kept counteracting itself. One stroke of bad luck followed by a stroke of fortune. She stared at the salt flats, eyes peeled for any sign of the men.

The curse of Umandu didn't seem like a curse at all. It seemed more like a challenge. Each stroke of misfortune — the *Christina* sinking, McGreenery pulling into port at Melbourne, the Hesky brothers and the *Juggernaut* explosion, and now, even the underground death trap — had each been trailed by a stroke of good fortune. The *Londoner* rescued them, Ira arrived to blow up McGreenery's ship, she and Oscar had miraculously survived the *Juggernaut*, and now the low water level underground. It seemed the challenge of Umandu was knowing what to do with the good fortune.

No sign of Oscar or Ira came with the setting of the sun. The whiteness of the salt flats started to bleed to a burnished orange, cueing Camille to make a decision: try and find her companions, or move inland to try and find the stone. The map was still in Oscar's pocket, she realized with a dip in spirit. Drawing up the image of it in her mind, she tried to remember all the etchings. She thought of the words only she had been able to see; the inscription that had told her only the worthy would be able to see Umandu. How could McGreenery possibly be worthy of the stone? Perhaps the worthy person was simply whoever found it first. Camille ground her teeth in frustration.

The next things she recalled from the map were the two triangles on the reverse side, joined at the base to form a diamond. What it meant eluded her, but the next etching she called up of the archway and fangs, did make sense. McGreenery had said cave-dwelling beasts protected the stone. She had nothing to fend off a beast with such fangs, and it would soon be dark. She'd need a fire before the cool night set in and froze her stiff in her wet dress. Or might the flames only draw the beasts?

Without answers, Camille climbed back down the tree, her woolen stockings snagging on the rough limbs.

Her father would have laughed at her right then, probably thinking she'd concocted some reason to be barefoot once again. How she'd loved his laugh.

The forest was a mix of leafy branches, draping mosses, and pitchy pines. Knee-high ferns blanketed the floor, along with saplings and rotted fallen trunks. The smell of rich soil intensified as darkness started to descend over the forest. The reality of a night spent in the middle of a creepy forest lurking with beasts made Camille long for the relative safety of the treetops. Then again, maybe the beasts could climb.

An owl hooted in the trees above. Grasshoppers played a droning, high-pitched tune. Other than that, the wood was silent. Camille cleared her throat and started humming the song Ira had sung to them one night along the highland path. The day Oscar had admitted he'd rowed to her instead of her father. She should have known it then. He loved her. A fire under her skin ignited, and she picked up her pace. Almost as much as she coveted the stone, she needed to find Oscar and tell him how sorry she was, how stupid she'd been.

"*Come all you gallant bushrangers,*" she sang softly. "*Da-da-dum . . . something, something, plains . . .*"

Camille took a step off a rock and landed in the middle of a foot trail.

"Hurrah!" she shouted, her voice scattering a flock of yellow birds from a shrub beside her. Dusky shadows cloaked both directions of the pebbly trail as Camille worked to steady her inner compass. She thought of which direction the salt flats had been, which direction she'd taken into the forest, but the direction in which to turn onto the path eluded her.

"Make a decision," she said aloud, her voice her only company. *Accept the challenge.* Camille turned to her left and continued on, her stocking feet soothed by the flatter terrain.

"I'll sing to you a story that will fill you with surprise," she sang some more. Her voice seemed so loud. Were there really creatures in the forest? She hadn't yet seen a cave like the one on the map. *". . . as he closed his mournful eyes, he bid the world adieu, saying—"*

"Convicts all, pray for the soul of bold Jack Donohue!"

She tripped over her own toes. "Ira?" she called into the gray night.

"Camille?" a voice answered.

Her skin tightened with gooseflesh.

"Oscar!" she shouted. "Where are you?"

A crash of leaves and branches came from up ahead, and two figures fell from a tree onto the path. She saw Oscar's tall frame, his wide shoulders, and the checked pattern of his shirt.

Camille ditched all levels of prudence in front of Ira and ran straight into Oscar's arms. He crushed her with his embrace, his hand against the back of her head, holding her tight to his chest.

"You're alive," he whispered, a dip in his voice.

"Thought you were a goner," Ira added.

Camille pulled away. She tried to see into Oscar's eyes, but the bluish dusk made it difficult.

"I was horrible to you," she said. "I'm so sorry."

She wanted to say more, that she'd been an arrogant prig worried about the laughter and hushed talk that would accompany any public announcement of their involvement. That her father's business would go under once Randall left, but that she'd risk it to be able to be with him. Bringing up something as weighty as that would darken the moment, though, and she didn't want to wipe the smile from Oscar's dimpled cheeks just yet.

"What happened to you?" he finally asked.

"It involves a long fall and lots of water, but I'll tell you later. We need to keep moving. There are beasts, you know. McGreenery warned me about them, and I didn't remember until after I fell," she explained, hardly taking a breath.

Ira whistled. "Well, ain't that the cherry on top."

Camille looked up into the branches from where they'd fallen. "Why were you up there?"

Oscar put his arm around her shoulders and held her close as they moved along the trail. "We heard something coming," he answered as Ira fell into step behind them. Granite rocks and spiked shrubs lined the foot trail, mossy canopies close overhead. Oscar looked down at her and grinned. "But we figured no animal would know the words to Ira's song."

Camille leaned against Oscar as they walked, their bodies knocking together and jiggling unevenly. But she didn't want to let go of him, and with his hand secure on her shoulder, she figured he felt the same.

Before night could fall completely, Oscar checked the map and compass.

"This can't be a good sign," he said, tapping the shallow glass face of the compass. Camille peered at the arrow, cutting her eyes through the encroaching night. It spun wildly, north, then west, then south, then west again, then over to east. The earth's magnetism must have been completely out of hand here. He tucked both the map and the compass away.

"'Least we haven't seen any of those beasts you were talking 'bout," Ira said just as Camille spied a granite outcropping up on their left. Blocky chunks of rock bulged from the side of a ledge, covered with moss and grass. Leafy shoots filled cracks in the granite, almost covering the entrance. She clutched Oscar's hand on her shoulder.

"A cave," she whispered. He stopped and found the craggy archway. The rifle was out of the bag and in his hand in an instant.

Ira groaned. "I always did talk too much."

The darkened opening was quiet and still. In fact, all signs of life—the trill of birds, the melancholy hoot of the owl, the hum of insects—had fallen placid. *They're hiding.* Camille pressed her nails into Oscar's skin.

"We need to get out of here."

TWENTY-TWO

Oscar kept Camille's hand in his as he continued up the trail, her tired steps quickly changing into a jog. She didn't know where they would be safe from whatever lived in the cave. The sun had disappeared and a gibbous moon brightened by the minute; they would have to stop and make camp soon. The path was too winding, rocky, and root-covered to chance traveling past dark with such little moonlight.

Without warning, Ira's fingers curled around Camille's shoulder and yanked her to a halt.

"What is it?" she asked.

"Hush!" He pressed a finger to his lips.

A low growl rolled out from behind the chest-high shrubs to their right. Camille couldn't see anything past the red berry–covered limbs. Another gurgling bellow came, and two orange eyes appeared among the choke-cherries. Oscar leveled the barrel of the rifle straight at the creature.

A catlike hiss startled her from behind, and Camille turned to see another orange-eyed creature perched on the ledge above them. It rose onto its hind legs, standing at double Oscar's height, covered in brown fur. The creature's arms bowed out at its sides, its feet and hands pawlike, its snout crumpled up in a snarl that exposed razored fangs. The beast vaulted from the ledge, claws spread and curled for the strike. Camille screamed and a shot rang out. The monster squealed and crashed to the ground.

"Behind you!" Ira shouted as the first creature hurtled over the shrubs. With one powerful swipe it knocked the rifle from Oscar's hand and hurled him against the rocky ledge. Camille reached for the fallen rifle, but the beast swiveled on its haunches and spotted her. Its solid arm caught her in the ribs, punching the air out of her lungs. Its claws tore at her back and threw her from the rifle.

Camille fought to stay conscious as the beast howled and took heavy, wet breaths. Her back burned and pain seared through her side. Lifting herself onto one elbow, she saw Oscar still lying limp at the foot of the ledge. God, what had she done? Oscar had followed her on this pursuit of hers. Ira, too. She'd led them both here. This was all her doing, all her fault.

The beast's sinewy shoulders heaved as it turned toward her. It blinked, the slits of its eyes snapping shut vertically. Whatever it was, the beast looked like a mixture of a bear, a wild dog, and a human. Slowly it came toward her, twitching its head, flexing its paws. It grunted and gurgled, fangs still bared.

She raked the ground with her hands, but her fingers closed on nothing but moss and small pebbles. With her stocking feet, Camille shoved herself away from the beast as it closed in on her. Her back hit the ledge. Nowhere else to go. Trapped, she watched it draw up its arm, claws extending. In the moment she had left, she looked toward Oscar.

He was gone.

A boulder struck the beast in the head. It yowled and craned its neck. From the rim of the ledge above her, Ira pitched another boulder, hitting the beast square in the chest. It crouched and then sprang up toward Ira. A *crack* split the air and the beast plummeted to the ground. Oscar stood behind the thrashing beast, the rifle back in his hands. He sent a last bullet into the beast's head, and its squirming stopped. Camille sucked in air, realizing she'd stopped breathing altogether. Oscar lifted her to her feet.

"What did it do to you?"

She couldn't feel anything, only a numb throbbing through her legs and arms and head. Camille buried her face in Oscar's chest. He tried to embrace her but instantly drew back his hands.

"Oh God," he said, and twisted her around to take a look at her back. The burning sensation returned as Ira ran up to them.

"Do you think there're more of 'em?" he asked. Camille could think only about the heat on her back.

"We need a fire so I can see this better," Oscar said.

Ira stole a look. "Holy gallnipper!"

Camille eyed him. "Thank you for helping save my life, Ira, but would you please stop saying that? I have no idea what a gallnipper even is."

"Mosquito. Big sucker," Ira explained.

"Come on." Oscar urged them forward, but Camille held him back.

"There could be more of them out there, Oscar. These two probably lived in the cave we saw. It might be empty now."

Ira picked up the bag of supplies. "You want to shelter in the cave? Love, that critter musta whacked you on the noggin, too."

Oscar took her arm and started back toward the cave, anyway, past the two dead creatures Camille still feared were going to leap up and attack again. Protesting under his breath, Ira followed. Camille tripped a few times over exposed roots and stumbled into crevices as the sky grew blacker.

She could barely see the entrance to the cave as they approached it.

"This is it," she whispered, but then doubted her idea to shelter there. Ira was right, there could be more of them hiding inside. Only two had attacked, though, and if they traveled in packs, as wolves did, they would have all pounced at once — probably.

They crept closer to the arch, stopping to listen for the wet panting the creatures had made. No sounds permeated the dark cavern except for their own choppy breathing. Moving under the cave's ceiling, she heard Ira rummage around in the bag, then the thud of sticks and logs on the rocky floor. He struck a match and a small light glowed; the sticks and logs ignited and the cave slowly brightened.

Skeletal remains littering the floor caught the light. Mostly small animal bones, though a skull and pelvic bone looked human. Two fetid heaps of moss and grass and weeds, most likely beds for the beasts, were the only other objects inside. Camille hadn't realized how cold she was until the warmth of the flames hit her in the face. She kicked a few of the bones deeper into the cave, out of the light, and crouched by the fire. Her hands shook as she held them close to the flames.

"I need to see your back," Oscar told her. Ira dug into the bag and pulled out the single pot and dried cod. He splashed some water from a canteen into the pot and threw in the cod to soften it up.

The wound's sting cut through her, almost unbearably. She braced herself as she faced the wall, slipped her arms from the sleeves of her dress, and undid the hooks and eyes down the front of her shredded corset. She peeled the ruined corset off and cast it aside, then shrugged the back of the dress down, the cotton sticking to her bloody wounds as she pulled.

"Holy gall—" Ira stopped. "Sorry, love."

"Canteen, Ira," Oscar ordered. Camille looked back at him.

"Don't waste the water. We only have enough for a few days," she said, but Oscar still grabbed it from Ira's outstretched hand.

"It needs to be cleaned," Oscar replied.

"Think there's venom in there?" Ira asked. Camille faced the wall again, thankful she didn't have to meet their eyes with so much of her skin exposed.

"Teeth normally release venom, not claws," she said as cool water dribbled down her back.

He snorted. "Normally, yeah. But what's normal about spiders the size of cannon shot, or holes in a dried-out lake? Or about whatever those freakish things were back there? This place is unnatural."

She heard the tearing of cloth as Oscar ripped off his sleeve. He gently dabbed her skin. Camille bit the inside of her cheek to keep from whimpering.

"How bad is it?" she asked.

"It's deep."

Normally she would have demanded a less vague answer, but Ira was right. This place knocked the normal right out of everything. Oscar tore off his other sleeve and tied the two into a bandage long enough to wrap around her back and bosom. He prudently let Camille drape her front, then tied it off. Still in pain, she pulled up the top of her dress. By then the fire was going steadily and the cod had softened enough to bite into. She thought about the next day and what they might encounter once they left the cave.

"How many more bullets do we have?" Camille asked.

"Plenty." Oscar's brevity did nothing to bolster her confidence. Ira swallowed a mouthful of cod.

"I say we pack up tomorrow morning and head back to the *Lady Kate*," he said.

"No!" she shouted. "I'm not going back without the stone. And not without my father."

He had been there for her in the depths of the underground pool, leading her toward escape. She needed to be there to guide him now.

Ira popped his last bite of cod into his mouth and, still chewing, said, "Listen, I know you want your father back and all. Even without knowing him 'fore he bit it, I'm willing to bet he wouldn't want you risking your own neck trying to bring his back."

Camille looked to Oscar for support, but he avoided her by staring into the flames. "If you want to go back to Monty's ship, I won't stop you," she said. "But I'm not going to let McGreenery get his filthy hands on that stone."

Ira shook his head but didn't say whether he was or wasn't planning to retreat the next morning. They agreed to take turns on watch throughout the night. First watch belonged to Ira, who sat alert by the entrance with the rifle. Camille tried leaning against the cave's wall, but it was too far away from the fire's heat, and her wounds couldn't take the friction on her back. Instead she lay on her side, lengthwise in front of the fire.

"You agree with him, don't you?" she whispered to Oscar. He tossed on another log, embers sparking into the air.

"I want your father back, too. But I'm not willing to risk your life doing it. That thing was playing with you, Camille. It could have killed you with that blow."

She remembered how its long claws had extended even farther as it had prepared for a second strike. They could have easily torn her apart.

"So you want to turn around? Give up on the chance of having him back?"

Oscar took a swig of his canteen, then capped it. He held her stare. "I just want you alive."

Camille glanced toward Ira. He sat far enough away to hear just the murmur of their voices. This was her only opportunity to clean up after the messy scene in the pantry. Where to begin baffled her. The cold manner in which they were now acting made it difficult to believe Oscar had held her so lovingly, her body curled into his. She'd felt his hot breath on her shoulder as he dipped into sleep and out again to bury his nose in her hair or trace her scar from the *Christina* with his finger. Camille had never wanted to leave that bed.

"I don't love him," she said with little fanfare. Plain. Simple. The truth. "He's a decent man, and things would be easier if I did love him. But I want what only you can give me, Oscar."

She couldn't imagine feeling warm and safe and loved in Randall's arms the way she had in Oscar's. She didn't know what would happen once her father returned to them or how he'd react. Right then, it didn't matter.

"Good night, then," she said when he remained quiet. Camille turned onto her other side, away from the fire. The immediate cold lashed at her. A moment passed before she heard the scrape of his boots on the ground. His footsteps rounded the fire. Without saying a word, he lay down beside her. Oscar pulled her close to him without checking to see if Ira was watching.

He kissed the crown of her head. "Good night, then."

TWENTY-THREE

The undeniable urge to relieve her bladder woke Camille. She sat up with a start. The damp cold of morning had settled in her bones, and she shivered as she realized Oscar had left her side. Spinning around, she saw him at the mouth of the cave, and a misty gray dawn outside. The healing wounds on her back stung from the stretch of her skin.

"Mornin', bright eyes." Ira crouched on the other side of the campfire, mostly smoke and embers now. He grinned at her. "Sorry for stealing your bedtime buddy. It was his turn on watch."

She blushed and got to her feet, the strain on her bladder painful.

"Where're you off to?" Ira asked as she hurried toward the outside. She shot him an annoyed glance. It wasn't obvious? However much she wanted to say something biting in return, his heroics the night before still held merit and she sealed her lips.

Oscar stopped her as she tried to pass. He unsheathed

one of Monty's knives from his belt loop and turned the handle toward her.

"Just in case. And don't go far."

Camille shoved the knife into her skirt pocket and ducked out to the left into the trees, off the path. She didn't want to see the two dead beasts, although inspecting them in the daylight drew on her curiosity. Would they look as vicious as they had at nighttime? Would she ever be able to sleep again if she looked too closely? She doubted it.

Out of sight of the cave, Camille lifted her skirt and squatted near the ground. With daylight, however dreary it was, coming through the trees, all fears of never reaching Umandu fled. They had plenty of bullets, Oscar had said so. The rifle would protect them from the unnatural beasts and maybe, just maybe, they wouldn't meet any others.

Talking her faith back into place, Camille started for the cave. A stick snapped behind her but she was so stuck on all the ways they couldn't possibly fail, she didn't turn fast enough. A gloved hand flew over her mouth and yanked her backward. Loud shouts at the cave drowned her muffled screams. Camille tried to see the cave through the trees, but the person heaved her backward, dragging her feet over the leafy ground. She struggled to pry the hand off her mouth, but another arm wrenched itself around her chest and squeezed her closer. Her back seared with agony. Tears stung her eyes. And then she remembered the knife.

Camille fumbled for the handle in her pocket. Finally she closed her fingers around it and thrust the blade behind her, striking flesh. The man howled and loosened his grip. Camille pulled the knife free and bolted for the cave, where the shouting had intensified.

A grunt from behind was the only warning she had that the man had regained on her. His hand buried itself in her loose hair and yanked her back again. Her scalp and back burned fiercely as the man shoved her to the ground. He rolled her over and she gasped at the sight of his long scraggly beard. The man who had broken into her bath in Melbourne and forced her to the *Stealth* kneeled on her legs and pinned down her arms. He slammed her hand against the ground until she released the knife.

"Get off of me!" she screamed, but he only laughed in her face.

Out of nowhere, a boot connected with his jaw. The man tumbled off her and lay still on the ground, out cold. Camille scrambled to grab the knife.

"It's all right! It's just me, Camille!"

Samuel reached out to her. Camille's breath wouldn't come, her heart hammering as she took his hand.

"Are you injured?" Samuel asked, pulling her up. "I didn't know my father was going to do this. We heard gunshots last night and he turned around. He told me he was concerned about the beasts harming you, but . . . but he . . ."

Camille didn't wait to hear the rest of Samuel's explanation. She ran for the cave, her brother on her heels. She came out of the woods, into the small clearing, and saw

McGreenery and his band of misfits had encircled the cave entrance. There were three of them in all, excluding Samuel and the man with the scraggly beard. The shouting had ceased, and as she approached, Ira tried to push past a brutish sailor holding a long speared pole to his Adam's apple.

And then she saw him.

Oscar writhed on the ground at McGreenery's feet. McGreenery stood over him, a bloodied spear in his hand. Her insides hardened as she ran to Oscar and knelt in the blood pooling around him. She clutched the chest of his shirt, the black-and-white checks now saturated by vibrant red blood. Oscar gulped for air, his eyes strangely blank and searching the sky above.

"Oscar, no. No!" This couldn't be happening. This couldn't be real. Her trembling fingers pushed a few wisps of his dark blond hair from his eyes. He furrowed his brow, anguish played out in the creases of his forehead. He grasped her fingers with his bloodied hand.

She keened at his side. "No, Oscar. I love you. You can't . . . you can't die."

He started to cough, and blood spurted from his mouth. Camille wiped it away with her sleeve, but more streamed out.

"Don't," she cried. "Oscar!"

Oscar's blood-slick hand slid from her palm and hit the ground. His lips turned up, almost into a smile, but his grin looked right through her. His body gave a long shudder, and his writhing stopped.

"Oscar," she gasped. Panic bubbled inside her chest.

She leaped to her feet and lunged for McGreenery, the knife Oscar had given her less than ten minutes before still clasped in her palm. She startled McGreenery with her speed and sunk the blade into his shoulder. He growled and cuffed her across the cheek, tossing her to the ground.

"Careful, Camille. That's how your beloved ape got killed." He winced as he extracted the knife and threw it aside.

Inside her, everything had been crushed. Her throat, her heart, lungs, stomach. She looked at Oscar, at him lying motionless, the blood, the vacant look in his eyes, still open. Not dead. Oh God, no, he couldn't be dead.

"Tie them," McGreenery ordered. One of the *Stealth*'s sailors wrenched her hands from behind and hastily bound her wrists. Another sailor bound Ira and then punched him in the stomach for good measure.

Samuel stepped up to McGreenery. "You said you were coming to help them."

McGreenery looked past his son as he pressed a handkerchief to his bleeding shoulder. Camille's hatred for McGreenery ran so deep and vicious that no death would have been too gruesome or painful for him.

"Do you want the stone, or don't you?" McGreenery asked.

"Not like this," Samuel answered.

McGreenery turned away from him and said to another of his men, "Tie him, too."

"What is this?" Samuel shouted as the sailor wrestled him to the ground. "I'm your son!"

McGreenery rolled his eyes to the clearing sky. "You sniveling little fool, you're nothing more than a mistake."

With his foot, McGreenery nudged Oscar's body and peered over him.

"Leave him alone!" Camille screamed, but McGreenery chuckled.

"My dear, if you weren't such a pain in the backside, I'd consider taking you with me. All that spunk could be enjoyable in other ways."

Camille struggled to loosen the rope around her wrists but managed only to cut into the old rope burns from the *Juggernaut*.

She spit on the ground by his feet. "I'd rather take my chances with the beasts."

McGreenery chuckled again. "Careful what you wish for."

His cronies knocked them down and bound their ankles. They then dragged all three of them together, back to back, and wound the rest of the rope around them.

"I haven't got all day," McGreenery snarled at his men and continued up the path without a second glance at Camille or his son. The men finished and hurried after him.

Camille closed her eyes. Tears streamed down her cheeks as Ira and Samuel bumped elbows, trying to loosen the ropes.

"They surrounded the cave, love. We didn't stand a chance," Ira said breathlessly. "Had us at the tip of their spears, they did. Oscar heard you screaming up in the woods and made to fight the lot of them."

Camille scrunched her eyelids tighter. Oscar had wanted to help her. Why had she screamed? She should have kept her mouth shut. He'd be alive if she hadn't gone so far into the woods. If she'd just woken up a few minutes later . . .

"That bastard didn't have to do it," Ira said. "He speared him from behind just for the hell of it. I shoulda blown him up in Melbourne along with his ship."

Camille opened her eyes. Oscar's lips were fast turning blue. His skin looked whiter than before.

"I should have listened to you," Samuel said to her, but she wasn't paying attention to him. All she wanted was to scream at the top of her lungs and pound on something. Every breath she took, every moment she lived while he didn't, was wrong.

Ira shuffled side to side, knocking her around.

"What are you doing?" she asked, her throat sore.

"Not only am I extraordinary at the poker table," he said as he stretched his wrists under his rear end. He cocked his head and winked at her. "I'm bendy, too."

He curled his legs up and slid his hands under his feet until his wrists were in front of him. Ira ripped off the rope tying them together and ran for the knife Camille had used to stab McGreenery. He sliced the rope around her wrists.

"There's no doubt in my mind that you can get that rock," he said to her. "It'll be tricky, but you have a better reason to get your hands on it than that prick does."

Ira looked at Oscar with visible grief before slicing Samuel's ropes. Camille knelt beside Oscar and covered his chest with her palm. She'd felt the strong, steady beat of his heart against her the night in Port Adelaide as he'd held her close. Now she rested her head on his quiet chest and wept.

Ira took her shoulders and pulled her back. He turned her to face him.

"Listen to me, Camille." She sniffled and gave him her full attention. He'd used her name, instead of "love." Ira was through jesting. "You have only one chance to get Oscar back. You can't do it sitting here on the ground beside him."

Camille wiped her cheek. "But what about my father?"

She made fists so tight her nails dug into her palms. Oscar had been faced with this decision that night in the dory: her life or her father's. Now the same choice had landed on her, but her heart would do the choosing. God, how would it decide? No matter what, it wouldn't be good enough. One of them would still be dead.

Samuel nodded up the path. "The mound of boulders isn't far from here. We saw it last night before sundown."

"We can't just leave him here," Camille said, still kneeling by Oscar's side. "We can't leave him for the beasts to take."

Ira helped her find her footing before he gripped Oscar under the arms and nodded for Samuel to take his feet. They moved him into the cave and then searched his pockets until Ira pulled out the map.

"It's the best we can do," Ira said. He held up the map to Umandu. "Let's go."

The cave looked dark and empty. She hated to leave Oscar there, unprotected. He'd said he wasn't willing to risk her life for the stone. But she'd risked his, and she'd gotten him killed.

Camille straightened her shoulders and took the map from Ira's hand.

"Right. Let's go."

Camille tore over the trail, the path's sharp incline burning her thighs, her stocking feet barely touching the ground. Behind her, Ira and Samuel huffed as they tried to keep her pace. Oscar had once accused her of being on a warpath for the stone. He hadn't known how close to the truth that statement had been. She did feel like a warrior, one set on revenge. With each stride, she pictured Umandu in her hands. The map had no description or etching of what the stone looked like. Just a triangle, pulsating at the crest of the mound of boulders—the end point of the perilous silver line.

Why couldn't her heart choose both of them? Because it would be too easy, she immediately answered herself, and nothing about Umandu was easy. Her father had been her world for so long; he had raised her, had loved her and given her everything. Life without him was unthinkable. And yet Oscar had rowed to her the night of the storm, changing everything she'd ever felt for him. It wasn't just lust or simple attraction. She loved him. She *wanted* him. Like her father, the thought of living without Oscar made her ache.

"There," Samuel called out as a hill of boulders rose behind green treetops. McGreenery and his men were nowhere to be seen, but Camille could feel traces of their passing, as if their rush for the stone still clung to the air and the sway of the branches.

She pushed on through the trees, toward the base of the mound. A slew of massive boulders, round, square, and misshapen, formed an uneven staircase. Once close enough, she shielded her eyes from the hazy sun and lifted her chin. Three quarters of the way up the mound was a small opening, similar to the arch of the beasts' cave.

The three of them arrived just in time to witness the last of McGreenery's sailors disappear inside. Camille stuffed the map into her skirt pocket and grasped the first boulder. Her arms throbbed as she scaled the boulders, her stocking feet treading on the hem of her skirt and tripping her. Glimpsing down, she saw Ira right on her heels and Samuel not far behind him. The distance to solid ground churned her stomach and made her dizzy.

"Keep lookin' up," Ira advised. She leaned her forehead against the boulder and took a few deep breaths before resuming her climb. At last, Camille's hands gripped the floor of the entrance. It wasn't a cave at all. Inside, the floor immediately descended again, more blocky boulders littering the 'way like wax dripping down the side of a tapered candle. The whole interior of the mound looked like a theater where rows of seating loomed over an actors' stage. She crawled inside and crouched behind one boulder, Ira and Samuel following her move.

McGreenery was already at the bottom of the cascade where the actors' stage was, in this case, a sheer oval slab. In its center, cradled by a mosaic of smaller rocks, Camille saw a brilliant, teal-colored stone, flecked with shimmering deposits of gold.

Umandu. Camille watched in horror as McGreenery laid down the spear he'd slain Oscar with and stepped up on the slab, a sack clutched in his hands. His sailors gathered around him in awe, one dropping the rifle taken from the cave; it clattered to the ground and its echo reverberated around the hollow dome. She darted out from behind the boulder before the echo ebbed, shrugging off Ira's hand as he tried to hold her back. As silently as she could, Camille moved down the cascade of rock. Shouting for McGreenery to stop would accomplish nothing. She needed to reach Umandu first. But how?

Halfway down the cascade, she saw McGreenery still hadn't reached the teal stone. Its magnificence increased, the closer Camille got. It was at least the size of a human head, and the blueness of it quivered the same way the map's surface had, like a lake disturbed by a skipping stone. McGreenery stared at it, entranced, now a single arm's length away. His men were too absorbed to notice Camille's descent behind a few more boulders.

Her eyes brushed over another, smaller stone similar to the ones cradling Umandu. It lay on the edge of the oval slab, as though cast out of the altar. Its smooth-cut triangular shape caught her attention, as did its soft amber sheen. There was something so familiar about it.

Camille carefully reached into her pocket. She unfurled the leather, and the amber flash that had lain dormant since the first time she'd held the map startled her again. It rolled across the surface, igniting the hidden letters once more. Her eyes caught on the first line: *Be not fooled by the first that you see, the stone is made plain to only the worthy.*

She flipped the map with trembling hands. On the back, ingrained in the worn leather, were the two triangles. Every time Oscar had unrolled the map she'd seen the strange symbol, but she'd never understood what it meant. Now the top, right-side-up triangle glowed the same radiant amber as the stone.

McGreenery had the wrong rock! A decoy. Renewed hope propelled her from her hiding spot. McGreenery and his men whipped their heads toward her as she hurried in front of the triangular rock. She didn't want to touch it yet, still afraid of her heart's decision.

At once, his four men rushed in her direction.

"Never mind her!" McGreenery shouted. The men pulled back. "She's insignificant now. You've managed to slink out of many tight situations lately, haven't you, Camille?"

She kept the rock behind her skirt, hiding it from plain view.

"Didn't I advise you to forget the stone? Didn't I tell you it would be mine? Look at everything you've lost." He threw the sack over the ornate teal stone, pulled a cord tight around the sack's opening, and lifted it from its resting place without placing a single finger on it. "And look at everything I've gained."

His sailors laughed with him. Camille spotted her straggly-bearded attacker. A fist-sized bruise from Samuel's boot discolored his jaw. Camille discreetly scanned the cascade, but didn't see Ira or Samuel. She returned her stare to McGreenery; only this time, it was she who smiled.

"I remember what you said. But I have the real map, don't I?" She held it up for him to see as the second wave of sparks, invisible to everyone else, rolled back over the map and erased the riddle. "Samuel copied the diagram for you, but there were things the map wouldn't show him. Things only the one worthy of the stone could see. And he overlooked something else, something he had no reason to believe was important."

McGreenery came around the shrine, the sack's cord cutting so deeply into his flesh, the skin whitened. Camille twirled the map around to show the glowing mark.

"This is the mark of Umandu." She stepped aside so he

could see the amber stone aglow at her heel. Shock drowned McGreenery's simper. "And you can go to hell."

McGreenery hurled the sack with the decoy toward her head. "Take her!"

Camille dashed out of the path of the flying sack and threw herself on top of the real Umandu, clutching it in her hands. The rock gave off heat and a subtle pulse, surprising her. She immediately understood Umandu was not just a rock — it was a life force. And now she had to choose to whom she'd send it.

Like the vision of her father that had come earlier, a new set of images flipped through her head, like pages of an open book blown by a gust of wind. One of her father at his desk aboard the *Christina*, another of Oscar laughing with Juanita in the kitchen; her father showing her how to record data in his log, and another of him tucking her into bed; her mother, clutching Camille's hand and begging for forgiveness; Oscar holding her that night in Port Adelaide; and the last image was of Oscar lying in a pool of blood at the cave.

An explosion of lustrous white light pierced Camille's clenched eyelids. The sudden hike in the stone's heat burned, but she couldn't have released the stone even if she tried. The rock drew her closer, sucking her inward, bonding her fingers to the stone so ferociously, she feared it might crush them. The stone's pulse thundered through her, and then what felt like a giant bait hook yanked her from behind. Camille flew backward and landed on her side, thumping the base of her head against a boulder.

She slipped to the cold rock floor, her vision spinning. The stone rolled to a stop a few feet away. In a great whistle of wind, the silvery white light gathered above her. It swirled into a luminous cloud and generated streaks of silhouetted lightning. Her hair lashed at her cheeks as she stared at the storm just above their heads. Thunder shook the dome. The tremors rumbled through her spine, her arms and fingers, through her legs and feet and toes. The wind pressed down with such force it flattened her and the rest of the men in the boulder dome to the ground. Sand and dirt circled through the air, scratching her skin, filling her ears, and whipping into her eyes.

Even though they watered something fierce, Camille kept her eyes upon a familiar shape as it congealed in the swirls of sand and dirt. Its lower jaw doubled in size and jutted out like a bulldog's, holding grotesquely pointed teeth unlike before. Its two eye sockets were no longer black voids, but balls of flaming red. Its giant maw sprang wide, and the skull roared at the white storm. The dual-pronged cyclone of dirt holding the skeletal face churned forward into the blinding white tempest.

McGreenery and his men covered their faces in an attempt to shield themselves from the grating wind, and Camille wondered if any of them could even see the horror happening right above their heads. Whatever this thing was, it was trying to beat out the light, the storm. It was trying to consume Umandu's power. Beside her, the stone's amber light flickered, threatening to go out.

Camille crawled toward the stone as the cyclone spun around the dome, chasing the white light with its barbed jaws. With sand abrading her lips and exposed skin, she grasped Umandu. Its heat immediately spiked, pulling her in once more. The growl of wind tempered as the cyclone stalled. Its eyes, two red-hot pokers, swiveled and found Camille pressed against one of the boulders. She held Umandu tight to her chest.

"I won't let you take it!" she screamed as the thing's pronged tail cut a path toward her, its teeth pried open like a bear trap. She squeezed her eyelids together, imagining how easily the cyclone could rip her to shreds, the whirling sand now more like a million tiny razors.

But then the wind shifted, and the brilliant light again seared through the skin of her eyelids. Camille opened her eyes to see the gleaming white tempest elongate into a funnel and spiral toward the skull-faced cyclone. The white funnel wrapped around the cyclone like ribbon, binding the cyclone and smothering its speed. Once it had fully enveloped the cyclone, the white funnel hurled itself toward Camille and the stone. The impact felt like it was melding her spine into the boulder behind her, but Umandu swallowed the light and wind whole. The noise in the boulder dome settled, and the rock's heat and amber glow fizzled.

McGreenery groaned as he lifted himself from the ground. Camille tried to move, but her limbs stayed put, paralyzed. She closed her eyes. Pain coursed through her head from where she'd hit the back of her skull, shooting through the back of one eye and down the bridge of her nose. On her back, blood from her reopened wounds was sticky and warm. Slowly, she bent her fingers, the tips still tingling from the energy of the stone. Its force pushed against the undersides of her skin, as though it longed to release itself once more.

Before she opened her eyes completely, she knew someone else was on the ground beside her. The person's presence sent a current of adrenaline through her. She blinked away schools of black dots and turned her head. Sprawled on the rock floor, bloody and pale, lay Oscar. Camille's eyes smarted, a sob caught in her throat and stuck fast.

She forced her legs to move, her hands to release the stone. Camille crawled across the floor toward him. He wasn't moving. His chest lay placid, his arms splayed at his sides, lips the color of ash. It hadn't worked. Umandu had brought him to her, but he was still dead.

"Oscar?" Her voice bounced off the boulders, the first sound since the thunderous white storm. She grabbed his hand. Skin like ice.

"Please, no," she whispered as she brushed his dingy blue cheeks with her fingers.

"You fool!" McGreenery seethed. He picked up Umandu and cradled it in his arms. "Do you have any idea what you've done? What you've unleashed upon yourself?"

Camille dropped her head to Oscar's chest and crushed

the collar of his bloodied shirt in her fists. She knew exactly what she'd done. She'd failed her father. Failed Oscar. Camille laid her forehead against his and wept.

"Frivolous little girl. If you thought you were cursed before, you're in for a new awakening," McGreenery said. She glanced up at him, her tears blurring his sneer.

"What do you mean?"

He boomed a heartless chuckle. "You've used the stone before joining it with its sister. Why not just slice your finger and jump into a pool of ravenous sharks? Perhaps I should put you out of your misery before you realize what you've done." McGreenery motioned to someone behind her. "Get rid of her."

Two hands gripped her shoulders and heaved her back. She tried to wrestle out of the man's grasp, but the fight fled her body.

"Leave her alone!"

Samuel jumped out from behind a boulder. McGreenery's man flung Camille aside to join the others rushing him. Ira hurtled out from behind another boulder and grabbed the rifle one of the men had dropped earlier. The scraggly-bearded man charged Ira instead. Ira fired two shots, hitting him and another sailor from the *Stealth*. A third grabbed Ira from behind and wrestled the rifle from his grip. It skidded across the floor as Ira bit into his opponent's arm.

The fourth and final member of McGreenery's crew tackled Samuel. Camille wrenched a smaller rock from the base of the cascade pile and ducked out of McGreenery's reach, bringing the rock down on the sailor's head. Samuel kicked him off.

She took Samuel's hand and pulled him up. "Now we're even."

Something hard and pointed nudged her in the back, stinging the wounds from the beast. "And so shall we be," McGreenery said with disconcerting calm. Camille faced him, the rifle he'd reclaimed from one of his men aimed at her chest. Samuel pushed himself in front of her.

"You can't do this."

McGreenery lowered the rifle, and a shot echoed off the boulders. Samuel screamed and sunk to the floor. He clutched his shin, blood seeping through his trouser leg.

"You're lucky I'm sentimental." McGreenery wheeled the rifle back to Camille. "You, on the other hand, are no kin to me. In fact, you've been a plague these last many weeks."

The blow to her head started to wear off and fear trickled in. He'd thought nothing of shooting his own son in the leg. Samuel lay curled in a ball of agony beside her as Ira and the remaining sailor battled behind the oval slab.

"If you're going to shoot me, do it. Do you think I'm afraid of you?" Camille asked. No bullet could hurt worse than the thought of her father drowning, or the sight of Oscar gurgling for air as he lay in a pool of his own blood. She stared into the barrel of the rifle. "You're a coward. Heartless and cruel, and the devil won't even want you."

A single shot and she'd be back with her father and Oscar. She'd have them both. Perhaps that was why Umandu hadn't worked; her heart hadn't been able to decide.

McGreenery pressed the cool steel against her throat. He bared his teeth, losing every ounce of composure and calculated grace. Camille threw a glance toward Ira, who finally jammed his knife into the ribs of his opponent. He pulled the blade free in time to see her at the end of McGreenery's rifle. But instead of running toward her, he stopped and stared. What was he doing?

McGreenery reeled forward. The rifle and stone clattered to the floor. His lips parted. "What — ?" he rasped.

Camille stared at him, equally bewildered. A sharp metal spike protruded from his chest and glinted in the single band of sunlight streaming from the dome's entrance. McGreenery collapsed to his knees and revealed his assailant to her.

Oscar placed a foot on McGreenery's back and kicked him forward, sliding him off the very spear McGreenery had used to kill him.

"Let's see how you like it," Oscar said and tossed the spear aside.

TWENTY-FOUR

*C*amille's eyes watered, her disbelief so strong it pulled her heart like an undertow. She touched Oscar's chest, the blood that coated his shirt still sticky. McGreenery had been wrong. She hadn't wasted it— Umandu had worked!

Oscar pressed her close to him, his skin still cold, but the pink of his cheeks and lips fast drowning out the blue. Camille pulled open his shirt without reserve. The gaping wound on his chest now looked little more than a scratch. He ran his hands through her hair and cupped her cheeks in his palms.

"You weren't supposed to choose me," he said.

Behind them, Ira approached, stunned and speechless for what must have been the first time in his life. He helped lift Samuel, whose cheeks had blanched as well. Camille prodded Oscar's arms and stomach and face. It was truly him. The unbearable grief over losing him flipped inside out. Her joy ran so deep and strong she thought she might burst from it.

"The night the *Christina* went down, you rowed to me,"

she answered, her throat knotted as she thought of her father. She forced it down. "This time, I must have needed to row to you."

Oscar kissed her, his lips still cold but filled with life. She leaned into him and hung on as though he might disappear. Ira let out a playful high-pitched whistle. Samuel coughed. Oscar and Camille reluctantly pulled apart and blushed.

"Holy gallnipper," Ira said. Camille grinned, not minding in the least that he was using that annoying turn of phrase again. "I can't believe that little rock . . . I mean you were dead, mate. Dead as this bloke right here." Ira kicked McGreenery in the leg. Oscar nodded, rubbing his hand over the fading red mark, as if to feel for himself that the deadly wound was gone.

"I was in the dory," he whispered. Ira cocked his head.

"Say again?"

Camille lifted her ear from his chest, where she'd wanted to listen to the smooth rhythm of his heart. She looked up at him before hearing its strong beat.

"The dory?"

Oscar nodded again, eyebrows creased.

"I heard your voice. At the cave," he said to Camille. "This force kept pulling me backward, away from you, like I was being sucked into the ground."

So this was how it had felt for him to die. She remembered the way he'd looked right through her and how it had chilled her to the marrow. Her own brush with death had been different, and somehow better, if death could even be measured in levels of bad or good. The image of her father had drawn her to safety, making her forget her yearning for air. He had been there for her, but she hadn't been able to do the same for him. All this time, all this trouble, and all she'd wanted was to bring him back, make him proud of the lengths to which she'd gone for him. In the end, she'd failed him miserably.

"And then you were gone. Your voice faded, and I was in the dory, adrift in the Tasman, the dawn after the *Christina* went down," Oscar continued.

Samuel and Ira glanced at each other with marked expressions of doubt and confusion.

"But I wasn't alone." He gently pulled Camille away from him and gripped her arms. "Your father was with me. He was sitting there, smiling. It all seemed so real. I could·taste the salt air, and . . . and I remember touching the water, and it was cold. It wasn't like in a dream, when you can't do those things."

Camille sucked in a deep breath, trying to inflate her crushing lungs. Oscar had seen him, too. She'd give anything to see her father again, to hear his voice, to feel at home by just being in his presence. At least, that's what she'd once believed. But Camille hadn't been willing to give up Oscar. Did that mean she loved her father less? Never. She could *never* love her father less. So then why hadn't her heart chosen him?

"Did he say anything?" she asked, anxious to know yet afraid to hear.

"It's all jumbled," Oscar said, again shaking his head and rubbing his chest. "I remember him saying a few things. Bits and pieces."

Camille looked to Ira and Samuel. Their parted mouths and bugged eyes hung on Oscar's every word. Oscar squinted at the ground and seemed to be working hard to piece together what her father had said on the other side.

"I'm still here to guide her?" he said, questioning his own memory. "It doesn't make any sense, I'm sorry."

She shook her head, eyes tearing up again. It had been real. He really had come to her in the black water of the underground pool.

"No, don't be sorry," she said, tears spilling. "It does make sense. It makes sense to me."

Oscar didn't seem to understand how, and she knew she'd need to tell him the whole story to explain.

"Did he say anything else?" Ira asked. Camille glanced at him, hoping he and Samuel, and even Oscar, didn't think she was horrible for bringing back someone other than her father. Though if they did, she wouldn't fault them.

"He did, but . . ." Oscar rubbed his chest some more, peeling back his torn shirt. Even the thin scratch of his remaining wound had disappeared. "I know William said more, but I can't put it together."

Camille wanted to know what her father had said, maybe even more than she'd wanted to read the rest of her mother's letter. Now wasn't the time to press Oscar, though. It would come.

Umandu had rolled from McGreenery's hand, and Ira now stooped to pick it up. He ran his hands over each plane of the triangular stone. Camille was certain he couldn't feel the heat or pulse that she had before. She'd sent everything special about Umandu straight into Oscar's lifeless body.

Oscar nodded toward the stone. "It doesn't look all that extraordinary. Not like the map, at least."

The crumpled map lay beside McGreenery's body. Camille must have dropped it when she lunged for the stone. She walked over, giving McGreenery's splayed limbs wide berth.

"We should make tracks," Ira said. He shoved the stone into the sack of supplies, and then offered his shoulder to Samuel for the climb up the rock cascade. "It's already midmorning, and we've got beasts to outrun, holes to avoid, and whopper spiders to squish before we make it back to the *Lady Kate*."

Camille picked up the map. Oscar took Camille's arm and helped her up the first boulder.

"Well, aren't we a sorry-lookin' lot?" Ira bellowed as they limped up the cascade, each one nursing injuries. As they climbed, their huffing and puffing and grunts of pain were both amusing and disheartening. They did have a long way to go before reaching the inlet. She was exhausted, too. Umandu had probably sucked out some of her life to restore Oscar's. The odd sensation of the stone's energy still pushed at the tips of her fingers, but perhaps it was just the excitement of having Oscar back.

Her father had said he would be there to guide her. Saying something like that didn't point to his being upset. In fact, she couldn't believe her father would ever begrudge her heart's decision. Camille only hoped she wouldn't. But already, the twist of her stomach was there. She still longed to be able to slide into a strong, reassuring embrace from the man who'd been everything to her for so long.

"Samuel, is your leg all right?" Camille asked. Her brother leaned on Ira's shoulder for support as he shuffled up and around rocks.

"Like my dear father said: I'm lucky he was sentimental."

Ira's laughter echoed throughout the dome.

"Will you be coming with us to San Francisco, then?" Oscar asked Samuel as he helped Camille climb the last boulder to the arched opening.

"If my sister will have me," he answered, taking her hand in his. "I'm sorry, Camille. You were right about my father. I should have listened to you. And to our mother."

She ruffled his hair, warming at the words "our mother."

"Samuel, I'm sorry. I know you only went with McGreenery to bring her back," Camille said.

Her brother grimaced as sunlight struck him in the face. "Yes, originally. Just as originally you traveled all this way to bring back your father."

The feeling of a hundred jagged shards of glass pierced Camille's heart. Samuel continued before anyone could notice she'd stopped breathing.

"But it's okay, Camille." He grasped her shoulder and gently squeezed. "It's okay. Life . . . life just changes, I think. It goes on."

Her brother released her shoulder, and Camille inhaled a ragged breath. Life just changes. *Like a stormy headwind,* Camille thought. First blowing the sails in one direction, and then, without any warning at all, shifting course.

"I think I'm going to like having a little brother," she said.

She and Samuel shared an unbreakable bond, even if the woman who linked them was gone. Death couldn't break an unbreakable bond. And death couldn't separate her from her father as long as she didn't allow it to.

Samuel and Ira started down the steep mound. Oscar slid his firm hand around the nape of Camille's neck. She loved how he did that, and she leaned into him. Together, they looked over the landscape, at the tree-covered hills, out to the cracked salt flats.

"It almost looks beautiful from here," she said. She couldn't see the inlet where the *Lady Kate* lay moored. Once they found their way to Sydney, they'd sail back to San Francisco, and Camille would face another world of unknown things. She'd need to tell Randall the truth, hurting him in a way he didn't deserve. She'd lose her home and her father's business, and once again she'd be the person everyone gossiped about in hushed tones.

Still, a thrill raced through her when she thought about the one thing she would have. Camille wrapped her arms around Oscar's waist and held him, breathing in his distinctive scent. It was such a small detail about him. She wanted to discover all the small details about him, and now she could.

"Don't ever die again," Camille whispered, pressing her cheek against the hard muscle of his shoulder.

"I'll give staying alive my best shot. On one condition." He lifted her chin up to look him in the eye. "Choose me."

Choice. She'd always had it, but strangely a life without the soft padding of money and reputation made her feel as though she had more freedom than ever. She could do whatever she wanted to do, be whoever she wanted to be. And the only person she wanted to find her way with was Oscar.

"I already have," she whispered, running her hands up his arms and over his broad shoulders. She still held the map in one sweaty hand. With a snap, she shook the damp, crumpled leather flat. Glittering dust filled the air. Oscar chuckled.

"What are we going to do with this?" he asked, running his finger along the emblem burned into the back of the map. The top triangle now looked as ordinary as before. Camille traced the upside-down triangle and wondered what would make that one come aglow. McGreenery had raged about how she'd unleashed something onto herself, some kind of new curse. She'd used

Umandu before joining it with its sister, he'd said. But she didn't care about the other stone, or the legend of the power-hungry goddess and the immortals Oscar had told her about. All she wanted now was to go home.

She rolled the leather neatly, tied it up, and shoved it into her pocket, never again wanting to see the lustrous ocean that had shone as brilliantly as sapphires, or the forested hills that sparkled like emeralds. Seeing them would only remind her of the task she had come so far to carry out but fell short of completing.

Oscar pushed a strand of her loose raven hair behind her ear, and Camille knew she hadn't completely failed. The man she loved, and who loved her, was alive when, under all normal circumstances, he shouldn't be. How could that be seen as failure?

"You know, and I know." Oscar paused to take a breath. "William would never have approved of us being together."

He held his eyes level with hers, as if trying to detect any flicker of doubt or apprehension in her.

"We won't be tying bait bags for a living, will we?" she asked, willing to give up her wealth, her good name, but never her dignity.

Oscar laughed. "No bait bags."

"Well, of that my father would at least approve. And even if he didn't," she said with a sly grin, "I do."

She rose to the tips of her toes and kissed him.

"Oy, lovebirds!" Ira shouted from the ground. He and Samuel had reached the base and now looked into the sunlight, shielding their eyes with the planes of their hands. "Should I build a campfire and start sending smoke signals? Here we are, beasties! Come have lunch!"

Oscar's familiar sarcasm slipped back into place. "No smoke signals needed, Ira, the shouting will do just fine."

He released his arms from around her waist, and Camille reluctantly let him go, too. He descended the first boulder. "I'll go first, in case you slip."

Oscar's eyes came level with Camille's ratty wool stockings. He looked up at her, his dimples as irresistible as the first time she'd seen them.

"Well, at least it's an improvement from bare feet," he said.

Camille wiggled her toes, laughing. She started down the mound of boulders toward the world that lay ahead, her footing sure and steady.

ACKNOWLEDGMENTS

My deepest appreciation to everyone who has helped me find my sea legs during this first voyage:

My husband, Chad, who supported my dream to stay home with our daughters, change diapers, and write books — now that's what I call true love. My agent, Ted Malawer, my editor, Jennifer Rees, and the entire team at Scholastic — thank you for the dedication and enthusiasm you've all shown *Everlasting* as it made its way into the world. My fearless band of critique mavens, supporters, research assistants, and merry mischief-makers: Amy Henry, Maurissa Guibord, Dawn Metcalf, Rose Green, Amanda Marrone, Susan Colebank, and Robin Merrow MacCready, among many others. My sisters, Lisa and Sarah, and all of my family and friends — there are simply too many of you to squeeze onto this one page! Lastly, I want to thank my parents, Michael and Nancy Robie. Your unconditional love and encouragement have been my constant guide.